The Viking Who Fell Through Time

MAUREEN CASTELL

CHAMPAGNE BOOK GROUP

The Viking Who Fell Through Time

This is a work of fiction. The characters, incidents and dialogues in this book are of the author's imagination and are not to be construed as real. Any resemblance to actual events or persons, living or dead, is completely coincidental.

Published by Champagne Book Group
712 SE Winchell Drive, Depoe Bay OR 97341 U.S.A.

~~~

First Edition 2022

pISBN: 978-1-959036531

Cover Art by Sevannah Storm

www.champagnebooks.com

Version_1
~~~

To Alan, for all your love and support on this long journey.

Dear Reader,

A few years ago, I attended an Icelandic festival in a nearby town. In addition to demonstrations of spinning and sword-making, there was a battle re-enactment (with commentary). That was also the year a fully-functional Viking replica longship sailed into the harbor. Needless to say, I was inspired and began writing about Vikings.

Of course, there was a twist. What if the Vikings encountered a spaceship, and what if that spaceship dragged them through a space-time portal to the distant past?

The Viking Who Fell Through Time is about time travel, Vikings, and, of course, romance. Since most of the action takes place in the ancient past, it could be considered a historical romance—except for that little matter of the spaceship.

I can't help it—my stories have to have that additional element of the unexpected. And a love story between two people born three thousand years apart? Well, you can't get more unexpected than that.

And this is only the beginning.

I hope you enjoy Tor and Kiana's story. Let me know what you think at http://www.MaureenCastell.com.

Maureen

Pronunciation Guide

If you are like me, you prefer knowing how words sound when read, especially if you are reading them aloud to someone else, so I have included my best estimate of how some of the less obvious words are pronounced, based on several sources. For multi-syllable words, the emphasized syllable is in all caps. Any errors are, sadly, my own.

Names

Ajmal (ADG-mal)
Beade (be-AH-dah)
Dyre (DEE-ray)
Emund (EE-mund)
Kiana (kee-ANN-a), formerly Nahid (naah-HEED)
Lida (LEE-dah)
Runa (ROO-na)
Vider (VY-der

Words

Á sér sitja (ah sair SEET-yah) - be quiet
Góðr (GOATH-rr) - Good or fine
Knorr (NOOR) - Viking ship used primarily in trade

Pronunciation Guide

Chapter One

North Atlantic, 982 A.D.

Tor Olafsson wrapped both arms around the groaning mast and shouted into the howling wind. "Curse you, Odin, punish *me* if you will but leave my people alone."

A huge wave crashed over *The Hammer*'s side, cascaded along the sloping deck of the ship, and swept a bleating, flailing goat toward the far railing. The remains of its tether dragged behind it. Tor lunged for the frantic animal and managed to snag the rope around its neck. They'd already lost one goat to the sea. He'd not lose another. They needed every animal they brought with them if they survived to make landfall.

"Got you." He pulled the goat to him and clasped it under one arm. His own tether tightened around his waist, but when he jerked to a halt, it snapped. His heart plummeted into his stomach. "No!"

His shout swallowed by thunder, he skidded along the deck, clawing for a hold with frozen fingers. A precious water barrel tumbled past him and crashed through the railing. His legs slid through after it. Tor grabbed the rail with his free hand, instinctively tightened his grip on the goat, and stared, mesmerized, at his legs dangling over the angry ocean. Shoulders strained; fingers slipped—

Someone grasped his wrist. For a moment he hung, suspended over the watery abyss. Time stopped. His rescuer dragged him onto the deck and back to the mast. Tor swiped wet hair from his eyes and nodded thanks to his best friend and first mate.

Vider held out a length of rope. "Never curse the gods."

Tor passed the goat to a crewman to join the animals in the shallow oar pit. After he attached the new tether, he focused his attention back on Vider. "They've done nothing to help us."

His friend shrugged. "They've kept us alive so far."

"Alive?" Tor ground his teeth and glowered at the battered longship, at his exhausted crew rowing and bailing for their lives. *My fault. They trusted me.*

"Perhaps we should also petition Jorvik's Christian god." Vider grinned at Tor's immediate scowl.

"If our own gods won't help us, why would his?" Not for the first time, he wished he'd left the priest behind. No matter he worshipped the one god—many of Tor's men believed the more gods they prayed to the better—but he also claimed to be a seer and spouted dire predictions before they set out on this journey. Why bother to come with them if he thought their exile doomed before it even began?

Tor again shoved wet hair from his face. The storm had struck with such sudden ferocity there'd been no time to braid the whipping strands that stung his cheeks and blinded him.

The ship lurched sideways. A wall of water rose on the right.

"To starboard," he shouted.

The crew strained at the oars while two helmsmen struggled with the steering oar and aimed the ship into the towering swell. The bow lifted, but not enough. They plunged through the wave.

Tor held his breath. *We're going under*. He and Vider clung to the mast and each other.

The ship, built by men familiar with these waters, emerged battered but afloat. When they straightened again, Tor glanced at the tent still anchored against the stern. If they got out of this alive, he'd add a hold or a cabin or…something…*anything* sturdier than cloth. At least Emund's trading vessel boasted a hold, now crammed with most of the livestock and his own family.

Tor raised himself to examine the surrounding sea. *Where are the other ships*?

After what seemed an eternity Emund's *knorr* appeared on the crest of a wave, the clumsy vessel recognizable by its width. A moment later, Beade's longship came into view farther away. His brothers were experienced seamen, but as the eldest it was impossible for Tor not to feel responsible for their safety. That the three ships still traveled together was a miracle.

"We're together still." Vider echoed Tor's thought. "Spring storms are always the worst."

"As if winter wants one last chance to conquer us," Tor muttered.

"This storm will pass, as all storms do." Vider helped Tor to his feet. "We have weathered worse."

The screaming wind failed to muffle the fearful wails of the women and children. Tor grimaced. "Not with our families aboard."

"True." Vider glanced at the flimsy hide tent that had

miraculously defied all attacks of the wild waves. "Look."

A tall blonde woman crawled from the tent. She remained on her hands and knees as she made her way toward him, her woolen dress plastered to her like a second skin. Tor clenched his jaw in an attempt to keep admiration from overwhelming his annoyance.

Even thus, crawling like a dog, her body heavy with child, his twin sister shamed the fiercest warrior with her courage. At least she had the sense to tie her tether to the lines strung from mast to stern.

When she reached the two men, Tor knelt beside her and wrapped one arm around the mast, the other above the bulge of her belly. Her skin was ice cold. She buried her face in his chest to avoid the stinging wind.

"I'll…go help the men bail," Vider muttered.

Tor didn't miss the longing glance Vidar threw over his shoulder before returning to the lower deck. If only he had been there to offer for her before she found herself carrying Ottar's spawn. If only Tor had been able to protect her from the bastard.

"Go back to the tent, Runa," he shouted into her ear. "It's not safe out here."

"It's no safer in that tent. The wailing is driving me mad." She flashed her annoying try-to-stop-me-brother grin. "If I'm going to die, it will be by your side. We took our first breath together, and we'll take our last the same way."

Pride warred with exasperation. His stubborn sister challenged even death itself to get her way. Tor hugged her. "We're not going to die."

Another wave, bigger and more powerful than the ones before, loomed over the ship. No time to aim into it. He tightened his grip on mast and woman. The wave fell. The world vanished in an endless flood of water. The ship tilted.

He lost his footing and dug his fingers into the wood. An eternity later, the wave passed, and he was able to breathe again, though he shook with cold.

"Go back." Fear for Runa's safety added a harshness to his voice.

She squeezed his waist. "My place is here, as always."

Gods, why did I go on that last trading voyage? It took him away from home for almost a year, and in that time… How could opening a new trade route compare with losing his father in a so-called *fair* fight with a man half his age, the same man who dishonored his sister and then cast her aside? Until she proved to be with child.

Tor wanted to keep Runa safe, but her will was as strong as his.

Hard enough to get his siblings to obey his lead, but when the most troublesome of them all was only minutes younger than he, authority was just a word. At least he had no wife or children of his own to worry about.

The ship lurched beneath them. He shouted orders to his oarsmen, who were already compensating. The deck tilted, straightened, then tilted the other way. He wanted to be down there, rowing with them, but they knew their jobs better than he. As captain, he hadn't lifted an oar in years, nor pitted his strength against the sea, and in truth one more oar would be of little help. Just keeping the ship from capsizing was a heroic feat.

Despair filled his heart. He touched his forehead to Runa's and whispered, "Odin has abandoned us."

She cradled his face in her hands. "Then we will spit in his face."

A bark of laughter escaped his lips. The corners of his mouth lifted, tugging at the scar on his left cheek. *Ah, Runa, ever the defiant one.*

A loud clap of thunder made her jerk away. Her eyes widened at something behind him. He twisted his head.

Black clouds filled the horizon. Between the clouds and the ship, the air shimmered as if with heat. Something smooth, shiny, and *big* emerged from the shimmer, first a stubby point like the edge of a shield, then a curve of metal, more, until finally the entire object hung in the sky before the three ships.

The shimmer dissolved.

Longer than all three of Tor's ships lined end to end, the object resembled a child's ball after being battered by a giant hammer. Around its edge lightning spun, shining with a blinding radiance. Strange metal spears bristled around the sphere, making it appear more war mace than ball. Without warning, a dark square appeared in the front part of the object and within that square Tor glimpsed startled faces. *People*? A moment later the square vanished, leaving smooth metal in its place.

The crew's shouts broke Tor's trance. Some cursed, others prayed.

Runa trembled in his arm and again hid her face in his shirt. "Odin, forgive me. I didn't mean it."

Anger flooded him. He staggered to his feet, hauling his sister with him. "I will not lie down like a dog to die." Using his body to brace her behind him against the mast, he drew his long-sword and waved it in defiance at the giant ball. "Come, Odin, do your worst!"

As if it heard him, the object shot straight up into the black clouds. A moment later it reappeared and dove toward his ship.

Runa screamed. The men on the oar deck scrambled toward the

stern. The object shot overhead and passed a hand's breadth above the mast.

The air shimmered again. A circle opened in front of *The Hammer*. Around the ship, waves crashed in fury, threatening to overturn the battered craft. Through the circle, far below—at least half the length of Tor's ship—the water lay calm, a bright sun shone among a few scattered white clouds, and a silver beach protected by high cliffs and a colorful tree-covered mountain beckoned.

"Asgard." The wind snatched his words.

The metal ball flew into the circle and dragged the churning water—and Tor's ship—behind it.

"Hang on!" He turned, gripped the mast with both hands, and pinned Runa against it with his body.

A moment later the ship tilted and rushed over the waterfall of storm water. A quick glance showed his brothers' ships pulled in his wake. At last, with a jolt that threw everyone to the deck, *The Hammer* landed on the calm water.

Everything stopped. The ship lay still. No roar of thunder or waves battered Tor's ears. *Have we all gone deaf*? Behind him, the circle vanished.

As if awakening from a dream, the men crept forward, staring at the heavens. Tor followed their gaze. The object had stopped its fall toward the beach. For an instant it hovered above the water before lurching inland. It shuddered once, then plunged into the mountainside, burying itself deep in the earth. The screech of twisting metal thundered through the air. A shock of sound rocked the ships, pressed against their eardrums as if to deafen them.

Then there was silence.

~ * ~

Farther along the shore

Kiana swung her sword at an invisible opponent, honing skills she had little opportunity to apply these days. Her prince's enemies were unlikely to find them this far north, but she was his sworn protector and thus responsible for remaining in top fighting condition. She gave a final stab at the imaginary foe and stepped back.

A sudden roar filled the air. Startled, she spun around, stared at the mountain looming over the village. Something too big to make out buried itself in the rock, spewing broken trees and dust into the air. The ground shook with the impact, but years of training helped her keep her feet and her weapon. With one final spurt of flame, the object disappeared under the collapsing peak.

Beren is up there.

She shoved the sword into her back scabbard and raced through the summer village. A mindless keening screamed through her head. *Not Beren.*

"Are we under attack?" Lida called from the training ground.

"Unknown," she shouted back, then slowed. *By the Lady, think. Don't dash like a raw recruit into danger. Always assume the worst.* "Set up guard around the village, just like we trained. Arm the nets."

Lida veered away to assemble her fighters. Most of the men were still at sea on a final fishing run, so only the few trained women defended the village. Fortunately the fishing nets proved strong enough to trap any enemy.

Miri ran from her hut, lacing her overtunic and struggling to keep her tangled skirts from tripping her. "I'm coming with you."

Kiana shook her head. "No. It's too danger—"

"Eskil's up there." Miri tightened her mouth in a stubborn line, a mother determined to rescue her son.

Beren and Eskil weren't the only children on the mountain. Young Eskil had gone with his friend and the older boy Arkin to clean the caves. "Try to keep up." Kiana signaled to two of her trainees. "Guard her."

Unencumbered by a skirt, Kiana soon outpaced the others. How bad was it?

Dear Lady, let it not be bad.

Arkin was a responsible lad for his twelve years—he'd look after the younger boys—and Beren was smart enough to seek shelter. If he had time.

She stumbled but bore down and kept going. *Hold on, Beren. I'll be there soon.*

~ * ~

Runa pushed against Tor's back and peered beneath his arm. "Where are we?"

"Dead." He stared at the perfect beach, the broken forest, the dented mountain. *Or mad.*

Why hadn't he been more diligent in the evening rites? The gods wouldn't welcome such as he to their paradise.

"We can't be dead." Runa shoved him again. "Look at the fish."

Puzzled, he turned his gaze to the breach in the rail and the water surrounding the ship. The salt tang of the ocean filled his nostrils, along with the stench of scorched metal, burning vegetation, and another smell, familiar but…

Fish?

He stumbled to the railing. Hundreds of fish floated belly-up on the waves, killed by the shock of the object's crash. *No. Wait.* As if waking from sleep, they stirred, flopped, and swam away. Soon the ocean was once again clear.

Not Asgard then. Even there, fish didn't die and come back to life.

Time to make some decisions. "We need to get to shore. We'll need food, water, shelter for the night, and we have no thralls to help us."

"But where are we?" Runa's question echoed the growing murmurs of the crew.

He had to stop the rising panic. Tor faced the crew and raised his voice. "Odin has heard our prayers and brought us to a land of peace."

"Aren't we dead?" one anonymous voice asked.

He'd thought the same moments earlier but the need to reassure his crew overrode his own fear. "Do you feel dead?" Tor straightened to his full height. "Do the dead feel pain? Are you not still wet and cold? Do your hands not bleed from the oars, your back ache from rowing? Wherever we are, we are destined to be here."

He studied the welcoming shore, the cliffs curving to either side of the cove—a natural harbor. To his right, the cliff jutted out a few feet from the beach, then dipped into shadow before it continued out to sea for perhaps a mile.

Tor infused his voice with all the confidence of a desperate man hoping to be right. "Ottar sent us into exile, to starve and die, but the gods brought us to a new home." He gestured to the beach. "We will survive. We will *thrive*."

The murmurs subsided. Someone gave a ragged cheer.

"Will we be safe here?" Runa rubbed her distended belly.

Tor smiled. "Safer than in that storm. Safer than under Ottar's rule."

He stared again at the land. A shiver of unease slid down his spine. There was something about the trees.

Colors. In spring, trees burst green with new growth, but these… A few spruce were scattered through the forest, but most of the trees were oaks, with some alder and maple mixed in. Orange, yellow, even red. The colors of autumn, of harvest.

How can that be? Three days ago it was spring. How can we lose a whole summer?

No, impossible. Think about it later. Right now they needed to make sure the land was safe for them. They couldn't stay at sea forever. "Let's get a scouting party ashore."

~ * ~

Even running, it took Kiana an endless fifteen minutes to reach the base of the mountain and begin the climb to the winter caves. Generations of villagers had smoothed the path, but to her the trail stretched forever. The acrid stench of burned leaves and pine needles stung her eyes and made her nose itch. Once she stopped to cough and catch her breath.

Thank the Lady this morning's rain quenched any fires.

When she finally rounded the familiar boulder, she skidded to a halt. A single entrance protected the series of caves the villagers used for winter quarters. That entrance—easy to defend and shore up against the blasts of ice night storms—no longer existed. Piles of shattered rocks filled the space, the fall so deep it covered half the plateau.

"Beren!" she shouted. She didn't expect an answer. How could anyone survive that avalanche?

"Here." A child's voice, weak and fearful.

Shocked, she spun in a circle. Not Beren. "Eskil?"

The thundering of her heart deafened her so she had to strain to hear the answering call. To her left. Oh, thank the Lady, to her *left*, not in front, not under that mass of earth and rock.

She squinted through clouds of lingering dust. There. A large rock marked the far edge of the plateau, and peeking from behind it, a pale shape. Relief and fear shot through her at sight of the child's ashen face.

"Here, Kiana." He waved to draw her closer. "We're here."

We. She swallowed the leap of hope and sprinted to the boy. When she rounded the rock, she understood why he hadn't run to meet her.

The rock leaned over his head to form a shallow cave between its bulk and the edge of the plateau. Somehow the boy had wedged himself into the cave. The angle of the balanced rock deflected most of the debris over his head and into the trees below, but some had fallen close enough to form a solid barrier that left an opening a hand's-breadth wide.

Eskil crouched close to the opening, the space behind him hidden in the dark. With Beren's dusky skin he'd blend into the shadows, and where was Arkin? Eskil shifted and a ray of daylight allowed her to glimpse the other figures huddled behind him.

"Beren." She breathed the word, terrified all over again when the figure didn't move.

"We're stuck, Kiana." Eskil's voice shook. "There was a fire in the sky, and Arkin carried us here but now we can't get out."

She squinted at the dark shapes in the shadows behind him. "Are you hurt? Beren, are you hurt?"

"He hit his head when I pushed him in here." Arkin answered this time. "Some rocks came down on his leg, but he breathes. I just can't move him. And we can't get out." His words ended on a squeak, and Kiana recognized the imminent panic. Young as he was, the boy had protected the two children half his age.

"I'll get you out. Eskil, your mother's not far behind, and she has some of the warriors with her, so we'll all get you out." She touched his hand to calm the boy. After all, at five he was just a year younger than Beren.

Eskil clutched her hand, but his eyes weren't quite so wide and white now, and when he spoke, the tension in his voice was noticeably less. "I didn't know if anyone would come," he confessed. "Arkin said so, but I didn't believe."

"Of course we'd come." She forced a teasing smile. "We need strong warriors like you to keep the village safe."

The boy said nothing, but his grip on her hand eased.

How badly was Beren injured? To distract herself, she studied the barrier trapping the three boys. Several large rocks blocked them in, but dirt and many smaller rocks and stones made up the bulk of the pile. Thank the Lady, it wouldn't take long to clear away.

"Tell me about the fire in the sky," she ordered, more to keep herself sane than to distract the boys. "How did you see it before it hit the mountain?"

"We were leaving, but Beren forgot his flute." Arkin's voice no longer trembled. "We turned back, but the sky… It was such a strange color, just for a few moments, then this big ball of fire came straight toward us and we dove under the rock."

The other women arrived, panting. No time to worry about the mystery of the object.

Miri ran to Kiana. "My boy?"

"Mama." Eskil pressed his face close to the opening, and his mother reached for him.

"Miri, stop. He's stuck." Kiana drew her away. "We have to loosen the rocks first or you'll hurt him."

Tears streamed down the woman's cheeks. "Thank the gods you're alive."

"Aw, Mama." Eskil sniffed and drew back.

"Eskil was very brave. He stayed with Beren and Arkin and looked out for them while they waited for rescue." It didn't matter Eskil had no choice about waiting, and the compliment soothed him some more. Kiana peered over his shoulder and winked at Arkin.

The older boy smiled.

Miri stared past Eskil into the shallow cave. "Arkin? Beren?"

Eskil answered first. "Arkin's all right. He saved us by pushing us in here. But Beren's hurt, Mama."

Kiana touched Miri's arm. "We need to lift these rocks. Can you help?"

Miri bared her teeth in a fierce grin. "Of course."

They set to work. It felt like eons before they'd cleared enough debris for Eskil and Arkin to crawl out. Kiana thrust her head and shoulders inside and let her vision adjust to the dimness. Beren lay on his side, his face toward the opening.

"Beren, I'm here." She didn't know if he heard her. His eyes were closed, but his chest rose and fell in a steady rhythm.

She skimmed her hand down his leg and discovered his ankle trapped under a large rock. Just one, thank the Lady, not a cluster. Let it not have crushed the foot as well.

She backed out of the space and turned to the other women. "All right, let's get the rest of this out of the way. Slowly."

When the opening was big enough, Kiana squeezed in and wrapped her arms around Beren's chest. "Now lift while I pull."

Ignoring his moans, she dragged the boy onto clear ground and bent to examine him. Blood on his forehead. A lump in his hair above his left eye. *He'll have a headache.* He wore the sleeveless tunic and short leggings of the locals. Scrapes and bruises on his arms and legs but nothing serious.

His ankle was another matter, swollen to twice its normal size. Kiana cut away the constricting hide boot and probed the flesh. She let out a breath when bone shifted beneath her touch.

"Broken, not crushed," she reported to the others. "We'll have to carry him back. I don't want that ankle to move more than it has to." *Can I carry him that far?*

"I'll do it." Kari, one of the trainees, fished with her father, heaving the loaded nets aboard his boat, and could easily manage Beren's slight weight.

"Good. Let me prepare the ankle first." Kiana needed to ensure it didn't move. Even dangling from gentle arms might cause a weakened bone to snap. "Get me some short branches, a dozen or so, about the length of my forearm."

The two trainees hurried into the forest. Miri, after settling Eskil and Arkin on a boulder at the edge of the plateau, approached. "Can I do something?"

Kiana studied her woven overtunic. The trainees, like Kiana, wore leather, too stiff for the purpose she needed. "Yes. Cut some long strips off your tunic to wrap around this leg."

Miri drew her bone knife from under her belt. When the other women returned with a handful of branches each, Kiana sorted through the offerings until she found the four straightest. Using those and the strips of cloth Miri handed her, she soon had Beren's lower leg strapped to the branches. Satisfied the ankle was safe from jolts and bumps, she backed away, nodded to Kari.

The woman lifted the boy in her arms, then headed down the trail with the other trainee. Kiana took a step to follow but a shout from Miri made her pause.

"Wait, Kiana. There's something you need to see."

Kiana wanted to brush her off, to rush after Beren, but the urgency in Miri's tone told her not to ignore the woman. "What is it?"

"In the cove."

From the edge of the plateau, the mountain curved toward the cove two miles north of the village. The air was still thick with settling dust, but clear enough to reveal three strange ships floating near the shore, easily visible from this height.

"Did they bring the fire ball?" Arkin asked.

If they did, the village was in more trouble than just the loss of their winter shelter.

Chapter Two

Tor stared at Emund's ship and cursed. With its deep hull, the *knorr* had run aground on a hidden sandbank, tearing a hole just above the waterline where the storm waves had weakened the wood. Tor hurried to the stern of his ship and cupped his hands around his mouth to shout toward his other brother's longship.

"Beade, drop anchor." The longships were shallow enough to clear the obstruction, but they'd be too far away to protect Emund if it came to a fight.

Beade nodded and turned to give orders. Tor's crew released their own anchor. Soon both ships bobbed close to shore in the protected cove.

"Right," he said. "Let's see what's ashore. Vider and…" He studied the crew huddled over the oars and pointed. "You three. Come with me."

Tor and the others jumped over *The Hammer's* side and landed waist-deep in water little warmer than what the storm had tossed at them. Five more men joined them from Beade's ship, although Beade himself remained aboard as war-leader in Tor's absence.

"What about Emund?" Vider stared at the beached *knorr* while they waded ashore.

"No." Tor didn't look at his brother's ship. "He'll need to inspect the damage. Besides, he's got all those animals, and they're bound to panic if water starts coming in."

Once ashore, Tor gauged the distance to the ships and studied the beach. Only a narrow rim of wet sand edged the water. High tide.

His spirits rose. "We can wait for the tide to withdraw, then unload the women and animals. Dry land will be closer to Emund then, and they shouldn't get too wet."

Recalling how they arrived there, Tor squinted at the mountain. No sign remained of the metal orb, now buried under rock and rubble.

Even the fires in the surrounding trees had burned themselves out.

What about the people in the orb. Did they survive?

He shrugged. They posed no threat at the moment. Once everyone was safe he'd take time to check it out, but practicalities came first.

"Ivar, take two men and search inland." To two of Beade's men, "Follow the shoreline north. Vider and I will head south." He turned to the remaining three. "Stand watch here. This land looks empty, but let's make sure. Shout if you see anyone."

With a nod, they strode off.

While he walked, Tor's mind crowded with problems. Mentally he counted them.

First, daylight. The sun, overhead not long ago, now edged toward the western horizon far out at sea. With luck they'd have time to set up a camp before full night.

Second, trees. It shouldn't be autumn, but the color of the leaves... He had pregnant animals on his ships ready to birth so any milk needed to be shared with the newborns if the flock was to grow. Casks held grain and seeds ready to plant, but no time to grow anything before winter.

So, third, food and shelter. If there were settlements, trade was a possibility, or outright theft if the natives proved hostile. Only then might his people survive.

As to how they lost a summer in getting here... Never mind. Time enough later to worry about that.

"I doubt there's a threat," Vider murmured after a few minutes. "We saw no smoke from settlements, and it's cool enough to need a fire."

Thinking of his third problem, Tor hoped he was wrong. "You can never tell."

Vider's gaze strayed to the mountain again. "It flamed. Why didn't the trees burn longer?"

"Feel the air." Vider sniffed, and Tor continued, "It's damp. Maybe just rained."

"We might have problems getting the wood to burn, then. Campfires will be needed tonight."

"Perhaps you should be leader instead of me," Tor teased. "You've a more level head."

Vider shuddered. "And deal with all those people? No, friend, it's you they followed into exile. I'm just glad I had no family to bring. You have more than enough, with those brothers of yours and their wives."

"Not to mention Runa," Tor added with a sideways look at his friend.

Vider shrugged but ducked his head. Tor chuckled.

They climbed the tree-covered hill bounding the southern edge of the cove. Vider stopped every few paces to mark their back trail by bending branches or carving a slice of bark from a tree trunk. Leaves crunched underfoot. The crisp air caressed Tor's skin and reminded him of the first spring day that promised the end of winter.

Or the first day of fall.

He frowned.

"Do you see something?" Vider drew his sword.

"No." Tor was unwilling to pursue that other worry yet. "Best to be wary."

They proceeded with more caution, swords at the ready. The hill descended in a gentle slope into woodlands. Trees closed over their heads and the sun dimmed to occasional shafts of light spearing through breaks in the leaves. Tor, in the lead, estimated they'd walked for half an hour without seeing so much as a curious squirrel or hearing the chirp of birds. No surprise with the presence of humans.

"Do you smell something?" Vider murmured.

Tor sniffed. "Wood smoke?" People.

He raised his sword and took another step. Without warning, the ground erupted beneath him. He lost his grip on his weapon and it flew out of reach before woven ropes closed around him and dragged him into the air. His arms and legs fell through the gaps, leaving his body trapped inside a strong net. Vider shouted and leapt forward. Another net sprang up around the first mate, but he managed to keep a grip on his sword and was able to hack his way out. He headed toward Tor, but a spear landed quivering at his feet, forcing him back. A second dug into the ground beside it.

"Go," Tor shouted. "Warn the others."

Vider paused. An arrow skimmed his ear, drawing blood. With a helpless shake of his head, he turned and ran.

The rain of spears stopped. The forest stilled. All was silent save for the creak of the ropes around Tor. A moment later, five women emerged from behind the surrounding trees.

"Who are you?" He regretted the question immediately. He should have stayed silent. Curiosity showed weakness.

The women crept forward without speaking. They were all as fair-skinned and blonde as his own people. Three were dressed in serviceable skirts and carried barbed spears. The remaining two wore men's trews and had bows strung and ready, aimed at him. One drew a knife and sliced through a length of rope stretched beside a tree.

His prison fell to the ground. He gathered himself to attack, but someone hit him from behind, enough to daze him. The women pulled his hands behind his back and secured them with leather thongs.

I don't believe it. On shore less than an hour and captured by a handful of women.

He struggled and cursed, but the women stood back until he tired of the fruitless effort.

When they at last hauled him to his feet and pointed their spears at him, he had no choice but to stumble along before them. Not a word was said. Their intentions were clear.

He fumed. *Stupid.* Blundering around a strange land with a single companion—what had he been thinking? Whether he freed himself or Vider came, Tor's pride was already lost.

Five minutes later they entered the village. A scattering of huts draped in hides sprawled over a sandy area leading to a shallow beach where several fishing boats lay. Like the cove with his ships, cliffs jutted out to either side of a sheltered bay. Farther out to sea, a white line of wavelets marked a reef, protection from the rougher water beyond.

Women, some with babes in their arms, lounged against doorways and stared at him with suspicion. Two old men paused in mending their nets, while several children ran toward the newcomers, dancing and pointing.

Tor fought a sudden impulse to duck his head in embarrassment. *This must be how a slave feels when first displayed to its captors.*

Instead he raised his chin and stared forward. His guards marched him toward a larger hut near the center of the village. *Few men in view. Good. Easier for Vider and my crew to take over when they arrive.*

One woman led the way into the large hut while two others pushed Tor through the entrance. Inside was dark, but he blinked until the room came into focus. The women pushed him forward, and two men, both of middle years, took his arms.

Several old men stood around the edges of the hut. In the center sat a massive wooden chair, with legs and arms shaped like the feet of a great beast, and a tall back carved into intricate lines and curves. It probably was meant to convey importance, but dwarfed the man who sat in it. This, then, must be their chieftain.

He appeared of an age with Tor's father, his blond hair and beard sprinkled with gray. The man's muscles declared him no soft politician, but if he'd ever wielded a sword in battle, he'd escaped with no scars. This was a man used to hard work, a farmer or fisherman, not a warrior. He wore clothes similar to Tor's, but around his shoulders draped a huge cloak of dyed wool decorated with a collar of claws, each the length of a short dagger.

A chill swept down Tor's spine. *What kind of animal has claws that long*?

The two men forced Tor to kneel before the great chair. The woman who preceded him into the hut now bowed before the chieftain, then whispered in his ear. When she finished, both stared at Tor, who bared his teeth in a silent snarl. The chieftain said something to the woman and waved her from the hut. She left without a backward glance. The chieftain glared at Tor and spoke.

The words were strange, familiar but…*twisted*…somehow. Tor remained silent. He guessed he was being asked where he came from, but even had he understood the words, he'd not give the man the satisfaction of an answer.

Several times the chieftain spoke, his tone louder and angrier with each phrase. Still Tor refused to say anything. He was prepared to wait until his men arrived.

This chieftain wouldn't be so confident once his village was surrounded by seasoned warriors.

~ * ~

The village was in uproar when the rescue party returned. Miri took charge, herding the children and the trainee carrying Beren toward the healer's hut. Kiana paused, wondering at the cause of this latest crisis.

A woman dressed like Kiana in men's clothing ran from the chieftain's hut. "You must come at once. Uncle Soren requests your presence."

"Not now, Lida. Beren needs me." Kiana sidestepped past her friend.

Lida shifted to block her path. "It's because of the prisoner."

Prisoner? Kiana stopped, heart pounding. *Has Ajmal found us*? She clutched Lida's arm. "This prisoner. Is he dark-skinned, like me?"

"No, yellow hair, light skin."

Releasing her hold, Kiana suppressed a sigh. *Not Ajmal*. She frowned when a more probable answer sprang to mind. The strangers in the cove?

"Chieftain Soren requests you go straight to the council hut when you return," Lida continued.

Soren *requested*, not ordered—a small victory.

The expression on Lida's face drew Kiana's attention. "There's more?"

Her friend cleared her throat. "The man wasn't alone. The other escaped."

"Ah." Kiana cursed under her breath. "He'll be back. Best gather everyone together and arm anyone who can hold a spear or bow."

Unable to do anything for Beren, Kiana was grateful for a task she *could* help with.

Her first sight of the prisoner after entering Soren's hut gave her pause. Two guards, the last men left in the village who weren't children or ancients, flanked the kneeling man. Tangled blond hair hung down his back to below his shoulders. With his hands bound behind him, arm muscles strained. She imagined those hands crushing an enemy's throat.

Kiana grimaced. This man brought danger to her new home, to Beren. He caused what the boys called a fire ball to batter a mountain onto the heads of innocent children. This wasn't a man to admire.

He was, however, a warrior, proud and fierce, and in another life one she might have gladly fought beside. Tall, even on his knees, he braced, shoulders back, chin raised. No doubt he glared defiance into the chieftain's eyes.

Soren sat in the great chair he'd purchased from a travelling merchant last summer. There was nothing like it in the village, but from the scowl on Soren's face it failed to awe this stranger with the chieftain's importance and power.

Kiana strode forward and bowed. "How may I be of service?"

Soren gestured to the man. "He doesn't speak nor seem to understand me."

She turned. Avoiding his face for now, she studied the man's clothes.

These were familiar, similar to those the village fishers wore—leather leggings over hide boots, a sleeveless leather tunic laced together with leather ties over a long-sleeved cloth shirt in a faded red. Salt stained his clothes in patches. A woven belt, tied at his waist, held a horn at one side and a loop for a sword on the other.

Good. Lida remembered her training and had taken that from him first thing. A hardened warrior, then. Kiana wondered how her raw recruits had managed to capture him. *Ah, there.* A few strands of thin rope were caught in his sleeve. The sturdy nets were used to haul in the largest sea beasts in these waters, not just seals but whales and even giant squid, so were strong enough to hold a man. Satisfied, she resumed her study and at last raised her gaze to the man's face.

Shock had her clamping her lips together to smother a gasp. *It's him, the man in mother's augury.*

Her heart thumped in her chest. *Breathe.*

Two years ago her mother had shown Kiana this man's face in her temple fires, a light-skinned barbarian with hair the color of the desert sands and eyes a brilliant blue. He looked older than her then-eighteen years, perhaps in his early twenties? She judged his features pleasing, even with a scar on his left cheek and covered by a thick beard.

Her mother's next words left her breathless. *He is your destiny.*

The priestesses were gifted prophets, none more so than her mother, but this? This was impossible.

Kiana had scoffed at the time. *My destiny is with Ajmal*. Ajmal was her future, not some stranger from who knew where. Ajmal.

Until he betrayed everything she held dear.

Now there knelt this same man, yellow hair, yellow beard, scar. He appeared the same age he'd looked in the smoke, but she was now two years older, and he didn't seem so ancient. In build and features he resembled her hosts, his skin pale beneath a sea tan. His eyes were a deep blue, reminding her of the waters of the inland sea her people had sailed for generations. His expression, however, was different, not the languid, smoldering stare that still haunted her dreams. The bared teeth and set jaw showed hatred and determination.

She made herself stare into those eyes, daring the man to drop his gaze. He did, at last, but not before a flicker of uncertainty creased his brow.

"Who are you?" There was no answer, and no flash of recognition for the language of her adopted home, nor for her own language or any of the other languages she knew. Nothing. She wagered the man understood none of them.

So it was up to her to learn his.

As a daughter of the king's wizard and the high priestess, she possessed a special gift, the gift of tongues. If she heard just a few words, the language blossomed full-blown in her memory as if she was born to it. That talent, perhaps more than her warrior's skills, had placed her in the queen's personal guard.

But to learn the prisoner's language he had to speak, and he refused.

"Hold him," she ordered the guards.

Each seized an arm with one hand and placed the other on one of his shoulders.

He tensed and frowned, wondering, perhaps, what torture they planned for him.

Kiana stood in front of him. Even kneeling his head was on a level with her own. She cradled his face in her hands and curled her fingers into his beard to keep his head still. While it appeared coarse, the hair was softer to her touch than she expected, and she itched to stroke it.

No, not now. Not yet.

She bent forward and kissed him.

A shock like lightning coursed from her mouth to her core. The touch of his lips on hers tingled with short bursts of fire. Only firm will kept her from reacting, even though she wanted to moan in pleasure. The man flinched. Had he felt it too?

It doesn't matter. I can't let this distract me.

She opened her eyes, surprised she had closed them, and found herself staring into the man's half-closed eyes, his expression dazed.

Languid. Smoldering.

Forcing down her uncertainty, she concentrated on the success of the first part of her plan. She kept a half smile on her face when she stepped back. The man focused his gaze on her, and his own lips began a slow smug curve upward.

Kiana yanked on his beard.

Chapter Three

The man roared—there was no other word to describe the sound—and reared back, but the guards' grip on his arms and shoulders prevented him from surging to his feet. Kiana released her hold, and his roar changed to curses.

She needed two or three words for her gift to give her the knowledge, but the words coming from this man's mouth made no sense. Oh, she understood them, but their grouping…dragons spawned from she-devils? Pigs with horns? Or…by the Lady, *fangs*?

At last the words she sought slipped into her mind, and she interrupted the man's tirade with a snapped order. "*Á sér sitja*."

He stopped speaking, and his mouth hung open.

Satisfied she'd used the right words for him to be quiet, Kiana faced Soren. "What do you want to know?"

"How many men does he have, and how long before they attack?" Having seen Kiana's talent at work when she first arrived in the village, Soren showed little surprise or even approval at her success.

She doubted the man would answer the question, but she turned to him, refusing to flinch at the raw hatred in his stare. "We hold your life," she began. "Do you understand your danger here?"

His eyes widened, then narrowed. "How do you speak my tongue?"

"Do you understand your danger here?" she repeated in the same flat tone, ignoring his question.

He was silent for a moment, then dipped his head in a stiff nod.

"Good. Answer our questions, and you may live. Refuse and we can make you wish for death." Not even the toughest fisher in the village had the stomach for torture, nor did she, but the man didn't need to know that. "How many men do you have?"

His mouth thinned even more. He raised his chin and shifted his gaze to stare over her shoulder. She sighed. *Why are men so stubborn*?

She expected more silence, but after a moment he swung his gaze back to her and curled his lips in a fierce grin, white teeth flashing through his beard. "Thousands."

Her heartbeat thundered in her ears. She gasped. She didn't believe the number, but that grin… That grin shot heat to her core, sweat to her palms.

Enough. She narrowed her eyes. "Those ships are too small to hold thousands."

He blinked, then flashed his grin again. "My ships are bigger than they look."

A twinge of admiration for his bravado threatened to undermine Kiana's resolve. *Focus*. She curled her fingers against her legs. "How many men?" she repeated.

He continued to smirk.

What to do next? He'd shown them no threat so far, but there was a chance he'd come to raid the village. This place was hers, at least for now, and she'd not allow another invader to drive her from her home.

Not even one who invaded her dreams.

She turned to translate the man's words, but at that moment Lida rushed in.

"Men in the woods, around the village." Her hands shook on her bow, but her voice remained firm.

Soren rose and jerked his head at the prisoner. "Bring that one." He strode from the hut.

The guards wrenched the man to his feet and shoved him toward the door. He towered over them, and had to bend to exit through the doorway.

Holy Inanna, even her dreams hadn't shown the true size of the man.

Everyone in the village gathered around the central hut. The injured and ill from the healer's hut huddled near the wall. Dangerous, keeping them all together, but easier to defend.

Beren sat with Inga, the village healer, unconscious still, a cloth around his head and his leg covered in thick wrappings. Anger filled Kiana. By the Lady, if these raiders planned to hurt her prince, her friends…

She drew her sword and strode to the front of the outer circle, between Soren and the prisoner, once again on his knees. She placed her sword at his throat. If his men attacked, he'd be the first to die.

Several strangers hovered at the edge of the forest, armed but their weapons sheathed. A movement in the woods drew her attention to the right. From the trees emerged three people. Two—no, *one* warrior.

The other man, perhaps twenty years older, with eyes that squinted in the sun and a body better suited to lifting pebbles than swords, was dressed in a plain brown robe. Between them walked…a very pregnant woman.

Their prisoner surged forward and almost impaled himself in Kiana's sword before his guards pulled him back. "*Runa.*"

~ * ~

Tor struggled against the men who held him. The woman's sword nicked his throat, and he stilled. Something in her stance, in the way she looked at him, warned him not to underestimate her. A shield maid, for certain, although he'd never met one who stirred his blood as this one did.

Runa approached, reminding him of the danger. He had no choice but to watch his sister stride into the middle of the enemy camp.

What is she thinking? She was no fool, but this action made him wonder if madness ran in the family. First his own lapse of judgement that resulted in his capture, now this. If a bargain needed to be made, why, by Odin's beard, weren't Emund or Beade here? Why weren't his brothers leading this…this foolish meeting, not his irritating sister? She should be back in camp, safe.

"Get out of here," he shouted.

One of his guards dragged his head back by the hair and shoved a dirty rag into his mouth before releasing him. Tor's protests turned into muffled growls. Runa spared him a glance, her expression warning him not to interfere, before turning her attention to the leader of these people.

The man might not be a war leader like Tor, but, despite the vanity shown by that ridiculous chair in his hut, he'd not be a man to cross.

Runa strode toward the chieftain, Vider on one side of her and Jorvik, thin and pale, on the other. Tor understood why Vider was there. His first mate was a warrior able to protect Runa to the death, but why Jorvik? Even as he asked himself the question, the answer came. The seer knew many languages, so perhaps not surprising Vider had brought him.

Runa paused before the chieftain. "We come in peace." She held out her empty hands. The woman beside Tor murmured to the chieftain, who stared first at Runa, then at the two men beside her, and last at Runa's belly. He said something in return, and Jorvik frowned in concentration.

"Well?" Runa asked.

"I'm not sure," he admitted with a frown. "The words are like ours or the Danes, but not quite. I think he asked about a child?"

"He said you must love your husband much to risk your child to his enemies," the shield maid corrected.

Tor glanced at her, at the tension in her shoulders, despite her seeming calm.

"You speak our language?" Runa asked in surprise.

The woman gave a brief nod but said no more.

Runa shrugged and bowed her head to the chieftain. "Please tell him we don't wish you harm. We are traders, not enemies. If my foolish brother has offended, we will make reparation."

Tor struggled, trying to shout a protest. Foolish? Reparation?

She shot him a quelling glance. "Let me handle this."

Anger and fear for Runa turned the world red. He sputtered, strained against his captors. Madness to risk her child.

The village woman spoke to the leader. Tor jerked his gaze to her. Strange. Was there less tension in her body now?

While the chieftain and Runa conversed through the woman's translation, Tor studied the surroundings. All the villagers clustered around this central area with few men in the group. Some women held bows or spears. He'd not underestimate women warriors, but these held their weapons loosely, as if unseasoned. The woman beside him, though, who now withdrew her sword from his throat…she'd not hesitate.

He returned his attention to Runa and the conversation. To his surprise, she was explaining how they arrived in this place. "We were in a great storm and a great metal ball of fire appeared in the lightning. It made a hole in the air and pulled us through to this land, or at least to the sea off this land."

Surprise, disbelief, filled the village chieftain's eyes.. "This fire ball—you didn't bring it to attack us?"

"*No*. It captured *us* and brought us here." Runa waved her hand at the village huts. "I didn't see it attack here. It went straight to that mountain over there."

After the woman translated the words, she and the chieftain conversed together for a few minutes.

At last Tor managed to spit out the rag. "Runa. What are you doing?"

"We need allies, brother. The more we tell them about us, the less they might be inclined to kill you." Her voice was dry with sarcasm.

His guards tightened their grip but didn't bother replacing the gag.

The chieftain turned to Runa, stopping any further conversation. "We have no wish to be enemies," he said through the woman translator. "We will speak further." He glanced at Vider and Jorvik, and for the first time a smile twisted his lips. "You may keep your protectors, but perhaps you should also have brought a midwife."

Runa grinned, a true grin, not feigned. "I still have some time. This child isn't ready to come into the world yet." She turned to Vider. "Send the men back to the ships."

"No." Odin's beard, Tor didn't know whether he wanted to strangle his sister or his friend. At least they had the sense to bring more men with them, but to now send them away? "This could be a trick." He glared at Vider. "And since when did you take orders from my sister?"

Vider opened his mouth, but Runa interrupted. "Since Vider is a warrior, and we need a peacekeeper."

The woman with the sword slipped it into a sheath on her back and nodded to the men behind Tor, who released his arms. She drew a dagger and cut his bonds. When he surged to his feet she stepped back. He wanted to…he didn't know what he wanted to do, but he'd not give her the satisfaction of being the one to break this truce.

The woman waved to the central hut. "Come."

He didn't want to *come*. He wanted to rage at Runa, at Vider, at anyone but himself. The gods knew he wasn't a prideful man, but these last few hours proved he wasn't the level-headed trader he considered himself. Coming through that strange hole from the storm must have addled his wits. It made perfect sense to deal with these people. Hadn't he wished for just that when he and Vider set out from the cove? Of course these people defended themselves. Why, then, was he so bad-tempered?

Yet one look at *that woman* brought the memory of that amazing kiss surging back, and all his common sense vanished. He glared at her and planted his feet.

She glared right back, then shrugged. "Come with your sister, then."

Turning, she marched into the central hut, annoyance in every line of her body. Ah, what a body. Similar to the women who had captured him, she wore leather trews and a sleeveless vest, but her skin, unlike everyone else in this village, was dark, almost golden, her arms strong with muscle yet still feminine. Instead of blonde curly hair, hers was black as night and hung straight as water in a tail down her back. It reminded him of women he'd seen in the Southlands. Even her eyes fascinated him…dark, mysterious, and that gaze so easy to fall into and be lost. Unbidden, another memory of her kiss came to mind and his lower body hardened. He dug his fingernails into his palms, the pain a welcome distraction.

Tor took a deep breath. No matter how fascinating the woman, he'd rather forget that moment of weakness. He'd deal with her later.

Right now he needed to find out what madness had taken his sensible first mate.

He strode to the trio still arguing in the clearing. Well, Runa and Vider argued, while Jorvik stood well back. Smart man.

"Go back to the ships, Runa," Tor ordered when he joined them. "We'll take care of these savages."

Runa glanced at him and placed her hands on her hips. "How? By attacking women and children? Don't be absurd, brother. We need them. We can't afford to make any enemies now."

"Of course I'm not going to attack them. What do you take me for?" He turned to Vider. "And why isn't Emund or Beade leading this…this…?"

"Rescue?" Runa finished. That wasn't the word he intended, but she carried on without giving him a chance to protest. "Because they can't." She hunched forward, her face flushed, gaze fierce. "Beade was injured in the storm, hit his head, and sees double. His wife is caring for him, and Emund stayed back to protect the families should I have misjudged."

"Misjudged?" Tor clenched his teeth. "Woman, we're standing in the middle of a village where I was held prisoner, still am if these people turn treacherous."

"They found two warriors wandering close to their wives, their children. What did you expect them to do? Welcome you with open arms?" He winced, and she held up a hand, closed her eyes for a moment. "I'm sorry, brother, but we *need* them. We have to try it this way first."

Tor turned to Vider, but his friend just sighed in resignation. "She has good reason, much as I hate to admit it, but I don't like sending everyone away. This could turn at an instant."

"Perhaps," Runa said, "but we have to risk it. We still need to make friends with them." She glanced at Tor, then returned her attention to Vider. "Have the men withdraw to that clearing we passed on the way here. They'll still be close enough to hear us if we need them."

Vider turned to Jorvik. "You tell them. I'm staying here."

Tor bristled. "I am still your leader."

"Then lead with your head, not your pride." Runa waved around them. "What do you see?"

He spared the surroundings a quick glance. "A village."

She sighed. "Around it."

Around it? "Trees." *Ah.* The reason he'd hoped to find a settlement in the first place. Autumn. Food.

He'd lived through one winter five years ago after a harsh summer where plants withered for lack of water, leaving a harvest too sparse to feed them through the cold months. Meat they had in plenty, and fish, but still, many of the elderly and children starved that year before an alliance with the Danes across the short ocean allowed them to trade for much needed fruit, vegetables, and bread.

They needed that from these people now.

Sanity returned, and Tor sighed. "Yes, we need them. Somehow we've lost a summer. Our stores won't last if winters here are as long as they are at home, and we'll need more than fish." He frowned. "All we have to do is think of something to trade with. We didn't leave home with much."

Runa stroked his arm, the familiar gesture soothing his worries. "We've been given a second chance at life here. We left Ottarshavn because of Ottar's bloodthirsty, treacherous ways."

"We left because he raped you and got you with child." Tor at once regretted the harsh words, and softened his tone. "And you'd not let me challenge him." That still hurt.

Runa paled, then firmed her lips. "I'd not have you die as our father did."

Tor closed his eyes. He didn't know how Ottar had defeated Olaf Strongarm, but not even the priest believed the fight had been fair. Why else did so many follow Tor into exile?

He opened his eyes and gathered his dignity. "Very well. I'll speak with them, and we'll find out if these people in fact do want peace."

"*I* will speak with them," she corrected. He stiffened but her expression softened, turned pleading. He wasn't fooled for a minute. "Tor, I know you. Your pride has been hurt and that may affect your skill with your tongue." She paused at Vider's snicker, rolled her eyes. "You know what I mean. You're not calm enough right now to negotiate."

Tor bristled. "I'm calm."

Runa just stared at him. Again he sighed. He hated it when she was right. This whole experience left him unsettled. Where had his trading skills disappeared to?

As if reading his mind, she stroked his arm again. "If you were silver-tongued like Jorvik we'd not be in exile."

"Then why isn't *he* doing the talking?" Tor shot Jorvik a glance, but that wise man had been backing away while they argued and now stood close to the trees. He cast Tor a sickly grin, then turned and fled into the forest.

Runa chuckled. "Because he has the courage of a field mouse."

Tor had to smile. She brushed past him to stride toward the central hut.

Chapter Four

His sister, not his wife.

The phrase repeated in Kiana's head without reason. What did it matter anyway? Why that twist of relief when the woman called the man brother? There might still be a wife somewhere and a dozen children.

Annoyed, she shook her head as if to banish the words, but still they echoed from afar. His sister, not his wife.

"Something troubles you, Kiana." Soren laid a hand on her arm. "Don't you trust the strangers?"

She hadn't trusted strangers in the last two years, even those she now called neighbors, but no need to speak of that. "Their tale is…difficult to believe."

"Yet something hit the mountain, and there was fire." He paused. "How are the boys? I heard your son was up there." *Your son*. As usual, the phrase sent a jolt through her. When they'd first arrived at the village, she'd tried to explain her relationship with Beren, but the villagers had grown tired of calling him *your friend's son* and simplified it. She hoped his mother would have understood.

"Beren's head was injured and his foot trapped in the rocks," she said. "I have yet to speak to the healer. Eskil and Arkin are fine, a few scratches."

Soren let out a breath. "Good. And the caves? How much damage was done?"

"We didn't have time to check, but it looks bad." She glanced at the mountain. "I'll go up again once this matter is settled."

The strangers entered the hut, and Soren said nothing more on the subject.

Kiana studied the sister. A strong woman, like Kiana herself, but not a warrior, not in that simple ankle-length blue dress, as like to trip her up as Miri's if she had to run. She wore her blonde hair in braids that fell from beneath a knotted head scarf. The man behind her… her husband? No. A husband walked at his wife's side, not behind or in front. Even her king held his queen as an equal, not another subject.

A shiver ran up her spine, and she pushed away the memory of Beren's parents.

The brother entered last.

All the breath left her body. His sheer presence filled the hut. It wasn't just his broad chest or thick, muscular arms. The man towered over her by a good head's height. Even Ajmal, the tallest of the royal guards, didn't stand more than two finger widths above her.

Another shiver skittered up her spine. At the memory of Ajmal? Or the sudden vision of wrestling this man in bed? Who was he? Why had his face appeared in her mother's augury smoke?

Kiana forced herself to breathe, to study the man as just another enemy, looking for weak spots and ignoring the fluttering in her belly.

To all appearances, he looked confident, but anger still simmered beneath the surface. No, not anger. Frustration? As if he wanted to be angry but strained to hold it in check?

Soren sat, gestured to the strangers to join him. Kiana and the man who accompanied the sister remained standing, arms crossed, the poses so similar she ducked her head to hide a smile. Beyond doubt, these people came from warrior stock, not like her current hosts.

"You wish to deal with us." Soren assumed the mantle of village chieftain instead of jailer. "What is it you want, and what do you have to trade?"

Kiana faced the seated warrior and translated, but it was his sister who replied. The warrior clenched his fists but said nothing. Kiana hid her surprise and reminded herself to listen to the words, to translate and not judge.

"First, mighty chieftain, let me make known to you who we are," began the woman. "We are Norsemen, from a great village many leagues from here. I am Runa, and this is my brother, Tor. Our father was Olaf, a chieftain of a great land across the seas."

"Anyone may call themselves chieftain," replied Soren.

When Kiana translated, Tor flushed in anger, but his sister just smiled. "That is true. Tell me, what weapons were our men holding when they came out of the woods?"

Puzzled, Kiana looked to Soren for direction. He shrugged and indicated she answer. She wasn't surprised. After all, she was the most familiar with weapons.

Staring into the distance, she envisioned the men surrounding the village, their companions in the center. "Your brother and your…guard?" She indicated the man standing across from her. "They carry swords, but the rest…" For a moment she closed her eyes to sharpen her memory. "They carried long sticks with blades on the end."

"Axes," supplied Runa, the word unfamiliar to Kiana even in translation. "The axe is a weapon for all our men, but the best warriors, the leading families, carry swords."

Soren frowned. "So because you carry swords you expect us to believe your words are true."

Tor scowled when Kiana translated, but Runa dipped her head in agreement. "Yes."

Soren stared at her, his expression unchanged, then he chuckled. He turned to Kiana. "She reminds me of you when you first arrived. Arrogant and stubborn." Without waiting for Kiana to comment, he turned to Runa. "Very well, continue your story."

She bowed her head in acknowledgement. "We and our brothers left our homeland many days ago, with families and friends, to seek a new land to settle. But we ran into a mighty storm. In the middle of this storm came the fire ball. It pulled us through a hole in the world into calm seas off these shores. My brother and others set out to explore. This is when you discovered him."

She gave her brother a look Kiana recognized as sisterly scorn. Her own sister had given her such looks, the sister she'd left behind to be slaughtered. Kiana crushed a pang of sorrow and guilt.

"What is it you wish from us?" asked Soren.

Runa took a deep breath. "Many of our stores were damaged in the storm. Winter comes soon here, does it not?"

"Most years within the next two months or less," Soren agreed.

Tor muttered a curse. His people faced starvation. No wonder his sister wanted to speak with Soren. The man behind Runa said nothing, but he stiffened and sweat beaded his forehead.

She looked at neither man but straightened her shoulders, as if the news confirmed a suspicion. "Then I fear we'll not have enough to survive and not enough time to grow and harvest more. We ask that we be allowed to share with you, to add our meager supplies to yours and winter together."

Tor growled deep in his throat, and Kiana agreed with his alarm. One in a weaker position didn't reveal that weakness during a negotiation.

"And in return?" Soren demanded.

Runa looked around the hut, then waved her hand at Kiana and the two other women who stood guard. "We can protect your village from attack, by man or beast. We have many warriors with us."

"We have warriors enough for that," Soren said. "Think you this is all?"

Runa frowned and turned to her brother to murmur a question. Their conversation was too low to hear, but if they were traders, perhaps they discussed what trade goods they had available.

"We can't let them starve, Uncle," Lida whispered on the other side of Kiana.

Soren turned to her. The hardness in his gaze softened, but his words sent a chill through Kiana. "We don't know how damaged the caves are. Until we check we have to assume the worst. We have no winter shelter other than this flimsy hide." He glanced at the walls of the hut. "I think, Lida, we have more important things to worry about than giving food to strangers. We haven't started stocking the caves, so we have food aplenty, but the first great storm will flatten these hovels. This is a *summer* camp, after all. We'll freeze in winter."

Lida paled. Few knew of the damage to the mountain. Kiana needed to confirm the extent and decide whether staying was still safe for her and Beren. South might be warmer, but more dangerous.

In the meantime, there were the strangers, *Norsemen*, people who had brought the flying fire to them, even if not on purpose. She understood Soren's reluctance to help them.

The fact remained, though, these Norsemen outnumbered the villagers. Until the men returned from their fishing venture—and even then, they were fishermen, not warriors—Kiana and her few trainees were responsible for protecting the village. Most of the time, their isolation kept them from the notice of enemies. They dare not anger the strangers or reject their plea. At least not yet.

She bent to Soren and whispered her concern. He nodded but said nothing.

Runa straightened and cleared her throat. "Perhaps a trade in furs? We are great hunters and have many fine hides."

After she translated, Kiana bent closer to Soren. "Hides will keep us warm over the winter."

"Not enough, but I think we'll get no better offer, for now." He studied their guests. "In the meantime, you will find out the extent of the damage to the caves. I trust no one else to be able to defend themselves should these Norsemen also search out the caves."

"Of course." She glanced at the strangers. "What do I tell them?"

Soren stroked his chin. "Tell them we accept their bargain, and they may begin building their settlement."

"But isn't that too dangerous? So close to us?" Kiana had trouble keeping her voice low. She didn't want the strangers to notice her surprise.

He gave her a knowing smile. "I said they may *begin* to build. I didn't say we'd allow them to finish. It all depends on what you find at the caves."

Kiana straightened, her mind filling in the rest of Soren's words. *And this will give us time until the men return and our numbers are more even.*

She relayed Soren's words. Runa looked relieved, but Tor's scowl deepened, as if he didn't trust them. Wise man. Kiana kept her hand on her sword, as, she saw with approval, did Lida.

"We thank you for your words of wisdom." Runa bowed her head to Soren. "With your permission, I'll take my foolish brother…" Tor stiffened, and Kiana managed to hide her smile. "…and leave you in peace."

When Runa started to rise, Soren held up his hand, and she paused. "If we're to be neighbors, we need to learn more of each other. Kiana speaks your tongue, so she will come to your camp at times."

Kiana started at that unexpected command. So did Tor once she translated.

Runa, however, nodded as though the request wasn't unexpected. "Agreed."

The man behind her helped her to her feet. Despite herself, Kiana liked this Norse woman. Tor stood in one smooth motion, then glared at Kiana. "My sword," he commanded, as if he expected her to obey him.

"He wants his weapon," she translated to Soren, who motioned to Lida. Lida went outside, returning a moment later with a leather scabbard in her hand. Tor reached for it, but she slipped past him and handed it to Soren, who passed it to Kiana.

Before handing it over, Kiana paused, struck by the weight of it, lighter than her own sturdy blade, and longer. Curious, she drew the sword from its sheath. The metal was unfamiliar, and several nicks along the edge made it clear it had seen hard use. She swung it through the air. Yes, lighter, and it flexed a little. Scratches along the flat of the blade caught the light. She squinted, trying to make sense of the obvious words, but although able to speak the strangers' language, that skill didn't extend to reading their script.

"It's called *Foe-Cleaver*," Tor snapped. "It's one of the greatest swords of my people."

She smirked. "You give your weapons names?"

He said nothing and held out his hand with the arrogance of one daring her to refuse him. Kiana yearned to keep the weapon, to study this sword so different from her own. However, she slid it into its scabbard and handed it over.

For a moment, their hands brushed. A jolt of fire slid up her arm, but she managed not to flinch. Tor jerked back, then drew the sword from its sheath and gave it a close inspection. Did he think her trainees had damaged it? Or was he trying to hide his reaction to their touch?

He clasped the sword in an expert grip, and for a moment Kiana doubted the wisdom of returning it to him—it was obvious the man hadn't forgiven her for that humiliating kiss—but then he slid it into the scabbard and the scabbard into the loop on his belt. Without another word or glance, he took his sister's other arm and all but dragged her from the hut.

From behind Kiana, Lida sighed. "That," she whispered in awe, "is a warrior."

Kiana agreed, but kept silent on the matter. "I need to check on Beren." She bowed to Soren and hurried out.

Chapter Five

After sending the waiting warriors back to the cove where the ships lay anchored, Tor, Vider, and Runa proceeded at a slower pace. Tor paid little attention to their route, his mind circling around the bargain they'd made. He'd have to check how many furs they'd brought with them before the village emissary came to visit.

The village emissary. Black eyes framed by long black hair filled his mind. How soon before he glimpsed her again?

Bah, why should I care? She comes when she comes.

Runa interrupted Tor's straying thoughts. "No grumbling, brother?"

"I don't grumble," he grumbled, pushing past her.

The sound she made wasn't a snort because she was too dignified to snort. A vision of her crawling across the deck of his storm-tossed ship flitted through his mind. All right, perhaps *dignified* wasn't the right word. All the same…

He crested the last rise and gazed down the steep slope to the beach. Emund's ship lay tilted at an angle on the sandbank. The other two ships bobbed in the gentle waves, but already people were ashore and several men waded waist-deep carrying wives and children through the receding tide.

Hatred for the man who had exiled them threatened to overwhelm him. Ottar had allowed them only a single day to provision the ships before banishing them. That deadline meant there was only time to load the bull, some goats, and a few breeding animals onto Emund's *knorr*, none of them intended as food. Fresh water had been their main concern, along with seeds for planting and a few barrels of apples and plums, cress and other herbs to tide them over until harvest time. Only now there wouldn't be a harvest.

Tor studied the trees behind him. "If the chieftain spoke true, blood month is due soon." He spoke more to himself than the others, so was surprised when Vider responded.

"We don't have any spare animals to slaughter."

He nodded, then glanced at the mountain. "We'll need to find out more about the fire disk."

"Why?"

"There were people on it. If nothing else, it might have supplies we can use." Tor started down the hillside.

Vider followed. "As good an excuse as any to explore it."

"Not so fast," Runa called. "Would one of you please help me down this hill before I fall down it?"

Tor glanced back. Runa rested one hand on a tree trunk, the other at the small of her back. Despite the amusement in her voice, her shoulders sagged with fatigue.

"Let me carry you." Vider sprinted back up the hill and halted before Runa.

She raised an eyebrow at his eagerness. "Lift me and we both end up at the bottom faster than we want."

Undeterred, Vider swept her into his arms and headed down the slope. Tor grinned at the sight of his first mate trying not to stagger. A moment later, Vider sat down with Runa on his lap and slid the rest of the way. Tor wasn't sure if it had been intentional or not, but Runa's laughter lightened his heart when the two of them skidded past. It had been a long time since he'd heard that joyful sound from his sister.

He joined them a moment later. Back on her feet, Runa helped Vider sweep the mud and dead leaves from his backside. Their laughter made it clear they enjoyed the task…perhaps a little too much.

"Anyway, we'll need to see what furs we have for trading," Tor continued, as if the previous few minutes hadn't occurred.

"Do we have enough?" Runa straightened. Worry clouded her gaze.

"I'm sure we do." He held out his arms, and she hugged him. "It was a good idea to trade the furs. What we don't have we can hunt for once we're settled. We'll be fine."

She sighed. "I hope so. I'm tired of travelling and storms and fighting." Weariness filled her voice. Her limbs trembled. "I want to stop, just stop somewhere and settle. Let's just settle here."

Odin's beard, why hadn't he noticed it before? She was close to weeping, his strong Runa. She had resisted for months telling anyone who fathered her child, knowing it meant death or exile for those she loved, and when the knowledge came out, instead of staying in the home of her birth, she snuck aboard *The Hammer* to join her family in exile. She faced so many new experiences, not only birthing a child but raising it away from familiar surroundings. At least there were other women there to help her through the days ahead.

He gazed around him with fresh eyes. This land wasn't so bad. Perhaps his first impression was the true one after all, not a paradise, but a good land. He needed nightfall to confirm where they were, but the angle of the sun suggested not much farther north than their old home. That meant game in plenty, trees to be cut for shelter, and a vicious winter.

A fresh start, a new home, away from Ottar's poisonous rule.

Tor held Runa away from him. "You're right, as always. I'll check the fire disk first thing tomorrow. Where there are people, there must be food, and mayhap there is something there we can use or trade."

"Do you think there might be survivors?" she asked, once again frowning in concern.

"Doubtful. Half the mountain came down on top of it."

"You'll take care though." Not a question, but a command. Runa turned to Vider. "You'll go with him."

"Of course." Vider didn't grin, but his lips twitched at the order.

What to do first? "Food isn't our immediate need," Tor decided.

Vider strolled over. "My stomach disagrees."

Runa ducked her head, but Tor didn't miss the grin. Good to know Vider still had the talent to make her smile.

"We'll need shelter. Huts or at least a longhouse we can all crowd into." He tilted his chin at Emund's ship. "If we can't find what we need in the fire disk, we can start with that. It won't sail again, not without lots of repair, and it can't protect us like the other two ships. We can use the wood to build a frame, then start cutting trees."

"Agreed," Vider said.

Runa nodded. "So." She cast Tor a sly grin. "Who gets to tell Emund he's lost his ship?"

~ * ~

Kiana ducked to enter the healer's hut. "Inga? How is Beren?"

The healer pointed to a pallet by the wall. Conscious now, the boy fisted his hands in the fleece covering him, but the pain in his eyes wasn't for his leg. "Kiana, I lost my flute."

That flute meant the world to him, the one thing he'd brought with him from home. She sat on the edge of his pallet. "It was lucky you did."

"It was?" He stared at her in confusion.

"Arkin told me if you hadn't turned back to find it, you'd not have seen the flaming ball and that gave you all time to take shelter before it hit the mountain." She stroked his hair away from his eyes.

"You're a hero, Beren."

He flushed, his dark skin turning a deeper gold at her praise. "I don't feel like a hero."

"No one does." She tousled his hair, then sobered. "I shouldn't have let you go in the first place." *He could have been killed. We should have left here months ago, when that southern trader came to the village.*

On the other hand, Beren was making friends, forgetting the life he'd led in Zamad. Was she wrong to stay, to give him the freedom of an ordinary boy? He was her responsibility, after all, her fault if he came to harm. It was a promise she'd made to his mother, but she hadn't expected to develop more affection for the child than was proper for a guard. So far the village had proved a safe haven, but they both might still be hunted. She wanted to wrap him in strong rope to keep him in camp, or tie him to her back so he was never far from her. She wanted to…she didn't know what she wanted, but none of this was his fault.

The misery in his eyes softened her scold. "You saved Eskil. He said you shielded him under the overhang."

"Is he all right? And Arkin?" The concern for his friends was evident in his tone.

The tightness in Kiana's chest eased. Even at six years old, the boy already displayed the qualities of leadership his father bequeathed him. He'd never rule as was his right, but Queen Siri was wise to insist he be raised as an ordinary child, not knowing what he lost, nor fretting for ambition no longer possible. His single sadness seemed memory of his lost parents.

"They're both fine," she soothed. "The worst Eskil has to survive now is his mother's fussing."

Beren grinned, then sobered. "I should have taken more care of him. I'm older."

"By a year. There wasn't time to do much of anything. You survived and that's enough, and Arkin helped you both." She paused, then gave voice to her fear. "I shouldn't have let you go there without me. From now on we go together or not at all. Understood?"

He lifted his chin. "I can take care of myself."

Ah, the stubbornness of youth. "Nevertheless. Promise me."

He thinned his lips, lowered his gaze, but then nodded. The tight knot of guilt in Kiana's belly eased.

After a moment, he looked up at her again, defiance replaced by curiosity. "Are the caves much damaged? We had the pens cleaned and set up."

"I don't know. I'll have to go back." She calculated the time. The sun had traveled too fast this day. She'd never get to the caves and back before nightfall. "I'll look for your flute tomorrow, if it's not too far inside."

"Yes, please," he murmured. He closed his eyes, lay back down, and slipped into sleep.

Kiana turned to Inga, one eyebrow raised. The woman held up a beaker. "It dulls the pain and will make him sleep through the night. His ankle is bad, but a clean break, thank the gods. I had to give him a strong dose to set it."

Kiana lifted the fleece cover from the boy's leg. Two straight branches from the healer's store framed the leg from foot to knee, bound with several strips of cloth to keep the leg straight for the weeks needed to heal.

Unable to stop herself, she blurted the question uppermost in her mind. "Will he have a limp?"

"I do better work than that, Kiana." Inga's voice held a trace of reproach.

Kiana bowed her head in acknowledgement of the rebuke. "Forgive me. I'm just concerned."

Inga relaxed. "Your son will be fine." She bustled around the tent, tidying up. "What of the caves? Can we still winter there?"

Little more than fancy tents similar to those in Kiana's homeland, the sewn hides that formed the village huts offered shade and openings for cooling summer breezes, but were never intended for the harshness of winter. For generations, the people took shelter in the numerous caves and burrows behind the entrance in the mountain overlooking their village, seeing no need to make the huts more sturdy. Inside the mountain was warmth and shelter, for both men and animals and the food that took them through the cold months. Even now, the men were catching their last net loads of fish, while women slaughtered the excess sheep and chickens, dug vegetables from the ground, plucked pods from growing plants, and ground the grain for making bread. The big storage hut was almost full.

Arkin had been tasked with cleaning out any vermin that had nested in the caves over the summer, and Kiana had expected no danger in allowing the two younger boys to help him. A decision she now regretted.

"I'll check tomorrow. The main cave is blocked but perhaps some of the smaller ones are still accessible." She glanced through the open door toward the mountain, hidden now by dusk and trees. *And I want a closer look at that thing that dropped on it.*

Chapter Six

Why do I have to be the eldest? Tor held up a hand, but failed to stem Emund's tirade. He sighed and waited for his brother to run out of words.

Emund hadn't taken the news well that they were going to cannibalize his ship, the only trading ship they had. Yes, it was damaged, but it wasn't beyond repair. Why did they have to tear his ship apart?

That was the complaint Tor *chose* to hear. He ignored the curses that made up every second or third word.

At last Emund closed his mouth and stood, panting as if he'd run a race.

Tor waited for more, but Emund remained silent. "I'm sorry about this, Emund, but there's no other way." He opened his mouth but Tor pushed on. "We need shelter for the winter. The tents won't work."

"My ship has a hold—"

"With a great big hole in the side," Beade broke in.

Their brother scowled.

Tor took a deep breath. "Even if it didn't, you know it's not big enough for everyone. It was crowded enough before. There'd be no room for the people from my ship and Beade's as well." He fixed his gaze on Emund. "As I said, our best chance is to build a great hall big enough for everyone to live in over the cold months."

Beade nodded and slapped Emund on the shoulder. "Tor's right. You know he's right. We don't have time to both fix your ship and build a longhouse. It makes sense to use the wood before we have to start cutting trees."

"By spring we'll have a better idea how many families want their own separate homes and how many want to stay in the longhouse. We can expand it then." *Assuming we survive the winter*.

Emund grumbled, but with two brothers against him, he at last agreed to the logic. The three men stood at the edge of the forest, staring down the gentle slope to the beach and the ships. A cloth was wrapped around Beade's head, but he claimed the dizziness had gone. Tor allowed himself to relax.

Most of the people who'd risked their lives following him into exile were farmers. The crews of the two longboats were warriors, but Emund's crew, working a trading vessel, knew no more than the basics of fighting.

"Meanwhile," Tor continued, "there's no time to build any kind of shelter before sunset. We'll have to keep the women and children on the ships for one more night."

"And the animals?" Emund asked.

"What about them?" Tor paused. "Oh. We can't leave them on your ship, and they won't fit on our longships with all the people. We'll have to bring them ashore."

"Then we need pens." Once convinced of the necessity, Emund turned his farmer's mind to the practicalities. "We can use broken branches and the tether ropes to tie them together. Since all the men are staying ashore, some of them can guard the livestock against wild animals."

"Agreed." Tor glanced at the women already on the beach. "Runa can organize the sleeping arrangements. That reminds me." Tor turned to Emund. Although the youngest brother, he hadn't been injured like Beade and was in charge of defense while Tor was gone. "What were you thinking, letting Runa come after me? She might have been killed." The memory still shook him.

Emund snorted. "Not Runa. Besides, Vider said she had the village surrounded first."

"Yes, *she* had." Tor's life wasn't worth risking his sister and her babe. "When did she become war chief? I know you both had other concerns, but, Odin's beard, why didn't one of you take the lead?"

Emund looked sheepish, and Beade hung his head.

Behind them, Vider chuckled. "They're scared of her. So are you, if you think about it."

When had Vider joined them? Tor whirled on him. "I am not scared."

"Oh, maybe not scared *of* her. Scared *for* her." Vider softened his tone. "You all love her too much."

Tor glared, but was unable to deny Vider's assessment. He glanced at Emund and Beade. Neither met his gaze.

Tor huffed out a breath. "Fine. But next time..." No, there wasn't going to be a next time. Not if he had any say in it.

"I'd...uh...better see to the pens," Emund muttered and hurried away.

Beade put a hand to his head. "I think I'll lie down for a while."

Tor waited until his brothers headed down the beach, then turned to Vider. "Any more words of wisdom?"

Vider grinned, ignoring the sarcasm in Tor's voice. "Not right now."

Tor grimaced. *Friends. Almost as bad as brothers. And why do I have to be the eldest*?

That night, determined to confirm his assumption, Tor studied the cloudless sky with Vider beside him.

"You should get Jorvik to look," Vider said.

Tor scowled. "I may not know as much as that seer, but I know enough to see we're in the North, maybe as far as Olafshavn."

"The sun showed you that."

"I know." Tor lowered his gaze, turned, and strode toward the camp. "It doesn't hurt to confirm."

Vider hurried to catch up. "Any idea where?"

"Not until we explore." Whether they were east or west of his old home was impossible to judge. "I'll send a crew in the spring to look for familiar landmarks. We all know these Northland waters so it shouldn't be hard."

"Not until spring?"

"Winter's too close. Less than two months, that village chieftain said. We need to get our people settled." *Where* they were wasn't as important as whether they survived.

Vider said nothing for a few moments, then, "Do you think we'll get enough food from those villagers?"

"Perhaps." Tor shrugged. "We still needed to discover what sort of animals live in these woods. We can use the meat, and the furs will be useful in the trade."

"Then tomorrow we hunt?"

"Tomorrow we hunt."

~ * ~

The next morning Tor set out with his sword, axe, and a borrowed bow slung over his shoulder. He sent some of his men in different directions, while he and Vider took the path leading toward the mountain.

They strode through the trees, slapped aside branches, and climbed rocks, all the while searching for tracks, for any sign of game. Tor marked the trail this time, with Vider taking point, until they paused in a meadow to orient themselves. The beach was out of sight, but the mountain loomed ahead above the trees. The tops of some of those trees still smoldered from the fire caused by the crash. There was no sign of the strange craft. Rocks and boulders slumped in a pile before what had once been a strong cliff.

Vider surveyed the surrounding forest. "You realize that crash may have driven any animals away."

Tor shrugged. "What choice do we have? We have to search." Movement on his right caught his attention. He whirled, caught a glimpse of antlers and a brown body vanishing into the brush. He smiled. "At least some of the deer stayed around."

They trailed the buck to a clearing and stopped inside the flanking trees. Their luck held. They'd come upon the clearing from downwind.

Tor slipped off his bow, fit an arrow to the string, held his breath, and let fly. The buck toppled, the arrow in its heart, dead before it hit the ground.

Vider strode past him. "Good shot."

Tor smiled. With luck, the other hunters were as successful.

Because he wanted to get the meat back to camp as soon as possible, Tor decided against field dressing the carcass. Instead he helped lay it across Vider's shoulders. With Tor guarding the trail, they made their way back to the cove.

After depositing their load with the boys tasked with gutting and skinning, Vider glanced at the mountain, then at Tor. "Didn't you say you wanted to look for supplies in the fire disk?"

"We've meat to catch. It can wait for another day." Despite his words, Tor studied the place where the mysterious disk had crashed.

"We'll keep looking on the way." Vider grinned. "If we find another deer, we'll kill it and come back. If we don't..."

"If we don't," Tor finished, "we may at least find answers."

They walked for a good twenty minutes without seeing another deer. At last they emerged on a plateau. Boulders and smaller rocks spread over the ground, most piled against the face of a cliff. Two of the boulders leaned against each other, leaving a narrow opening into the mountain. A foot stretched from that opening and a moment later someone backed out. Tor and Vider stopped, hands resting on their swords.

Tor was the first to relax. The someone was slim, with a backside he itched to palm. He wiped damp palms down his trews. *Kiana.* She rose to her feet and tossed her tail of black hair over her shoulder. He wanted to slide his hand down that length. Was it as soft and silky as it appeared?

She clutched something long and thin in her hand, but at sight of the two men, she shoved the object into her belt and drew her sword.

He stared at the weapon, curled his lip. True, the blade was sharp enough to prick his skin, but it wasn't made of steel. He drew his own sword and held it by his side instead of at the ready, an insult to show she posed no threat. The woman didn't back down, just crouched into a swordsman's stance. Vider stood back, leaving Tor to the confrontation.

Kiana bared her teeth in challenge. "What are you doing here?"

He raised the bow in his other hand. "Looking for game." He pointed at the stick in her belt. "What have you there?"

She ignored his question and raised her sword higher. "There is no game here. You need to search lower down, where the forest turns to the north."

He raised an eyebrow at the information. "You're most helpful."

She shrugged. "This is no place for you. Go away."

He slung his bow over his shoulder, took a firmer grip on his sword. "But I like it here. Nice view." He stared at the woman.

A dull flush crept up her neck. Was she blushing? Hard to tell with that golden skin, but good to know she was as unsettled by this meeting as he. At least his own skin didn't betray him.

"I think," Vider murmured, "I'll keep looking down this other trail."

Tor blinked. He'd forgotten the other man was here. He glanced at his friend. A knowing smile curved Vider's lips, but Tor refused to be baited.

He shrugged. "Fine. I'll be along in a minute." In truth, he was intrigued by this woman. Perhaps if they were alone together he'd be able to get some answers from her without the intimidating presence of another warrior. He turned back to her, studied her. "You're not like the others. Not as…timid."

She narrowed her eyes.

Her suspicions cheered him. Perhaps having his own sword in his hands boosted his confidence.

He paced forward, glanced at the opening behind her. "What's there?"

"Nothing for you." She shifted her position, blocked his way.

He didn't stop until his sword clanged against the flat of her blade. She braced. He added more pressure, but she resisted. Muscles on her arms flexed under the sleeveless vest she wore. His sword didn't move any closer to her. *So, no weakling this one.* Admiration coursed through his body and something else…anticipation.

He drew back, then whipped his sword forward again. She caught it with the edge this time, but when they drew apart again there was a nick in the metal. “Poor workmanship there,” he taunted.

She sucked in a breath, more annoyed, it seemed, than dismayed. “This is the finest bronze my people make. None better.” She glared at the nick and muttered something too low for him to hear.

He smirked. “And yet my blade can take a bite from it.”

Her face flushed again, but she held her ground. Good. This one was a true shield maid, refusing to let herself be bullied.

Tor tapped the edge of his sword to hers. “Where did you learn to use that?” When she tightened her lips, he shrugged as if he didn’t care about the answer, and raised his sword in salute. “Very well. Keep your secrets. I have no wish to fight you, woman. We are supposed to be allies.”

Kiana stared at him for a moment, then sheathed her weapon. “Allies don’t fight each other,” she agreed. “Your sister is either very brave or very foolish to propose such a truce.”

He shoved his sword into its sheath. “My sister is never foolish. The truce was a good idea, but I wonder if her condition sometimes addles her wits.”

The corner of her mouth twitched. “You think pregnant women have no sense?”

He grimaced. “No, just sisters.”

The smile broke through, and he stopped breathing. Odin’s beard but she was beautiful when she smiled.

Kiana stared at the ground. Shy? No, more as if avoiding his gaze. “What kind of name is Tor?”

The sound of his name on her lips had him catching his breath. He swallowed, willed his heart to stop pounding. Did she have an interest in him? As more than an ally? He stopped himself from puffing out his chest. “A fine Norse name.”

She looked up. “What is a Norseman?”

He stared. All in the Northlands knew of the Norsemen, the sea wolves who ruled the ocean and coastal lands. “Where are you from that you don’t know of us?”

She shrugged. “South.”

For a moment, neither said anything, then Tor glanced up the hill. “I want to get a closer look at this thing that brought us here. Do you wish to come?” Now why had he asked that?

Kiana nodded. “I, too, wish to see this thing.”

Tor turned away and sought a path up the cliff. He found a faint game trail leading to the east. She fell into step beside him, keeping her hands tucked close to her body, as if reluctant to touch him. What if he touched her? The answer he imagined made him smile.

They walked in silence for half a mile. The trail meandered up the cliff side, keeping to a path that allowed for an easy climb.

Unable to ignore his curiosity any longer, Tor cleared his throat. "It looked as if the mountain crushed a cave back there. What is that stick you risked your life to get?"

She fingered the object. For a moment he didn't expect her to answer, but at last she said, "A flute."

He raised an eyebrow. "You play a flute?"

She shrugged. "Not me."

When she said no more, he sighed. They continued up the trail until they rounded a boulder and found themselves facing a jumble of rock and a metal wall.

Tor stopped and stared. He'd never seen anything like this before. A wall of metal? *Is the whole fire disk made of metal? What kind of blacksmith constructed such a thing*?

Kiana approached, her gaze on the wall. Suddenly, a man appeared before her, hands raised in a warding gesture. She crouched and drew her sword.

Odin's beard, where did he come from?

Tor's sword appeared in his hand before he was aware he'd drawn it. Without thinking, he placed himself in front of Kiana, but she slipped from behind him to stand at his side. He didn't have to look at her to sense her irritation.

Tor braced for attack, but the man never moved. *Where are his weapons*?

Still on guard, Tor studied him. The man's hair was dark, cut short like a priest's. His eyes, too, were dark, but his skin lighter. He wore light-colored trews of a linen-like material, a dark shirt that fastened up his chest in some mysterious manner, and boots made of hide, not sturdy fur-lined boots like Tor's. But strangest of all was his color. He was gray from head to foot, different shades of gray, his clothes, his hair, even his skin.

All this Tor noted in an instant. A moment later, the man spoke. "Warning. Keep back. This ship is guarded. Keep away."

Chapter Seven

Tor grunted in alarm. The voice was clear, but the man's lips didn't move.

His palms slippery with sweat, Tor tightened his grip on his sword. "This man is no Norseman, yet he speaks my tongue as well as I."

Kiana ignored him. Sweat dewed her forehead, but her voice remained steady when she spoke, the language strange to him, fluid and…exotic.

"What did you say?" he demanded.

She shook herself, but never took her gaze off the man. "I asked him how he knew my language. I haven't heard that tongue in over two years."

"Your language?" Tor repeated, confused. "But he spoke *my* language."

She stared at him. "What?"

"His words. They were in my language." When she frowned, Tor huffed out a breath. "The language you spoke to me in the village. The language we're speaking now."

She narrowed her eyes. "No. He spoke *my* language, not yours."

What sorcery was this? He turned back to the man. "How do you do that?"

The man remained still. "Warning. Keep back. This ship is guarded. Keep away."

"Wait." Kiana circled around the man. She kept the point of her sword aimed at him. When she stood behind him, opposite Tor, she drew it back, ready to attack. "Look at him. He has no color, and he's flat."

Tor studied the gray man again. It was true. The man wasn't even solid, more like a thin haze of smoke through which she was visible. "He is…an image," he decided. "Like those drawn in ink. Not a real person."

She resumed circling. Without warning, she thrust her free hand forward, as if to strike the man. Her arm swept right through his head but he didn't even flinch. She didn't jump back. Instead, she tilted her head and gazed at the man with sudden focus. She muttered something in that fluid language of hers.

Tor tired of her mysterious actions. Perhaps she was used to such apparitions, but he was not. "What did you say?"

"An augury of some kind. A vision," she repeated in Tor's language.

He recoiled, raised his sword again. *Witchcraft*. As much as he tolerated their seer, he refused to trust anything unnatural, and this *ship*, this *image*, were unnatural. "Keep back," he warned.

No change.

Tor sidled around the image. He faced the man's back, drew his sword and sliced through the gray man's chest. The sword swished as if through air, and still the man didn't move.

"Ghost." Tor suppressed a shiver.

She tilted her head. "Perhaps, but I've seen no ghosts like this."

He shot her an incredulous look. "You've seen ghosts?"

"A few. In the temples." She continued to study the image. Unsettled, Tor backed away, closer to the metal wall.

The man vanished. A moment later, his voice came from behind them. "Warning. Keep back. This ship is guarded. Keep away."

Tor spun. The man now stood between him and the wall. Tor sheathed his sword and stared at the metal wall. He wanted to run away from this strange apparition, but refused to show weakness to his companion.

"That is like no ship I've ever seen." Kiana strode up to stand beside him. They craned their necks, but trees and dirt and boulders hid the top of the wall.

"Nor I. Hmm." The flaming ball from yesterday came to mind. "A ship that sails the skies, perhaps?"

"Crewed by gray men," she agreed.

Still, even gray men needed to eat. Perhaps his idea for supplies was yet possible. "I wonder what it means by *guarded*."

He stretched out a hand to touch the wall, but Kiana grabbed his arm. "No." Her touch sent tingles down his arm, and his breath caught. He stared at her fingers, grateful they clutched the sleeve of his shirt. If she had touched bare skin… At the mental image of her hand on his, blood rushed to his lower body.

As if sensing his thoughts, she jerked her hand away. "I…I mean, we don't know what could happen. If they sent this gray man, perhaps they…whoever sailed this thing…have bite to back up their warnings."

Tor swallowed and shifted his gaze from Kiana's hand. This was no time to be distracted. "Agreed." He stared at the wall once more, then backed away. The man disappeared.

She let out a breath. Tor glanced at her. A light sheen of sweat glistened on her brow. Was it the gray man who unnerved her? Or Tor?

"What now?" he asked.

Instead of answering, she bent and picked up a rock. She stared at the wall, eyes narrowed. "I want to know how it is guarded."

He shrugged. "Does it matter?"

"Perhaps not. Still." Without warning, she drew back her arm and launched the rock at the ship.

The gray man flickered into view a moment before the rock clanged off the metal wall. Sparks shot in all directions from the point of impact, a local lightning storm centered around the rock. When the sparks cleared, Tor blinked his eyes and stared. There was no sign of the rock. A pile of broken shards marked the place where it had fallen.

They both drew in a sharp breath at the same time.

"So," Tor said, proud his voice didn't shake. "Now we know."

"Now we know." Kiana turned away from him. "You saw the sky ship, now go away. I have things to do."

He'd planned on leaving anyway. He still needed to rejoin Vider to continue the hunt. Perhaps he'd return another day. There had to be a way into this…sky ship, despite the ghost's warning.

Yes, he'd planned on leaving, but her words spawned a quiver of mischief. "Perhaps I'll keep you company."

She glared at him, then sprinted into the woods. He cursed and took chase, but no matter how fast he ran or how many bushes he crashed through, she stayed well ahead of him. Fleet of foot, knowing this land better than he, she slipped around trees and rocks with ease. He wasn't surprised when she disappeared from sight.

He staggered to a halt and leaned against a boulder to catch his breath. *Odin's beard, the woman can run.* He could battle for hours without stopping, tend a ship through days of storm without sleeping, but a simple sprint upland through wooded land defeated him.

Tor rested his hands on his knees and gasped in shallow breaths. When he had his breath back, he straightened.

Vider lounged against a nearby tree. "She's fast."

Tor scowled. "How long have you been following me?"

"Long enough. You didn't think I'd leave you alone in a strange land again, did you? Even with the warrior maid you are so interested in?" Vider grinned, then sobered. "I saw that gray ghost man."

Tor's heart slowed to a more normal pace. "I'm surprised you didn't rush in to join me in battle."

"You had it under control." Vider looked around the clearing. "Now what? More hunting?"

The gleam in his friend's eyes told Tor Vider was just as curious as he. Hunting was important, but if there was a chance this ship held supplies… Resigned to the inevitable, Tor shook his head. "I'm too curious, now. I want to find an entrance to that ship."

Vider chuckled. "Then we'll keep looking."

~ * ~

Assured she'd given Tor the slip, Kiana slowed to a walk and resumed her exploration along the path she'd set herself. She didn't need the man distracting her. This was more important.

The main cave was gone. The thigh-high tunnel framed by two slabs of rock leaning against each other, where she'd managed to retrieve Beren's flute, opened for ten child-sized paces, then ended in a solid wall of broken rock. The sole entrance to the cave complex was blocked now.

What of the smaller caves? Did they survive the collapse? Had another entrance opened? She sped up. *There has to be a way in. Our lives depend on it.*

The main cave was for stores and clan gatherings, the others for sleeping rooms. Last winter she and Beren had been treated as a family and had their own cave.

She remembered that winter. Desert nights were cold, but nothing compared to the bite of northern *days*. Even their first winter after they'd fled the palace wasn't as bad as that. Of course, they were farther south then and hadn't yet arrived at this tentative sanctuary, but still…

She followed the curve of the metal ship and the mountain and tried to ignore the worry burning in her belly. She needed to concentrate. The gray man flickered into view whenever she neared the wall, but after his third appearance she ignored him. She now knew what sort of magic protected his ship, and as long as she didn't touch it, she ought to be safe.

When she passed the last crumbled cliff face, she stopped and dropped onto a fallen tree trunk. The evidence was undeniable. There were no new cracks in the rock, no hoped-for entrances to the caves. They were gone. All gone. The burning in her stomach turned to a hard knot, and her hands shook. Panic stole her breath. Her heart drummed in her ears, and her vision grayed.

The summer huts weren't built to stand through winter. The villagers would scatter to friends and relatives in other villages, but Kiana and Beren had no one to go to. This was a disaster, a death sentence. To come this far to safeguard her prince, only to fail in the end…

Had she been too hasty in shrugging off the Norseman? The villagers had been reluctant to take in two strangers, and she had no contact with other settlements. It was a risk even talking to the peddlers who visited last spring—she'd not want word of Beren's whereabouts getting back to the wrong ears—but one had carried the boiled sweets the boy loved, and she'd weakened enough to trade one of the queen's plainer gold rings. She'd managed to also secure a dagger and a woolen cloak for herself and leather boots for the boy to replace the ones he'd outgrown.

She'd not made friends elsewhere, at least not close enough to reach before winter. If she was unable to find a place for herself and Beren in another village, there'd be no choice but to beg the Norsemen for shelter.

Frustrated, angry, she returned the way she'd come, faster now that she took the straight path. She arrived at the plateau outside the main cave without encountering the Norseman, and decided to keep going. There were no caves in the other direction that she knew of, but perhaps an opening…

Again she walked, again the gray man appeared to warn her away every time she glimpsed the metal ship. One more clearing, she told herself. If she still found nothing, she'd head back to the village, to tell Soren, to think.

To decide what to do.

She edged around a boulder on a strip of bare rock, shouldered through bushes and past torn-up tree roots, and broke into another open space. The metal wall facing her appeared different from the rest of the ship, duller, *flatter*, somehow.

Her heart raced. A vertical gash the height of her shoulder and an arm-length wide split the metal. Forgetting caution, she hurried forward, but stopped short of the opening. *What am I doing*? *Remember that rock you threw earlier*?

As she studied the clearing, she realized what was missing. *Wait. Where is the gray man*?

Backing away from the opening, she picked up a stone and tossed it. When it hit the metal wall it made a loud clang before dropping to bounce twice on the ground.

No sparks. No lightning.

An opening into the mysterious ship.

Were there people inside, injured, needing help, able to help her? If no one survived, was there space inside to shelter?

What choice did she have?

She stepped forward.

~ * ~

The distant clang stopped Tor just as he passed the clearing where he'd met Kiana. Alarm shot through him. "What's that woman found now?"

Vider shrugged. "One way to find out."

They ran in the direction of the sound. It took less time than Tor expected before he emerged from the trees into another clearing. The gap in the metal wall ahead of him wasn't hard to miss, nor was the woman half in and half out of it. He hurried forward.

"What are you doing?" he shouted. "Are you mad? You'll get yourself killed."

She paused and glanced back at him, frowning. "This is not your business. Go away."

He stopped. Not his business? When she'd found what he'd been searching for, a way into this *ship*, and a possible solution to their food shortage? "It's as much my business as yours. I'll stay."

She huffed out a breath, then turned away. "As you wish." She disappeared into the ship.

Tor stared suspiciously at the surrounding metal. "Where's the gray man?"

Instead of answering, Vider tossed a stone at the wall. They both sucked in a breath when nothing happened.

"Go on," he said. "I'll stand guard."

Tor approached the narrow opening and leaned through the gash. Ahead of him, perhaps two paces away, was another metal wall. To the left a narrow passage curved into distant darkness. A similar passage on the right ended a few paces away in a jumble of metal rods and buckled sheets of wall. There were no openings big enough for Kiana to fit through, let alone himself. Left then.

Tor thrust the rest of his body through the opening and stood to his full height. The ceiling was a mere hand's width above the top of his head. A sliver of light shafted through the gash, but did little to penetrate the darkness ahead.

He drew his sword and, holding it before him, rested his left hand on the wall to guide him forward. Faint scuffling sounds came from ahead, proof he was heading in the right direction. The sounds stopped, and then came an unearthly shriek. Despite his racing heart, he resisted the urge to sprint forward. Instead, he clutched his sword and crept toward the sound. *What sort of monster has that woman wakened in here*?

The hallway curved to the right, revealing a faint light, flickering like fire, but blue. As he approached, the light grew brighter until one final step revealed the source.

The passage ended at a wall, but with a narrow gap the width of his hand cutting the passage from floor to roof. Kiana, wedged in the opening, strained against the end of the wall. To Tor's surprise, the wall moved, a few finger lengths at a time. Instead of swinging in or out like a door, it vanished into the side of the wall opposite. With each push, the metal wall screeched against the floor.

Not a monster, thank the gods. Tor's heart slowed to a more normal rhythm.

He sheathed his sword and rested his hand above Kiana's. "Let me."

She backed out of the way, and he replaced her in the gap. Tor gave a mighty shove, and the wall slid several hand lengths more, leaving an opening now wide enough for even him to fit through.

He slipped into the room beyond, Kiana behind him. Both drew their swords again, but the sight that met them had Tor doubting if swords were of any use there.

Several paces ahead another wall blocked his view, but to the right, the room opened into an enormous cavern, so large his curse echoed. A faint blue glow lit the walls. Large metal shelves filled the space, blocking his view. Each shelf climbed to the high ceiling, at least twice his height, and each held identical metal boxes the size of his war helmet, fastened down by nets, scores of them in the immediate area ahead of him. One of the nets had ripped and several boxes had fallen from their shelf. One lay on its side in front of him. From it shot a beam of light.

"By the Lady," Kiana whispered. She stood to the side of the beam, staring at a bright circle no bigger than her head that appeared reflected on the nearest shelf.

"Stay back." He strode forward. He had seen what was inside the circle, and his blood ran cold.

"But what is that place?" She ignored him and approached the reflection. "Is it another image?"

Within the circle thrown by the fallen metal box, a life-sized stone room appeared. They stared into the room from a point several paces from a wooden trestle. Atop the trestle sat clear ropes, like strands of woven icicles braided into loops and curls. Within the tubes a reddish liquid flowed from one bubbling flagon to drip into another. Nothing else stirred in the room, but there were sounds—the gurgling of the liquid in the flagon, the *drip-drip-drip* of the droplets, a faint hum in the background.

When she circled behind the image, she disappeared. The swish of her sword sounded and the tip appeared at one side of the circle, slicing sideways with no effect.

"Stand back." Tor raised his own sword and plunged it into the circle.

"What did you do?"

"Stabbed into the hole." He waved the sword around.

"It didn't come through the back."

She returned to Tor's side and they both stared at the sword, hilt-deep inside the glowing circle, the tip a hand's breadth from the wooden trestle.

Tor closed the distance and tapped the point on the trestle. The *thunk* of metal on wood echoed through the chamber, and the shock from the solid surface vibrated up his arm. Startled, he withdrew the sword from the circle.

"That is no image," he muttered.

"But how?"

More sorcery? He backed away and stumbled over the box on the floor. Without a sound, the beam and circle disappeared. "Odin's beard."

Kiana sheathed her sword and knelt beside the box. Drawing a knife from her boot, she then used it to prod the box, turning it around, flipping it over. Colored circles and short metal sticks covered one side. One of the sticks had snapped in half, held in place only by a thin strand of metal.

"You broke it," she whispered.

Shaken, Tor skirted the box and walked down the room, keeping near the wall. The rows of shelves disappeared into the distance. "There must be hundreds, thousands of these boxes here. But what are they? What are they for?" Was this sorcery a danger to his people?

As Kiana studied the cavern, she narrowed her eyes, and when she spoke, it wasn't to answer his question but to ask one of her own. "Can we move the shelves?"

Chapter Eight

Tor jerked at her words. "What?"

Kiana laid a hand on the first shelf. "Can we move the shelves? Take them out of here or shift them to the side."

The cavern was big enough for the entire village to winter in, but the shelves were too close together. There was space for her huge Norse companion to walk between them without brushing them with his shoulders, but not enough to provide a practical barracks or camp.

On the good side, the narrow passage by which they'd entered was easy to defend, and the villagers had nets woven through with branches and leaves to hide the entrance and protect it from the winter storms. The room was warmer than outside, as if the blue light heated the space as well as lit it. It was perfect.

Or might be.

Tor tensed, ready, she supposed, to question her sanity. To forestall his protest, she gave the shelf a push. It didn't even wobble. She grasped a metal bar at the end and tried to pull it, muscles used to swing a sword now proving their use in another way.

To her surprise, Tor placed his hands above hers and added his strength. Kiana froze.

Breathe.

His scent filled her nostrils, sweat and spice and a lingering pine from the forest. He strained to pull the shelf, muscles flexing, but even the two of them together were unable to shift it.

Defeated, she stood back. She wanted to kick something, pound her fist on something. *Scream.*

"Why did you want to move them?" Tor still rested his hands on the shelf.

She shrugged. He didn't need to know the problems the village faced. "I was curious."

He narrowed his eyes, then turned away and wandered down one of the aisles between two shelves, from time to time shoving at one side or another.

"They're all the same," he said when he returned, confirming her suspicion. "They won't budge, and all have the same boxes on them."

Kiana studied the space one last time, then sighed at the loss of such a perfect solution. "We don't know what they are or what they do. I can't fathom what they're used for, but they don't *seem* to be a threat."

"As you say, of no use, at least until we find out more about them." Tor sounded disappointed, as if he expected more from this discovery. With one final look at the space, he turned back toward the door and disappeared through the entrance.

She stared after him for a moment, surprised she missed him already. What was it about him? Was the prophecy just that she was destined to meet him one day, or that he'd come to mean something to her, as her mother interpreted?

"I have no time for this," she muttered, and followed in Tor's wake.

When she emerged from the gash, he was speaking to his friend, and a moment later both men clambered back into the metal ship. She shrugged. Let them figure out the mystery. She needed to get back to the village with her bad news about the caves.

First, though, she returned to the plateau outside the collapsed cave entrance and stood at the western edge to peer down at the distant cove where the strangers' ships bobbed on the water.

No, two were still on the water, close to shore, but the third had been dragged onto the beach. Curious, Kiana squinted to bring the activity into focus. People surrounded the ship, crowding close, then walking away carrying something.

Unable to resist, she slipped back down the trail toward the cove. The trail crossed a wider track that led in a more direct path, but she didn't make the mistake of going down it. At this time of year the bears were preparing for their winter sleep, However, unlike the bears in the South, who begged scraps from the towns and villages in their territory, these were vicious, even when not hungry, and they were big, much taller than the Norseman, with claws the length of daggers.

Kiana had joined a hunt the previous autumn when one came too close to the village. She'd been impressed by how well the men worked together to bring it down. The hunter who made the kill claimed the fur hide for a cloak, a sign of prestige among the villagers, and the claws now decorated Soren's ceremonial robe.

I'll have my own cloak one day.

When Kiana was close enough, she peered around the thick

trunk of an oak. Men stripped wood from the sides of the beached ship and piled the boards close to the tree line. Did they plan to build a fire? When nothing else happened, she turned away. Soren needed time to prepare what to tell everyone. And she needed to decide what she and Beren were going to do.

~ * ~

After his initial astonishment, Vider plunged into the depths of the metal cavern. Tor leaned against one wall, amused, while his friend examined the shelves and boxes with gleeful enthusiasm. Vider had a passion for building or repairing objects around the camp. He'd repaired the dragon at the prow of Tor's ship, broken during a storm two winters ago. Last summer he'd invented a thin, hooked hammer for Petter to carve the more delicate designs on the swords after removing them from the heat of his forge. The metal boxes were impossible for Vider to resist.

Sure enough, once he'd finished his exploration, Vider returned and lifted the box that had fallen from the shelves. He studied the metal sticks and blobs. "You say this opened a hole and there was a table inside?"

"Yes."

"Like the hole our ships fell through?" Vider persisted.

Tor blinked. He hadn't made the connection, but… "Smaller."

"So…" Vider continued to study the box. "There's a room. And we can toss something into that room or take something from it?"

Tor frowned. "One of the sticks is broken. I don't think it will work anymore." *Why does it matter? There's no food in this cavern, and we can't eat metal.* He clapped a hand on Vider's shoulder. "Don't worry. Perhaps one of the others will work. Anyway, there's no time to find out what these do—at least not yet. Perhaps Petter can melt one down to make more weapons."

"There are lots of boxes to melt if we can," Vider agreed. "It's a big cavern."

"I suppose if it's on a ship this is probably a hold," Tor mused. "It might have served as shelter, but not if we can't get these shelves out."

Vider contemplated the shelves, then replaced the broken box on the floor and pushed against one. Tor added his weight, but even with both of them, the shelves didn't stir. Vider wiped his brow. "Pity. It's a good space."

"Never mind." Tor headed for the door.

"I'll take this one back with me." Tor turned to see Vider wrapping the metal box in his cloak. "I'd like to see what we can do with it."

If his friend wanted to waste his time… "If you want."

Vider grinned and hurried after him.

Upon their return, Jorvik met the two men at the tree line. They'd managed to kill a buck on the way back, and Tor now carried it across his shoulders while Vider carried the metal box.

"There is something strange about this place," Jorvik muttered to Tor. The priest's face was creased into even more wrinkles than usual, making him look much older than his forty years.

"This place is in autumn, and we left in spring. Four days ago." Tor shifted the buck on his shoulders then strode past the man, who fell into step beside him, trotting to keep up. Vider veered off toward the beach, where the smith was helping out.

"Not that." Jorvik clutched his familiar priest's robe about him. "The night sky isn't right."

Tor sighed. Of course the night sky wasn't right. Hadn't he just pointed out it was an autumn sky, not spring? He hadn't wanted to bring the priest with them when they'd been exiled, but the man had insisted on coming. Some claimed he was a seer, and he did nothing to deny it.

He had warned Tor not to flee from Ottar, that he'd never return home if he went into exile. That part had come true, but he doubted the priest had foreseen the sky ship or even the ghost who guarded it.

Seers. They were as bad as witches.

Tor's silence must have tried the man's patience, for Jorvik huffed out a breath. "We have been changed," he pronounced with all the authority of his shaky voice.

Now Tor did stop, his heart speeding up. "Changed how?"

Pleased he had Tor's attention, Jorvik's tone became smug. "The gods haven't revealed that to me yet, but they have told me we are…marked."

Disgusted at the vague warning, Tor resumed his march. "When they see fit to tell you more, talk to me again." On impulse, he spun on the man. Jorvik stumbled and tripped over his robe. Tor grabbed his arm to steady him while managing to keep the buck balanced on his own shoulders. "Say nothing to anyone else." He caught and held the other's gaze to avoid any misunderstanding. "I want no panic. We have enough to worry about now without vague threats about being marked by the gods."

Jorvik threw back his shoulders. "It is no threat, merely truth."

Tor glared at him. "Until you can show me proof, it is *merely* the ravings of a madman."

The priest stopped, his mouth agape. The man had lived a life of privilege at home, and Tor suspected he was dumbfounded anyone doubted his words.

Runa insisted they needed a priest in their exile, but why, in the name of Odin, had Tor allowed *this* one to push his way in? He had no time for fear-mongering. He strode away, leaving the old man behind.

Vider joined him a moment later. “Let me take that.”

He transferred the deer from Tor’s shoulders to his own and strode away. Before Tor could follow him, Runa called and he veered aside to see what she wanted.

“You seem distracted, brother.” She sat in the doorway of the tent that had been on the deck of their ship.

They had relocated the tents to allow the women and children to sleep on solid land for the first time in days. The rough pens holding the cows and sheep and goats now shared space with another for the bull. The ships were fine for raiding and trading, but when it came to living on them with families and livestock, any alternative was better than those crowded conditions.

Tor jerked his head back at the priest. “He annoys me, with his false predictions and tales of doom.”

Runa smiled. “What has he done now?”

He sighed. He didn’t want to worry her. This was his burden to bear. “Just being his usual self. We should have left him behind.”

“We need a priest to bless our new life,” she reminded him.

He scowled. “There were others.”

“None willing to come with us, and Ottar didn’t let us take a healer.” She clenched her fists in her skirt. “At least he didn’t know Beade’s wife was also a midwife, and Jorvik has some healing skills.”

“Healing?” Tor rolled his eyes. “He can clean a scratch and that, badly.”

She relaxed her hands and grinned. “Come, brother, you know you just don’t like anything that can’t be fought with sword or spear. Admit it, he frightened you when he said you’d marry a woman more than twice your age.”

Tor growled. “He didn’t frighten me. It’s madness. What makes him think I’d wed an old woman?”

Runa chuckled. “She must be a very special old woman.”

He scowled, and with her laughter chasing him, joined Vider at the cook fires, where he drew his knife and bent over the deer.

Vider, already slicing into the skin, glanced back at Runa. “Your sister is in a good mood this morning.”

Tor grunted. Together they began the task of cleaning the carcass, working alongside the boys and hunters butchering the rest of the day’s harvest. A pale sun shone overhead. Had they only been gone a few hours? He'd lost track of time in the hold of that sky ship.

"Why don't you go find out for yourself?" he muttered.

Vider concentrated on the pelt he was cutting. "Just making a comment."

Tor paused, regarded his friend through narrowed eyes. "She doesn't hate men."

Vider jerked as if struck. His gaze, when he raised it to Tor, held anger. "She should," he snarled. "I would have challenged Ottar myself—"

"You think I didn't want to?" Tor stabbed his knife into the carcass, the memory of that blood-lust making his hand tremble. "She begged me not to."

"She can't have affection for him," Vider protested.

"No." Tor dragged his knife through the skin and ripped it in a ragged line. He stopped, sighed, and carried on in a calmer voice, "No, she feels nothing for him, but everything for her family. If I'd challenged Ottar, or Emund had or Beade, or…," he raised his gaze to Vider, "or even you, we'd have died."

"He's not that good," Vider protested.

"No, but he's that sneaky. Do you think he kept people around him who were honorable? Who wouldn't stop at a knife in the back if it raised them in Ottar's favor?" He still doubted his father's defeat in lawful challenge had been honorable.

Vider stabbed at the carcass, perhaps imagining Ottar's throat, then sighed. "Ah."

"Yes. Ah." Tor stared at the deer, at the torn flesh and ragged skin. A chuckle escaped him. At Vider's confusion, he gestured. "We'd best let someone else work on this before we have more of a mangled mess."

Vider glared at the deer, then sat back on his heels and shook his head with a rueful grin. "Perhaps not the best conversation to have at the moment."

"No," Tor agreed.

He called over one of the boys working beside them, then led Vider to the edge of the water and stared at Emund's ship being taken apart. Neither wanted to talk further about Runa, but what to say next?

Vider broke the silence. "Those things, those boxes… Perhaps they have value in trade."

Tor shuddered. "I'd not want to touch them."

"Not to use," Vider agreed. "I grant they may be too dangerous for that, but Petter thinks he might be able to melt down the metal. We can always use more axes or even nails for the longhouse."

"Yes." Tor studied the pile of wood salvaged from Emund's trading ship. What else was needed? "I didn't see any food in that ship. What if those villagers change their minds about trading?"

Vider tilted his head. "You gave your word to Runa we'd honor the truce."

"And give them furs in trade. Yes, I know." Tor dug the toe of his boot into the sand. "Damned women. Why do they always have to interfere? What we needed was a good fight to settle it without all this *negotiation*."

Vider chuckled. "You don't mean that. Aren't you the one who says trade is easier on survival than war?"

Tor scowled. Yes, he'd said that, but why did his friend have to remember?

"Besides," Vider continued, "you negotiate for trade goods. Runa was negotiating for your life."

He avoided his friend's gaze and faced the sea. "If she'd been born a man she'd be challenging me for leadership of this tribe."

"If she'd been born a man we wouldn't be here." Some of the anger crept back into Vider's tone.

Tor rubbed the back of his neck. "Women."

"Yes." Vider fell silent.

After a moment, Ivar called from the shore. Tor sighed, and with Vider beside him, headed toward the beached ship. Time to plan on a lengthy stay.

Chapter Nine

"Are you sure?" Soren glared at the mountain as if willing it to bow to his will. "Are there no caves at all?"

"None." She'd reported to Soren as soon as she returned to the village. In addition to the destruction of the caves, she'd also told him of the gray man and the sky ship.

He scowled once more at the mountain. "So the fire ball, this…sky ship…is our doom."

Her heart sank. "The metal cavern—"

A slash of his hand quieted her. "You said it was impossible to remove the shelves." At her reluctant nod, he continued, "Then we go to Suudrun."

The next village south? "Will they take you in?"

He glanced at her, and the scowl vanished to be replaced by a fatherly smile. "Don't worry, child. You and your son will both be welcomed." He turned toward his hut. "They'll not turn us away if we bring our own food."

"What?" She hurried after him. "But what about the strangers? We made a bargain."

"That was before." He didn't stop.

"But they have women, children. Without food they'll die." She'd rather slaughter them all in their sleep, a more merciful death than slow starvation.

"Why all the shouting?" Soren's wife emerged from their hut, brushing dust from her overdress.

"Nothing important," the chieftain muttered.

Without thinking, Kiana appealed to the other woman. "Ragna, he'll let the strangers starve."

Ragna glared at Soren. "Explain."

The mighty chieftain squirmed under that look. Reluctantly he told her the results of Kiana's exploration and his decision. "We have no choice. We have to go."

"I'll not have the death of children on my conscience." Ragna wagged a finger at her husband. "Find another way."

She marched back into the hut. Kiana found her mouth had dropped open and quickly shut it. Ragna had stood up for her when she and Beren first arrived in the village, but this was the first time she'd seen evidence of how much influence the woman had over the chieftain.

She glanced at Soren. He straightened his shoulders and, without looking at Kiana, strode away.

In the end, the council decided the best way to protect their people from the winter cold and storms was to gather them all together in one large hut. Over the next three days, everyone worked to take the village apart, hut by hut, using the hides to expand and add thickness to the walls of the council hut. A hole left in the central roof allowed smoke from the cook fire to escape.

"It's not unlike sewing torn skin," Inga remarked the first day when she showed Kiana and some of the older children how to sew the separated hides together. The children grinned ghoulishly at the comparison but to Kiana it brought memories of slashes and torn limbs she'd sewn on injured warriors.

She changed the subject. "At least food won't be a problem with our stores still safe in the cook hut."

"True." Inga tilted her head toward one of the farmers. "Did you hear? Skara suggested putting the livestock in the main hut with the rest of us. To keep us warm, he said."

Kiana grinned. "Imagine the smell."

"Oh, I'm sure someone did. They're building a second hut instead. We can put some of the grain in there that won't freeze and the fish once the fleet returns. We'll salt them as soon as they're back."

Even with the sea on their threshold, ice flows made fishing dangerous, if not impossible, during the coldest months. Before Kiana's arrival, no one knew how to preserve food for longer than a few days. Now the salting process she'd observed in the palace kitchens allowed meat and fish to keep all winter.

"I'm glad it helps," Kiana responded. "Beren and I need to eat as well."

Inga chuckled, and they returned to their task. Kiana hoped it wasn't in vain. Well on its way to becoming a snug shelter, only time would tell if the altered hut was as reliable a protection as the mountain caves.

Two days later the fleet returned, swelling the number of men in the village. However, they were just fishermen, and though a few hunted, animals were not men. It was almost impossible to train battle-killing into those not raised to it, so the number of actual warriors stayed the same.

Despite her experience stitching up wounded soldiers, Kiana was terrible at sewing and hated the domestic task. Her skills lay with sword and bow, and after three days of bleeding fingers and Southland curses, Inga finally took pity on her clumsiness and complained to Soren.

"This might be a good time to visit the strangers," he said after calling Kiana aside. "Find out if they truly intend to honor our bargain."

Grateful for the reprieve, she hastened to the hut she shared with Beren, though she suspected if anyone reneged on the bargain it wouldn't be the strangers.

He laughed at her grumpiness. "It's your fault for telling Chieftain Soren you were a fleeing soldier when we arrived, instead of the daughter of a great wizard."

"It seemed prudent at the time." She shoved arrows into a hide quiver and tested the string on the bow. "No one must know who you are."

"I don't see that it matters." The boy sighed, his tone petulant. "We're never going back there, and everyone we know is dead now."

His words brought an image of Yasmin the last time Kiana had seen her little sister, all misty-eyed with first love.

She tamped down a pang of grief, remembering even as she did so that Beren's words had a more personal meaning for him. He'd lost his parents, and that was what he missed most, not his palace or the servants. Children, especially Beren, were resilient, and he'd become part of the village. Despite not having Kiana's skills, he'd had no trouble picking up the local language. She was still considered an outsider, but him…everyone liked Beren.

She was grateful the women whose children were too old to fuss over enjoyed mothering him, fixing rents in his clothes, feeding him the plumpest berries, even giving him clothes their own children had outgrown.

She patted the stiffened hides along his leg. "Don't go running any races," she teased.

When a tiny smile twisted the corners of his mouth, her spirits lifted. She slung the bow over her shoulder, ducked through the doorway, and headed toward the ridge. The plaintive notes of Beren's flute followed her from the village.

So there she was, stalking through the woods, ready to spy on a potential enemy. Or a potential ally, if Soren changed his mind about staying.

Thank the Lady, he was willing to stay. Even if there was still time to leave with Beren for another settlement, the boy's injury prevented him from walking. He needed to rest in one place until his leg healed, and that meant waiting until spring.

More time for their enemies to find them.

She banished the thought. There was no help for it. She'd have to be more vigilant, pay attention to anyone asking after them.

The closer she came to the encampment, the more irritable she became. She didn't like the Norsemen. They were too big, too good-looking, too…

She slapped at a low-hanging branch. *Be honest, you don't know what those other Norsemen are like. Just him. Tor.*

He was arrogant and pushy, and like many men, one who imagined he always knew best. Men who believed themselves privileged annoyed her, but this one… Lady, why did this one get under her skin? Of course, it had nothing to do with her mother's augury. No matter what the high priestess had seen in the mystic smoke, Kiana didn't believe this…*Norseman*…was her future.

For a short while they'd been allies of a sort against the gray man, and in that strange metal cavern, but she knew nothing about him…about any of them. Their tale of being dragged through a hole in the world had to be just that, a tale, too fantastical to believe.

But then, so was a sky ship with a ghostly protector, lightning in its walls, and boxes that opened windows into stone rooms.

At the top of the last ridge, she gazed down on the beach and caught her breath.

Near the tree line, where last she'd seen men piling lengths of wood taken from the beached ship, stood the foundations of an enormous hut. The base was even bigger than the ship they'd scavenged the boards from, a ship that no longer existed.

The beach was crowded too. Three tent-like shelters ranged high above the tide mark, the side flaps lifted to reveal the interiors. Women tended fires, children dashed among the adults, playing the same mysterious chasing game known to children in every village, and the men…

Some practiced with wooden swords on a cleared space near the beach. Closer to hand, one man had set up what she recognized as a crude forge and was busy doing something puzzling with bits of metal piled on the ground at his feet. Kiana was too far to tell whether the metal was fodder for the forge or the result of its efforts. Other men worked on the large hut, banging rocks against wooden walls.

Off to one side a pen of branches and rope held several different animals: sheep, some pregnant cows, a few goats. In a separate pen roamed a young bull—in its first season, if Kiana was any judge—and beside it more pens had been erected for the other male animals. A rooster strutted around another enclosed area, inspecting his hens. Three dogs ran loose along the beach, snapping at the waves and chased by five small boys. They reminded her of Beren and the puppy he'd owned. He'd been heartbroken when it fell into an open well the summer he turned three.

There were as many people there as in the village, more perhaps, for several men worked among the trees. Yet the hut they were building, judging from the foundation, was big enough to house twice as many. How did they plan to finish it? They'd used all the wood from the beached ship to create the base. Unlike in her homeland, clay wasn't strong enough for use in this harsh northern climate. If they planned to use hides to complete the shelter, they'd need to kill a lot of deer to cover such an enormous frame. Perhaps they intended to cannibalize the remaining ships.

A steady, rhythmic *chud-chud-chud* came from the forest. She squinted. One man, a big bear of a warrior, had stripped to the waist. Muscles flexed with every swing of his arms back and forth. Each forward swing stopped with a jerk, accompanied by that strange *chud* sound.

"You don't have to spy on us," said a feminine voice behind her.

Kiana slapped her hand to her sword and swung around. Tor's sister, Runa, stood a few paces away. Her dress was bunched in one hand and in the dip formed by the fabric lay dozens of ripe bilberries, the lush fruit so dark a purple as to look black.

Runa smiled. "You were invited here, after all."

Kiana cursed under her breath. Why hadn't she heard the woman? She'd become careless these last few years, but Runa's smile was genuine, and Kiana found herself relaxing. "I...didn't want to intrude."

"You're not. Kiana, isn't it? Come, you can walk me back. The slope is quite steep, and I could use a steady arm on the descent." She gestured to her extended belly with another smile. "My balance isn't what it used to be."

So Kiana found herself entering the Norse camp at Runa's side. Several people raised their heads when they passed, but returned to their work without questioning Kiana's presence. The children, however, were honest enough to gather around and point until Runa shooed them away with a mock scowl.

"You deal well with them," Kiana observed with not a little

envy.

She chuckled. "Just practicing for when I have one of my own to bully."

Kiana remembered the trail she'd crossed a few days ago. Still walking, she turned to Runa. "I must tell you, it's not safe for you in the woods at this time of year. You or any of the women or children. There are bears."

Runa threw her a smile. "Thank you for the warning, but we have bears where we come from also. The children know to stay in camp, and I didn't go far for these." She twitched her berry-laden skirts.

"Good." Kiana still wasn't happy, but at least she'd delivered her warning. "Good."

A cat sunned itself on a bare rock. What were you supposed to talk about with pregnant women? Her female companions back home had been fellow guards, and Queen Siri was her ruler. After a moment, she remembered overhearing her mother talking to a friend she hadn't seen in several years.

"Um…is this your first?" There, that was a good question.

Runa rubbed a hand over her belly. "Yes."

"Your husband must be happy." She tilted her head at Tor's friend on the beach.

"I have no husband," Runa snapped, but smoothed her expression when she saw where Kiana looked. "Oh, Vider." She sighed, shook her head. "No, he isn't my husband." Was that regret in her voice?

Kiana wanted to ask whether he was the babe's father, but the sadness in Runa's eyes warned her she'd not get an answer. Instead she shrugged and let the matter go.

Runa stopped at one of the tents where several women sat kneading dough for bread. One woman handed her a wooden bowl, and she dumped the berries into it before handing it back.

She straightened from her task and turned to Kiana. "Are you thirsty? We have some mead left from the cask we brought with us or there's water from the spring we found."

"What is…mead?" The word didn't translate into anything familiar.

Runa grinned. "Ah. Let me show you." She led the way to a large cask. The boy who tended it poured a golden liquid into metal cups.

Kiana studied the cup, more fascinated by the strange metal than the liquid inside. "I've never seen metal like this. Is it like the swords?"

Runa sipped her drink before nodding. "Yes, although the steel in the swords is stronger, of course."

"Steel?" Another word that didn't translate.

Runa pointed to Kiana's sword. "What is yours made of?"

"Bronze. The best our people produce." Kiana grinned with her boast, until she remembered the blade did have several nicks, the latest from Tor's sword.

Her smile faded. Bronze wasn't meant to meet an enemy sword edge to edge. It engaged on the flat of the blade or not at all. She'd been trained to avoid direct contact when possible.

Better to stab into a gut than risk damaging your weapon. "What type of sword do you carry?"

Runa raised her eyebrows. "I don't carry a sword."

"Then how do you protect yourself?" Most of the women Kiana had encountered on their flight north were the same, and she had puzzled at it.

Runa shrugged. "The men protect us."

"And if the men are killed in battle?" They'd be defenseless against enemies, human or animal.

"Then we run." Runa glanced at her belly and shrugged. "Or we die fighting with whatever we have. Do all your people—the women in your village—do they all know how to use swords?"

"A few were willing to learn weapons work. We're isolated here, and I'm told no enemies have attacked in a generation. Where I come from, though, my people all know how to defend themselves, men and women alike. Even the children carry knives." Kiana broke off. She hadn't meant to say so much.

"Oh, we carry knives." Runa patted a bone knife at her belt. "For cutting fruit or cloth." She studied her. "Your people…you bear the skin color of the southern climes, but not as dark as the Africs. Are you from the Spanish states or the Arabies, then?"

Kiana shrugged, not understanding the names. To cover her discomfort, she took a swig of the mead.

It burned all the way down her throat, and she gasped for breath. "What…?" She coughed, swallowed, tried again. "What is this?" Whatever it was, it had the strongest kick she'd ever tasted. Not even the king's finest wines were this potent.

"Mead." Runa slapped her on the back. "It's made from honey."

Kiana took another cautious sip. The burn wasn't as bad the second time. "That's not honey."

Runa laughed. "It's fermented with herbs and water. Vider found a hive yesterday so we're in hopes of making more. We brought dried herbs and fruit with us just for that purpose."

Kiana licked her lips. "I don't taste any fruit."

"You won't. We use dried grapes from the South to give the

honey and water flavor, but it won't taste like grapes, just more…*more*, I suppose." Runa shrugged. "Once it's mixed, it's left and can be used after three or four days, although there's no harm leaving it longer. I'm no expert in the process, but I do know we use all parts of the hive, even the bees themselves sometimes."

Kiana paused before taking another sip. Even the bees? Squinting, she studied the liquid, but no dead bodies floated in it. "Your bees have more secrets than ours, then," she muttered.

Runa chuckled. "We'd have brought wine with us, but water was more important, and mead is easier to make in a hurry. Do you have wine where you come from?"

"Oh, yes." She didn't want to think about palace life. "You asked where I came from. The villagers call them the hot lands, but not the places you named."

Runa tilted her head. "What brings you this far north?"

The murder of my family. The slaughter of my people. Forcing down the helpless anger, she shrugged again. "We wanted a change of scene."

Runa snorted. "Very well. Keep your secrets. Now, what were you looking at from the ridge that had you so entranced you didn't hear me lumbering up behind you."

Unable to stop herself, Kiana laughed. "Oh, Lady, you don't lumber."

Runa squinted at her swollen belly, then laughed herself.

"What's so amusing?" a male voice asked.

They turned at the words. Tor strode toward them. He, too, like the big man in the woods was stripped to the waist. His muscles weren't as big as the other man's but…oh, the sight of all that tanned flesh—arms strong enough to lift a horse, a chest she itched to pet—left Kiana speechless.

Sweat dripped down his face, and one droplet traced a path from his neck down his taut stomach and lower, until it disappeared into the waistband of his leggings.

She swallowed, trying to restore moisture to a dry mouth, and raised her gaze to his face. Somehow, even the scar on his cheek made her palms sweat. Kiana was powerless to look away from the man, while he stared anywhere but at her.

Runa answered for them both. "Women's jokes, brother." She glanced between the two of them, then pressed a hand to the small of her back and stretched. "That little walk fair tired me out. I'm going to lie down for a while. Tor, why don't you show Kiana around the camp?"

Without waiting for an answer, Runa returned to the tents.

Despite her complaint, her stride was graceful…and not at all fatigued.

Tor turned to Kiana. "I guess I'm supposed to welcome you to our camp." He sounded nervous.

The idea that she made this big, brave warrior uneasy helped Kiana regain her composure. She tilted her chin at the wooden base near the trees. "That's more permanent than a camp."

He started toward the foundation, and Kiana had to trot to catch up with him. "We plan to stay." He indicated the timber half-walls. "There's no time before winter to build more than just one structure. This will be the longhouse. All our people will stay together for the winter months, and in the spring we'll build more."

So, they had the same idea as Soren. She studied the foundation. Up close the space was even bigger than she expected. The ground inside had been packed down by what looked like many feet and was as hard as stone. "That will be mud in the first rainstorm."

He shook his head. "We'll cover it with straw, then wood on top. They tell me that keeps the cold from your feet."

"Wood on top?" Kiana furrowed her brow. "But you've used all the wood from that broken ship."

This earned her a puzzled stare. He gestured toward the forest. "What is that, then, but wood waiting to be cut into planks?"

She followed his pointing finger. "You're trying to cut the trees?"

The South held few trees, the land around her home barren and dry, desert sands and tumbled rock. What trees grew were spindly and bent with the winds. *These* trees were tall and straight, with trunks so wide she'd not be able to touch her fingertips if she hugged one, but the villagers didn't harvest them.

"Not trying. Doing. You've never seen trees cut before?" For the first time since she met him, Tor smiled, not a smirk or twist of the lips but a true smile.

It transformed his face from grim to…well, breathtaking. Despite the thick beard…or perhaps because of it…she found herself fascinated by his face: hair stringy with sweat flopping over a high forehead, beard braided into three points that emphasized high cheekbones, a crooked nose that must have been broken at one time, firm mouth with full ripe lips.

Her gaze stumbled to a halt on those lips. Her own tingled. In memory? Or anticipation?

Stop staring. She lowered her gaze to the piles of thick logs stacked at the edge of the forest. One man strode from between the trees and threw another three logs onto the pile.

What had he asked?

"No, I've never seen people cut trees." In their travels north she and Beren passed through many villages, and those huts…yes, those huts had some wood.

For the most part, though, they were a mixture of stone and earth, and what the locals called thatch, but they had doors of wood. Once she and Beren settled in the village, where the huts were made of hide and bent twigs, she hadn't given the building materials another thought.

Now, studying what the men were doing, she noticed a pattern. The men swinging their arms held long sticks with blades on the end. She knew those blades, had seen them before, but surely these weren't the same? "What are they using?"

"Axes." Tor sounded amused at her question. Or was it at the preceding silence?

She blushed, but ignored the heat in her skin. "But you said axes were weapons, not tools."

He smiled. "They're both."

Intrigued, Kiana approached for a closer look. The axes cut into the tree trunks like soft gruel, and as soon as a tree fell, other men swarmed over it, cutting branches to pile to one side, chopping the thicker branches and the trunk into logs. Still more men took the logs from the pile one by one and split them, again with axes, into thinner boards.

She studied the foundation again. "You plan to build this all of wood? No hides?"

"We'll use hides inside, on the sleeping benches," he confirmed, "but the walls…yes, all made of wood and some stone. Come."

He led her to the foundation, his reluctance to show her around vanished. He stepped over the knee-high wall and headed for the middle of the space. The area was longer than wide, and a circle of stones was arranged at each of the ends. "The fire pits will go there and another in the middle. We have winter storms at home so we'll build to withstand them. They can't be much worse here."

Kiana noted the pride in his words but said nothing. Despite herself, she was impressed.

After a few moments of silence, Tor cleared his throat. "So, did you come here for a reason?"

"Hmm? Oh, no particular reason." There was no hurry. If Soren's plan worked, she and Beren had no need to come as beggars yet. Still, she needn't return empty-handed. "Tell me, is it possible to take some of the mead with me?"

He grinned. "You like it, do you?"

"Well…" She gazed at him from under her lashes, something her sister did often when she wanted to get her own way. "It does taste better than water."

At Tor's explosion of laughter, she allowed herself a wide grin.

Chapter Ten

Kiana reported to Soren what she'd seen. When she stopped talking, he said nothing for a few moments. She waited, certain he hadn't finished with her.

"Tell me again about this hut they build," he ordered.

"It's big, perhaps eight or ten times bigger than that." She flicked a hand toward the frame of the council hut, already stripped and ready for the sewn hide cover.

Soren stared into the distance. "Big enough to hold all their people?"

"As well as the animals they brought with them, with much room to spare." She paused, wondering how much more to say. "Tor—their leader—told me they plan to stay, and if they do use that building for all their people in winter, then it makes sense for them to build it big enough to take more people. There are several pregnant women so a few more mouths to feed and bodies to shelter before spring."

Soren focused his attention once more on the village. "It is interesting, this news." Then, waving his hand in dismissal, he strode away, calling his advisers into the smaller hut he'd taken over while the council hut was being enlarged.

After making her way to the healer's hut to check on Beren, Kiana found the boy leaning against the central support post, upright but braced on one leg. In one hand he held a sturdy branch as tall as he.

She hurried forward. "Foolish boy. It's too soon for you to be up."

He clung to the pole and his branch, ignoring her outstretched hand. "Inga said I have to get used to being up. She said if I keep lying down my leg will die, and she'll have to cut it off."

The leg was that bad?

Forcing herself to show nothing but calm, she accepted his refusal, then left the hut in search of Inga. She found the woman in

Birgitte's hut, helping in the final stages of birthing. Despite her own misgivings, but not wanting to miss a chance to speak to the healer, Kiana waited just inside the doorway, mesmerized by the sight.

Birgitte panted with pain and exertion, but, unlike the women of Kiana's country, the mothers in this village never gave voice to their pain.

One more push, and something red and wrinkled fell into Inga's hands. A moment later, the baby hauled in its first breath and let it out in an explosive wail. Inga finished the job of detaching the child from its mother, then wrapped it in cloths and laid it in the woman's arms.

Kiana wiped damp palms on her leggings and cleared her throat. "Healer."

Inga concentrated on the woman before her. "One moment."

Blood gushed from between Birgitte's legs, then other—stuff. Kiana had wrapped field dressings on men with limbs cut off or hanging by a thread, had held the hands of warriors with their guts spilling on the ground while they died, but a battlefield didn't prepare her for this…this messy birthing process. She had been old enough and curious enough to sneak into her mother's chambers when her brother was born. She remembered the hours of suffering, the pain her mother endured, only to lose the child before he took his first breath. It made no sense, but ever since, Kiana expected death with every birth she witnessed, and no matter that most were successful, she never shook that illogical belief.

Unable to stand it any longer, she ducked out of the hut. She inhaled the crisp air and decided she'd never have children of her own.

Inga emerged from the hut to stand beside her. "It's not as bad as it looks."

"Of course." Kiana swallowed bile, took another deep breath. She waved at the hut door. "How do they stand it? I mean, I can understand them going through that with the first one. They don't know any better. But this is Birgitte's fifth."

Inga laughed. After wiping her hands on a damp cloth she'd brought out with her, she patted Kiana's arm. "The gods make them forget the pain and just remember the joy."

Kiana shook her head in disbelief. "If you ask me, the gods are addled in the head."

Again the healer chuckled. "Gods are men. What do you expect? Now, what is so important you'd brave a birthing hut to talk to me?"

The memory of Beren clinging to the center pole in Inga's hut banished the unpleasantness Kiana had just witnessed. "Beren. How bad is the leg really?"

"Ah." The healer strolled away, gesturing Kiana to walk with her. "It will heal, but not if it doesn't get enough blood. I gave him instructions to help it, but he decided he liked being waited upon. So I told him what would happen if he didn't move his lazy hide."

Relieved, Kiana had to grin. "Ah. I hoped it might be something like that." The grin faded, and she placed a hand on Inga's arm, echoing the healer's gesture a few minutes earlier. "Thank you."

"Don't thank me." She grinned. "You're the one who's going to have to bully him from now on. I'm releasing him back to your hut."

"Oh." Kiana dropped her hand, but panic threatened. "I can't look after Beren. I have too much to do, and I may not be there all the time. I have to visit the strangers, the Norsemen, for Soren, and there are bear tracks near the cove so we'll need to send out a hunting party, and we still need deer for the winter."

The healer smirked. "All the better. If you aren't around to care for him he'll have even more incentive to move around on his own." She winked. "Especially if he wants to eat. I told him he'd have to make his own way to the campfires. No one is going to wait on him."

Kiana laughed. "No young boy can go for longer than an hour, two at most, without something in his mouth."

However, it wouldn't be easy. As the dwellings were taken apart, everyone shared the few left with their neighbors, so she'd have to find somewhere other than their own hut for Beren to rest. Huts built for two people now housed six, and even one of the storage lean-tos had become a temporary home for three hardy old men. Perhaps she'd settle him with Lida in her family's hut for a few days. Even that short time might make him more independent.

"Kiana," one of the chieftain's advisors called and waved.

Saying goodbye to Inga, Kiana headed toward Soren's hut. When she entered, she found the chieftain alone. He motioned her to a pile of hides on the floor and sat on another pile across from her. His great chair remained in the council hut, too heavy to move. "When you came to us two winters ago, I saw the value you'd bring to this village."

Kiana held her tongue. The chieftain had been the most vocal in insisting they not take her and Beren in, until his advisers, prompted, she suspected by Ragna, pointed out the advantage of having an actual warrior in residence.

"And you have proved your worth in many ways, validating my decision to let you stay." He paused, cleared his throat. "These…axes…the strangers have…"

"Yes, Chieftain?" Perhaps he'd heeded her words after all.

Soren rubbed his chin. "I'm not convinced the council hut will serve our purposes as planned, but if it was reinforced with wood sides…" He paused.

Kiana understood. "You want to bargain for axes as well as the furs?"

"We've lost the caves. If we're to stay, I believe we need something stronger to live in."

If we're to stay… A knot tightened in Kiana's stomach. They *had* to stay. She and Beren wouldn't survive a winter by themselves, not unless they made their own bargains. *What do we have to bargain with*?

She fought the panic from her voice. "I'll see what I can do."

On her way back to the hut, Kiana saw Lida sharpening her spear, and Kiana had an idea.

~ * ~

The next morning, Tor lowered his axe and wiped the sweat from his face and chest. The number of cut logs headed for the longhouse remained constant, finished planks thrown on one end of the pile even as builders took them from the other. While the height of the walls increased with each passing hour, still it seemed too slow.

Vider strode past and deposited a bundle of boards onto the growing pile. He grabbed a water skin and gulped the contents before wandering over to Tor. "You know, I never appreciated what went into building a longhouse."

Tor grinned. "I know what you mean. I thought they just tied the boards together, but it's more complicated than that. At least we've got Petter making nails."

The blacksmith melted the metal they'd scavenged from Emund's ship and shaped it into hundreds of nails, which were then pounded into the boards and bent to hold them in place.

"Any more ideas what we can trade to the villagers?" Vider asked.

"Just furs."

The hunt had been good so far, but not enough meat filled the salt-chests piled near the trees. There were fish in the sea, but again, not enough to catch before winter. Besides, they needed more than meat. Grains for bread, herbs and fruits and green things to keep away the sickness that preceded starvation.

"There has to be something else." Vider stared up the mountain at the metal sky ship. "What about those boxes?"

"Not without knowing how they work. Any luck getting Petter to melt them down?"

"No." Vider sighed. "He's too busy making nails and axe heads to waste time on a whim." He grinned at Tor. "His words, not mine. I left it with him, and he promised to try if he gets a spare moment."

"Pity." Tor bent to his axe again but paused at Vider's next words.

"She's back."

Tor followed Vider's gaze toward the southern tree line. *Kiana*. Heat flooded his body, and his breath quickened. Sweat dampened his palms. He set the axe aside before it slipped from his fingers. As she emerged from the trees, a forest nymph in battle armor, he smiled in anticipation. The restlessness vanished. The day had become more interesting.

She strode into the village as if she belonged. Bow slung over her shoulder, sword at her back, she looked like a warrior ready to face battle.

She was accompanied by five women, dressed like Kiana in trews and shirt and carrying bows and spears. Tor recognized two as among those who had captured him when they first arrived. Kiana looked around, then her gaze lit on Tor. To his amusement, she stumbled—because of him?—then regained her balance and hurried forward.

"Welcome," he said when she was close enough to hear.

She nodded a greeting, her gaze on his face. "Some of my warriors wanted to see how your men train."

Tor studied the women standing behind Kiana. He raised an eyebrow. "Warriors?"

She stiffened, her shoulders straightening. "Do you not believe women can be warriors?"

Gods, he admired the way she bristled. It was so easy to tease her. "Of course they can, but I'd not call your companions warriors." Tor gestured to the bustling camp behind him. "Most of our women cook and care for their men and their children. They're to be protected, not given a sword to fight battles. Some choose to be shield maidens and are trained with the men, but I doubt your women have such training."

"Do you object to us watching the practice?" Her voice was as stiff as her back.

Tor glanced at Vider. His friend's hand covered his mouth, and his eyes sparkled with laughter. He turned away, winked at Vider, then turned back, his expression composed into the gracious host. "I don't object to you and your friends watching. Are you looking for husbands?"

Her eyes opened wide. "What?"

He shrugged and indicated several young women who stood at the edge of the practice area, cheering on the warriors. "It's what our maidens do, watch and judge who will make the best husband."

Vider made a strange choking sound, but Tor's attention was on the flared nostrils and red flush on Kiana's face. Odin's beard, she was beautiful when angry.

"Actually," she said after a moment, her tone still stiff and formal, "my *warriors* are here to give yours some tips."

She marched away, leading her five companions to the practice area. Tor made sure she didn't hear his low chuckle.

"I think you may have just lost any chance of making an ally of that one," Vider murmured.

"It was worth it." He studied the women with a critical eye. "You don't seriously believe those village women are trained warriors, do you?"

Vider shrugged. "Maybe not, but Runa said—"

"Aha!" He might have known his headstrong sister had something to do with Vider's attitude.

Vider ignored the interruption. "Runa said it made sense for *all* the women to learn how to fight, not just the shield maidens. What if the men are killed in battle? And sometimes the women can't run away. Look at Runa. She'd never get far in her condition. And mothers are slowed by their children."

Tor was struck by the wisdom in that. The gods knew Runa was more vulnerable than most at present. She had never mentioned learning knife or sword, and it never occurred to him she might want to.

If she'd been able to defend herself when Ottar had taken her…

"It makes sense," Vider persisted. "These villagers, their men are away, you saw that. Who was left to defend the village? Young boys and ancients. So why not have the women prepared to defend themselves as well?"

"Hmm." Tor stroked his beard. "I suppose it can't hurt."

Vider stared after the women. "Good," he said in amusement, "because Runa isn't waiting for your permission."

"What?" Tor whirled.

One of his men handed Runa his sword, and Kiana showed her how to hold it. Annoyed, Tor strode toward the women. Frowning in concentration, Runa held the sword in both hands—*Odin's beard, she'll cut herself if she's not careful*—and stabbed it toward Kiana. Tor broke into a run. *Cut herself? She'll kill someone.*

Kiana sidestepped the thrust and used her own sword to deflect the blade. Tor arrived in time to hear her say, "It'll take time to get used to the weight. This is too long. Can you have something shorter made for you?"

"She's not having anything made for her." Tor glared at his sister and snatched at the sword. *What is she thinking, in her condition*? "She's going to go rest before she does herself an injury."

To his shock, Runa held the sword out of his reach, turned her back on him, and spoke to Kiana. "I'll see about it. So what do I do if someone pushes my sword out of the way like you did?"

Kiana twisted her hand. "Then you—"

"Stop." Tor thrust himself between the two women and faced Runa. "You'll not do this."

Runa raised her chin. "Why not?"

"Because…because…" *Because you are with child, and I don't want you to get hurt.*

Some of Tor's men had gathered around. Aware that more than his sister's folly was the subject of their interest, that his leadership might be at stake, he glared at Runa. She glared back. Outrage threatened his control. Didn't she realize she might be hurt, even with training swords? Didn't she understand he'd never forgive himself if anything happened to her?

However, that stare calmed him down. His sister wasn't one to take on a task at a whim.

"Brother." She laid a hand on his arm. Her gaze softened, leaving no sign of her anger. "It doesn't diminish you."

Kiana spoke up. "The men of my homeland are proud to fight next to us, and knowing we can defend ourselves makes it easier for them to concentrate when they go away to battle. But…" She paused, her gaze swinging from Tor to Runa and back. "I don't wish to go against your wishes if you don't want me to teach your women. Know that I'll not teach them battle skills, just enough to defend themselves at need."

He remained silent a moment longer and forced himself to consider the logic through his fear. Her words made sense, and he didn't object to the other women learning, but the idea of Runa having to fight…

No, not fight. Defend herself. That argument he approved. One glance at his men showed most agreed, the rest not hostile to the idea. Fine, but he'd still take precautions.

He turned to Vider. "Find out if Petter has some training swords the women can use." Boys as young as eight sometimes joined the warriors. He turned back to Kiana. "They're short and light, made of wood. Our women don't need the longer swords." Now wasn't the time for teasing. This was serious. "But, if you teach women in Runa's condition, you'll do nothing that endangers them or their babes."

She smiled. "Agreed. Gentle exercises. No long swords." She paused, swallowed. "Um, does your blacksmith also make your axes?"

Puzzled at the change in subject, Tor nodded. "When there's need for them."

She straightened her shoulders "We will add thirty loaves of bread to our trade, in return for six of your axes."

Axes? What did her people need with axes? Still, thirty loaves, although a cheap payment, allowed them to conserve their less perishable food stores. *But let's not look too eager*. "Make it forty loaves."

"Agreed." She looked over at the training field. "Women may not have the strength to lift your large swords, but we're quick and sometimes that more than makes the difference. Would you let me and my companions train with your men, so we may exchange skills?"

Tor hesitated, but there wasn't any reason for him to object, and it might be amusing. "Agreed."

~ * ~

Kiana stood beside Tor at the edge of the crowd encircling the training area on the beach while two unarmed, bare-chested warriors grappled with each other. Her trainees seemed impressed by the display, but she had seen men wrestling all her life. She admired the muscles rippling on strong bodies, the suppleness needed to slide out of hand holds, the near impossible contortions to subdue or escape a competitor. But the moves themselves? Those she recognized. There were only so many ways for a body to bend, after all.

Then one man did the unexpected. He grasped the waistband of his partner's leggings and yanked down, revealing the startled man in all his glory. The crowd roared with laughter, and Kiana wasn't surprised to hear the women, both Norse and villagers, cheering the loudest. The ploy served its purpose, and the other man vanquished his distracted opponent with no further resistance. Once released, the loser hastily pulled up his leggings, shot the crowd a sheepish grin, and rejoined his fellow warriors on the sidelines.

Kiana glanced at Tor. "A fine trick."

"One of many." He signaled his men, who tossed various items into the arena: a pitcher, a stick, a belt.

She raised an eyebrow. "You can use those as weapons?"

"Not just those. We also use the sun. Watch."

Two men stepped into the space. They drew their swords—sharp metal, not dull wood—and crouched, facing each other, then proceeded to demonstrate how to use the common objects to distract an opponent. At one point one of the men, on his knees and seemingly at the mercy of his opponent, angled his weapon so the sun reflected into the other's eyes, blinding him. He then took quick advantage and soon stood the victor.

Kiana glanced at her bronze sword. Even polished it couldn't produce a reflection bright enough to blind, and she now understood why they hadn't used wooden swords for this display.

Tor caught her eye, then looked at the now-empty space. He'd finally—*finally*—put on his shirt, but the sight of his naked chest, sweat dripping trails through the dust, remained clear in her mind. It had taken all her inner strength not to follow those trails down to— She caught herself before the memory repeated in real life. His shirt covered the trails, but she still imagined them.

She swallowed and dragged her gaze away. The empty space. Why had he…? Oh yes, her turn in the training area. Or at least for her trainees to show what they knew.

With one last peek at Tor, Kiana turned to Lida. "You and Kari show what you can do with spear and net."

Lida grinned. There were no swords in the village, so one of the first things Kiana taught was how to use what they had as weapons. Spears and nets were common fishing tools, and as even Tor had to admit, they were also formidable on land.

Lida and Kari strode into the middle of the training area. Kari carried the barbed spear used to harpoon the seals and whales that ventured too close to shore. Lida left her weapons with Kiana and instead swung a net over her head. When she reached the center of the area, she feinted to the side, then flung the net at Kari, who ducked and lunged with her spear. Lida rolled under Kari's feet. She leaped to avoid being tripped, but Lida had reached her net and now rose, swinging it side-to-side.

Kiana smiled in approval. Lida had proven the most adept of the trainees, and now showed how well she'd absorbed her training. Net fighting was impractical in actual battle. The net needed to be large enough to engulf a whole man, and to cast such a net required lots of space and the use of both hands. The enemy, meanwhile, was free to throw javelins or charge, or once the net was thrown, deflect it with those same javelins. As traps, though, they were very effective. When Kiana decided to use them as weapons, she'd adapted the smaller nets.

At the same time Lida swung the net, she rotated it through her hands. In a matter of seconds, the net became a thick rope, and this she snapped at Kari, entangling her spear and jerking it from her hands. There the demonstration stopped, for the next stage called for both to draw knives and close for more lethal battle. Lida and Kari bowed to each other, and the crowd erupted in cheers.

"Clever," Tor said.

Kiana fought the urge to preen. "It's an effective defense when there's just one enemy."

He grunted. In agreement? "Perhaps a display of aim and

accuracy now?" He twirled his hand in some kind of signal, and the circle opened at one end. Tree branches had been gathered in piles near the water, the whole as large as wide-spread arms and covered with cloth. The center was marked with a large X.

"Our bows against yours?" Kiana judged the distance to the beach and raised her eyebrows in surprise. Fifteen paces? Even the weakest bow shot over ten times that far.

"Our axes," Tor corrected. "I've seen the accuracy of your bows." He glanced at Vider, who raised a hand to finger his ear with a rueful grin.

Axes. That made a difference. Fifteen paces may be nothing to a bow, but to throw a clumsy axe that far and with accuracy? Kiana wasn't sure it was even possible.

One of the Norsemen strode into the open area. Short and wiry, he didn't appear as strong as most of his companions. He flexed his fingers, drew an axe from his belt, and caressed the handle before wrapping his fingers around the smooth wood. He stood square to the target, one foot in front of the other, lifted the weapon over his shoulder, took a breath, stepped forward, and swung the axe. It rotated through the air, head over hilt, before the tip of the blade landed in the middle of the X.

His audience applauded and cheered.

"The axe is a good weapon," Tor said.

She turned. "I thought you preferred swords."

He hooked his thumbs in his belt. "I do, but few have one. Remember what Runa told you? Only the leading families carry swords."

She remembered. "Are the rest forbidden?"

"No." He chuckled. "You need a lot of gold for a sword, but even the lowliest farmer has an axe for cutting and splitting wood."

Ah, for fires. That made sense.

"Are you as good with your sword as you pretend to be?" His tone held underlying amusement.

She refused to be baited. It had been a mistake to cross swords with him before. Hers was better suited to cutting and stabbing, not striking another blade. Training was intense, and fighting more like a dance than a skirmish, but oh, she so wanted to show this man what a true warrior was capable of. There were tricks every soldier learned, to compensate for a weakness or to take advantage of their own strengths. Good with a sword?

She hid a smile and inclined her head. "I am. Are you?"

He gave a short laugh. "Shall we see?"

At some point in the past few minutes, Vider had returned from wherever Tor sent him. He held several wooden swords under his arm. Good, they'd do well for the women to practice with. Tor took two of the swords from Vider and tossed one at Kiana.

She caught it and studied the weapon. This was good. They'd not have the familiarity of their own swords, so it didn't matter whether one was superior to the other. This was down to skill alone.

Tor paced into the center of the circle, which had again closed together. Kiana swung the wooden sword a few times to test its weight and balance, then joined him. They faced each other, and the crowd quieted. She sensed no hostility there. Yet. What if she defeated Tor?

She crouched into a fighting stance and waited for him to make the first move.

As he had at the plateau, he swung his sword at her. This time, however, she didn't bother intercepting it. Instead she ducked under the blow and rushed forward, sliding the edge of the wooden blade along his arm as she passed. When she came to a stop behind him, he pivoted to face her. His incredulous stare made her want to laugh. A thin red line traced her sword's path down his arm. If the blade had been metal, she'd have sliced through muscles and tendons, making the limb useless.

Tor narrowed his eyes. This time he stabbed his sword toward her, but Kiana was ready and danced out of the way. They settled into a rhythm, taking turns thrusting and battering at each other. Kiana used her size and agility to stay out of reach—deadly if she allowed him to land a blow—but Tor kept her moving. He was bigger, stronger, with greater endurance. She wasn't tiring yet, but soon.

Time for one of those soldier tricks.

Tor rushed toward her once more. She dove to the ground and rolled under his legs, tripping him. Her head brushed the ground before she flipped to her feet. Tor scrambled up and turned to her. Perfect. Just where she wanted him.

She somersaulted toward him. At the arc of her jump, she jerked her head and flicked the sand clinging to her hair into his face. When she landed, he was already stumbling to his knees, one hand scrubbing at his eyes while he blindly swung his sword.

She pressed the point of her sword to his neck and said in a sweet tone, "Is that good enough?"

He froze, then lowered his hand and raised his head. Silence gripped the onlookers. Kiana sensed the tension. Sweat trickled down her back. Had she gone too far?

Tor loosened his grip, and his sword fell to the ground. He peered at her over his shoulder, eyes red and streaming, then used two fingers to carefully push her sword away from his throat. He was breathing as hard as she, his cheeks as flushed, but when their gazes caught, he nodded.

"Good enough, shield maid." His tone was warm, not grudging. He clambered to his feet, and now the audience cheered.

Kiana staggered back to the sidelines. Lida handed her a flagon of water. She dropped her own sword and took it in trembling hands.

"That was well done," Lida whispered.

Kiana gulped the water. "Better than I expected."

She assumed Tor would be angry at his defeat. Instead, he stood, surrounded by his men, accepting commiserating slaps on the back, and not looking upset at the laughter. In fact, when he glanced her way a moment later, he inclined his head. A sign of respect. It occurred to her that he might have let her win, but that nod put her suspicions to rest.

Tor slung an arm over Vider's shoulders and propelled him toward Kiana.

"The rest of the swords." He handed her the remaining wooden weapons. "I'd like to see more of what your…warriors…can teach us." This time the word *warriors* wasn't delivered with scorn.

"We know several tricks you may not have seen before," she admitted.

The rest of the afternoon passed in similar vein. Kiana's trainees worked with Tor's men, exchanging skills, while Kiana split her time between studying the mock combat and teaching basic tactics to the Norse women. In a way, the day was successful. However, the idea had been to *offer* skills, not *exchange* them. Now how did she ensure shelter for herself and Beren if Soren left them behind?

Chapter Eleven

Four days later, Tor headed toward the training grounds, a bundle under his arm. Shouts and laughter filled the air, not all of it masculine.

Over the past few days he'd grown accustomed to the sounds and the sight of men and women facing off against each other. At first he'd expected the pairings to be more social than serious, with the women using *training* as an excuse to be close to his men, but after observing a few sessions—and his initial sparring with Kiana that first day—he had to admit the women from the village were as skilled in their way as Kiana claimed.

Runa and the other women of his own people who had taken up the offer of learning defense were also gaining skills. Already most of them used the wooden training sticks without hitting themselves or tripping over them. Some, in fact, had graduated to exchanging blows with the men—even Runa, as his own bruises showed.

Kiana had surprised him the most. Skilled as her companions were, she made them appear beginners by comparison. Her demonstration with him that first day had shown a mere taste of what she was capable. She claimed she'd fought beside men in battle. Now, watching her spar against Havard, one of the biggest of Tor's crew, he believed her.

She dodged Havard's strikes with ease, got in a few blows of her own, then danced out of the way. She didn't pit her strength against his, but used agility and, yes, guile, to fight him. He came at her, and she leaned to the side, as if to dodge that way, but when he twisted to compensate she shifted the other way and slipped under his guard. Tor had never seen deception used so well. Truth be told, he was learning a few tricks himself.

A few minutes later, Kiana and Havard parted, stopping by mutual consent. When she turned away, her gaze lit on Tor, and for a brief instant her expression lightened. A moment later, she schooled her features into blandness and strolled over. Sweat gleamed on her face and exposed arms.

The scent teased his nostrils. He itched to slide his fingers over the dampness, savor her heat. He knew of other ways to make her hot and damp and sweaty. Better ways.

He tightened his grip on the bundle until his fingers ached and fought the urge to drag her into the woods and show her those ways.

"Come to learn something, Norseman?" She drew a cloth from her weapons bag and wiped at her face.

He shifted the bundle lower. *Act normal. She'll expect you to tease her*. "The day I learn anything from a woman is the day I walk into Asgard." At least his voice didn't tremble.

She tilted her head. "Asgard?"

"The home of the gods." He looked around the camp. "We've decided to call this place New Asgard, in their honor, for if not for the gods we'd not be here."

"The gods and the sky ship," she corrected in a low voice, as if reluctant to remind him of their accidental arrival.

He scowled at the mountain. Already the shape of the metal ship was impossible to make out. More of the mountain had collapsed on it over the last ten days after it settled. Some of the bushes and trees, bent by the force of the crash, now straightened and strained toward the weak sun, striving for their previous position. Had the entrance been covered up yet? At least her talk of the sky ship had eased the tightness of his trews.

"So what have you there?" Kiana drew his attention back to the bundle he held.

"Ah." He waggled his eyebrows to emphasize the mystery and led her away from the training area to a pile of logs near the tree line.

There he laid the bundle on the ground and opened it. Two other bundles lay inside. He opened one to reveal six short steel swords, each with a delicate hilt and guard small enough for a boy's—or woman's—hand.

Kiana gasped in delight and lifted one out. She swung it, testing the weight. "Good balance, and it's so light." She narrowed her eyes. "I thought you wanted your women to use the wooden swords. Do you now trust them with real ones?"

He wanted to squirm. No, he didn't trust them with real ones, but if it ever came to defending themselves, they'd need every advantage. Not that he'd ever admit that.

"The wooden ones often break, and we don't have time to keep making new ones." There, that sounded reasonable. "They might as well use these and be done with it."

She relaxed. "Yes, these will be perfect for your women." There was a gleam of envy in her eyes.

"Would you like one?" he asked on impulse.

She looked up. For a moment, the envy was replaced by avarice. She hesitated, then laid the short sword back with the others. "My own sword is good enough for my needs, but thank you for the offer." She stared at the second bundle. "More swords?"

"No." He smiled and drew back the cloth.

"Axes!" Kiana lifted one out. Even though the shaft was of wood, the metal head made it heavier than a sword, but she hefted the weapon with ease. After a few experimental swings, she replaced it with the others. "These will do well."

He had to know. "Why do you want them?"

She traced a finger over the smooth handle. "Soren wishes to have wooden walls, like yours." She gestured at the half-completed building, already as tall as Tor's waist.

He remembered the arrogant village chieftain. If he believed owning a few axes made it possible for his people to copy the longhouse, he'd be disappointed. "It takes skill to build such walls. Anyone can swing at a tree and cut it down, but the walls need logs that are shaped just right. Does your chieftain have people with such skills?"

She hesitated then said, "I'm not sure. Can it be learned?"

Something else to trade, perhaps? He shrugged. "We shall see."

Kiana gestured toward the beach, where several boys played Catch the Stick. "They're getting along well."

Two boys tossed a stick between them, while a third jumped to snatch it out of the air when it passed over his head. Unlike the adults, the village children hadn't hesitated to take advantage of new playmates and had been coming to the camp for several days now. Only their clothes differentiated them from the Norse.

"It's good to hear them laugh." He'd been surprised how fast the youngsters who'd come with them into exile recovered from the hardships of the journey.

She shrugged. "Children always find a way to escape the attention of adults. Beren will want to come too, once his leg is healed. I think they get bored with companions they've grown up with, and new faces are a challenge."

Who was Beren? Did she have a child of her own? "Was…Beren…injured?"

She looked away. "He and some friends were on the mountain

when the sky ship hit it."

He straightened. "Was anyone killed?"

Kiana shook her head. "No, thank the Lady. Some of the falling rocks broke Beren's leg, but the healer says it will mend. It could have been worse."

Tor's heart tightened. "Is Beren your son?" *And where is your husband*?

She hesitated before answering. "His mother…died, a few years ago. I promised to care for him. Everyone calls him my son because it's simpler."

He frowned. "She had no other family to look after him?"

"Not anymore." She stared into the distance and lowered her voice. "Neither of us do."

So, no husband. Guilt shot through him. If she had a husband once, she'd lost him. She was alone. Tor wanted to put his arms around her, to comfort her. Instead, he returned his gaze to the children. "You're not worried about them playing here?"

She glanced back at the boys. "They were careful when they first came but children…well, they tend to be ignored. And curious."

He raised a hand to touch her face, but drew it back before she noticed. "Did you want me to send them home?"

"No. Let them play." She returned her attention to him, then sighed. "I'd best get these axes back to the village."

Tor rewrapped the bundle. "What of the swords?"

This time she flashed him a grin. "I'll let you have the honor of giving them out to your women. I'm sure Runa, at least, will be delighted." She turned to the bundles. "Again, thank you for the axes." She lifted the heavy bag, settled it on her shoulder then strode into the forest.

A small piece of him went with her.

~ * ~

For the next ten days, life in the camp fell into a routine. The longhouse rose taller with each day, its sturdy wooden walls reinforced with beach stone to fill the chinks and provide strength. With everyone except the hunters working on the building, a task of a year or more was being accomplished in mere weeks. Of course, this wasn't as complex as most great halls Tor was familiar with. There'd only be one open space and the usual sleeping benches lining the sides, but no trestle tables for eating.

Each day more villagers visited the camp, some to take part in the training. Mothers brought their children to play with the Norse children and sat with the Norse women baking and sewing and picking up more of each other's language. Even some of the men ventured from their village, the extra help welcome in raising the longhouse.

Kiana came often, sometimes helping with translations, sometimes training with Tor's men, sometimes teaching the women while the men looked on in fascination. She seldom spoke to him, and he found himself spending more time on the training ground watching her than out hunting or working on the longhouse.

This morning, though, Kiana was waiting for him. When he arrived, she strode from the training area to join him. "I wanted to show Runa a new move. Is she nearby?"

Tor nodded at the forest. "She went picking berries this morning with some of the other women. Something about eating fresh and saving our stores for the cold days."

Kiana stiffened. "I told her to keep everyone out of the forest."

"*You* told her?" Irritation banished his mellow mood. "She doesn't answer to you."

She frowned. "Didn't she tell you about the bears?"

Had she? "What bears?"

"They don't often come this close to settlements, but there are tracks nearby." She swept past him.

Bears in Tor's homeland were timid creatures, but what did he know of those in this land? "She knows enough to make noise in the woods," he soothed. "The bears will keep away." *Wouldn't they*?

"Not the ones here," Kiana explained. "They'll eat anything that crosses their path, this time of year more than others."

"Your village women come and go with no problems."

"They know the signs and take the direct route." She frowned. "Searching for berries could take your women anywhere. The bears stay away from settlements, but unarmed women in their territory—"

Memory of the chieftain's cloak filled Tor's mind. Those claws… He cursed. If he'd known, he'd have sent warriors with the pickers. The women weren't unarmed, but the bone knives they carried for cutting branches were no defense against a determined predator.

He shouted orders to his men and led the way toward the trees, trying to remember if his sister had said where they'd be gathering berries today.

~ * ~

Runa was in trouble. Kiana was sure of it. Blessed Inanna, let the woman not be harmed. Kiana had much in common with the Norse woman, both far from their homes, thrust into situations neither had asked for. Perhaps, with time, they might even become close friends.

If Runa lived.

Tor led several men with Kiana into the forest. They'd not been on the trail more than a few minutes when, to her relief, several women appeared, laughing and swinging full baskets of berries.

Tor eyed the group. "Is Runa with you?"

"She wanted to see the gray man." One of the women pointed back up the trail. "She sent us back with the berries."

He cursed again.

"Does she know where she's going?" Kiana wanted to curse as well, but someone had to keep focus.

"The general direction." He pursed his lips. "I was blind. She kept asking questions about him after we warned everyone."

"You couldn't have known." The woman struck Kiana as someone who pursued her own path.

After impressing on the women the danger of the bears, he sent them hurrying back to the village with two warriors to guard them. He then split the remainder of the men into groups of two and sent them in different directions in case they missed the signs. That left Tor and Kiana. She followed him to the woods, where he cast around for a trail.

After a few minutes, she huffed out a breath and elbowed him aside. "You may be master of the seas, Norseman, but even my Beren tracks better than you on land."

He didn't argue but let her take the lead, where she soon picked up the trail. At one point they passed a wider trail leading to the side.

She stopped and showed him claw marks in a nearby tree. "Bears."

Tor spread his fingers over the mark, which dwarfed his hand. He paled. The mark was at his eye level.

"Ten feet tall," she murmured. "Maybe more."

"If Runa ran into this…" He clenched his fist.

"She didn't." Kiana glanced at the muddy ground. "No footprints."

Tor didn't seem reassured and when she drew her sword, he drew his. They walked in silence. On guard, he studied the surrounding trees while she led the way. After twenty minutes, Tor stopped.

"She can't have gone this far. Not in her condition." He turned back. "We must have gone the wrong way."

As if in answer, a low moan sounded from up ahead. They glanced at each other, then crouched, swords in front of them, and sidled forward.

The trail stopped a few paces on, but the undergrowth had been beaten down on the right. Kiana led the way, looking for any sign the trail had been made by anything bigger than a human. She pushed through a clump of bushes, then came to an abrupt stop. Tor arrived beside her.

Ahead, on a bare patch of ground beside a bush ripe with berries, lay Runa. She rested on her side, her back to Tor and Kiana.

He strode forward and bent to touch her shoulder. "Odin's beard, what are you doing lying down here? You had us all worried—"

Runa turned onto her back, and Kiana swore under her breath.

Chapter Twelve

Runa's face was pale and covered in sweat. She panted as if she'd been running, but the ripple in her swollen belly told the true story. She gripped Tor's hand. "Thank the gods. I thought…I thought I'd have to…deliver him…myself."

To Kiana's amazement, Tor went as pale as his sister. He cast a panicked glance at her. "We have to get her back to the village."

She shook her head. "No. We can't move her. We'd never get her back in time."

"Then…then I'll get the midwife, bring her here—" He half rose to his feet.

Again she shook her head, her own panic held by a thin thread. "No time."

"You," Runa whispered. She gasped, squeezed Tor's hand so hard the white of bone showed through his skin. "You must deliver him."

"Me?" Tor's voice came out as a squeak, and Kiana breathed a sigh of relief. At least she'd not be the one to deliver this baby.

"I'll try to find some water," she said, anxious to get away, anywhere, with any excuse.

"No, don't…go." Again Runa gasped, then arched her back and moaned.

She can't be comfortable like that. Kiana had seen enough women give birth to know this wasn't the way to do it.

She shoved her terror aside, knelt on Runa's other side, and looked at Tor. "Get behind her, cross your legs, and sit her up on them. Let her lean back against you."

He blinked at her. "What?"

"Do it," she snapped. To break through panic on the battlefield you had to remind the recruits of their training. Obey orders. Don't question, just do. If this wasn't a battlefield, at least Tor's reaction was satisfying.

As if in a daze, he eased his hand from Runa's grasp and positioned himself as directed. Kiana helped spread Runa's legs over his, fortified herself with a deep breath, and peered beneath Runa's skirts.

"What are you doing?" he asked, his voiced edged with the same terror Kiana felt.

"This is what the village healer does, and the healers in my homeland." *What in Inanna's name am I supposed to be looking for*? Unnerved, she fought for calm.

Runa slumped back, panting with exhaustion, but the worst of the contraction had passed, and she breathed easier. "What...do you see?"

Kiana straightened. She swallowed, then knelt between Runa's legs and rested her knees on Tor's ankles for balance. She looked again. Was that the baby's head? She gave Runa what she hoped was a reassuring smile.

"I see your son." Ah, Lady, why did *she* have to do this? She tried to remember everything she'd observed in the birthing room. "I want you to take shallow breaths, fast shallow breaths, until I tell you to stop. All right?"

Instead of replying, Runa began the shallow pants. To her surprise, the woman's private parts relaxed, then her belly rippled in preparation for another contraction.

"Now, push," Kiana ordered.

Runa pushed. And screamed. Again. And with one final push, the baby slid out, right into Kiana's hands.

For a frozen moment, she stared at the small creature, terrified she was going to drop it. At last, it opened its eyes and mouth, breathed its first breath, and howled at the top of its lungs.

Runa, crying and laughing, raised her head. "Is he safe? Is he whole?"

Kiana reached for the cloth Runa had been using to collect berries. No, too rough. Too stained. Her gaze lit on Tor.

"Take off your shirt," she ordered, cradling the baby against the warmth of her body.

"What?" He stared at her, his eyes glazed in shock.

Kiana snapped her fingers. He blinked.

"Just—" She stopped, drew a shaky breath. No need to bite his head off. The time for panic was long past. "I need something to wrap the baby in. Your shirt is soft."

"It is? Oh." He fumbled at the ties of the shirt with one hand while supporting Runa with the other. After he struggled out of it, Kiana wrapped the child in the cloth, and he eased back, letting Runa lie down.

Kiana placed the babe in her arms.

"He's beautiful," she whispered.

"Yes." Kiana's heart slowed to a steady beat. "I hope you're not disappointed."

Runa looked up, her smile radiant. "How could I be disappointed?"

Kiana lifted the shirt. "Well, I'm afraid your son is a daughter."

Runa's smile, if anything, grew brighter. "A daughter." She stared at the child's face, touched her cheek with a tentative finger. "He wouldn't have wanted a daughter." She stared over her shoulder at her brother, a fierce satisfaction in her gaze. "And now she is all mine, none of *him*."

Tor's face was still ashen—Kiana expected hers was too—but he stroked his sister's hair with a tenderness that tugged at her heart. "Yes," he agreed. "All yours. And we'll raise her together."

~ * ~

After cleaning up Runa and the child, Tor gathered her in his arms for the trek back to the village. Kiana strode ahead of him, her sword at the ready. There was still the threat of bears to worry about.

The chill air raised bumps on his bare chest, but his attention wasn't on the cold. When he'd first lifted Runa and started walking, his gaze kept sliding to his niece, but after stumbling twice, he forced himself to pay attention to the trail, not this newest addition to his family.

He hadn't thought much about babies. He'd *never* imagined seeing one born. That made this one all the more precious. *Thank the gods Ottar can never get his hands on her*. If one good thing had come from falling into another time and place, it was the finality of their exile. Runa was safely out of Ottar's reach.

Tor peeked at the babe in his sister's arms before returning his attention to the path. The child wasn't beautiful—all that fuzzy white hair and wrinkled red skin—but he supposed she might grow out of that when she was older. If not a beauty, well, he'd not have to worry about randy warriors lining up to steal her away from him.

He'd have to make sure, come spring, that his own house was big enough for both Runa and a growing child. Assuming they survived the winter.

He glanced at Kiana. He'd have to speak with her after they got back to camp. Somehow, he must convince her to plead their case with her chieftain. She had to convince him to share their winter stores, even if the trade fell short.

A shout up ahead had him raising his head. Kiana tensed, but relaxed her guard when Vider and two other men dashed around the bend.

Vider skidded to a halt in front of Runa, anger and panic clear in his wide eyes and bared teeth. “What were you thinking leaving camp when you’re so close to your time? What if something had happened to you? What if you’d given birth out here in the forest?”

His first mate scolded Runa as if he had the right. Tor opened his mouth to put him in his place, but Runa raised a hand, stroked Vider’s cheek, and drew his attention to the bundle resting against her chest.

“You…gods, you did.” He collapsed to sit in the middle of the trail, breathing hard.

Tor and Kiana exchanged amused glances, but Runa regarded him with annoyance. “Oh, get up. It’s just a baby. Tor and Kiana were excellent midwives.”

“Tor and Kiana?” he echoed, as if the words made no sense. He stared at his captain. “Tor?”

“Get up, Vider.” He gave his friend an encouraging smile. When Vider was again on his feet, Tor handed Runa to him. Despite his surprise, Vider tightened his grip on her, and she settled against him. “Get her back to camp. I want the midwife to check her over and the child.”

“But…your sister…” Vider looked at Runa and seemed struck dumb with awe.

“Is now in your capable hands,” Tor agreed. Vider’s gaze went blank. “Is that not what you wanted, my friend?”

Vider nodded, gazed at Runa and opened his mouth, but she pressed a finger to his lips. “Now isn’t the time.” She looked at Tor. “Thank you for this, brother.”

He smiled. Perhaps he didn’t need a bigger house after all. It was about time Vider stood up for what he wanted. He was sure to speak to Tor before long with a formal request.

The other two men, grinning at the exchange, now spread out to guard and lead them back to camp. Vider turned and Runa peered over his shoulder at Tor. “Aren’t you coming?”

He gestured to his clothes, his hands and arms and chest streaked with blood and…other smears he didn’t want to think about. “I’m going to find a bath first.” He switched his attention to Kiana, whose clothes were no cleaner than his own. “Do bears go near water?”

She shrugged. “If they’re thirsty, but if we take turns, one guarding while the other bathes, it’ll be safe enough.”

Take turns. Of course she’d also want to bathe. His mouth went dry, and he had to swallow twice. “We crossed a stream up ahead.”

This time she smiled. “I have a better idea.”

She led the way to the stream, where they parted with Vider, he to carry Runa back to camp while they followed the flow of water upstream. After a few minutes, Tor and Kiana came to a clearing backed by a cliff. There a waterfall fell into a deep blue pool, while the stream exited from the far end.

Perfect.

"It'll be cold," he warned.

"Yes." Laughing over her shoulder, she dropped her weapons, then began to strip off her shirt. She paused, glanced at him. "You're supposed to be keeping watch, Norseman."

He turned his back, drawing his sword to guard for bears he had yet to meet. They'd had no trouble with them so far. There'd been signs, that slash in the trees earlier, tracks a few days ago of enormous paws, but the softness of the mud allowed prints to easily spread out and exaggerate the size. He didn't doubt her word but preferred to know what he was up against.

Water splashed, and he no longer thought of bears. His imagination took over. Was she cleaning the muck off her leathers? Perhaps if he offered to help her... *After all, how will she wash her back?*

A boot landed at his feet, then its mate. Tor stared at them, uncomprehending, until her wet shirt landed a few paces away, then her trews.

He heard the splash when she leaped into the water, then the moment she came up sputtering and gasping. Unable to resist, he peeked over his shoulder. She stood hip-deep in the pool, her back to him, that long tail of hair dipping into the water. His trews were too tight. His *skin* was too tight. When had she started to mean something more to him than an ally? When they'd explored the hold of the sky ship together? Faced the gray man? Or was it that first kiss?

He swallowed, his gaze sliding down that fall of hair. Shoulders, soft yet strong, gleamed golden on either side of the black strands. The skin narrowed at her slim waist, then flared at her hips until hair and skin disappeared beneath the surface.

She glanced over her shoulder. She didn't scream or duck under the water. Instead she laughed. "If you want to make yourself useful, Norseman, spread those out so they dry."

She gestured at the damp shirt and trews, then swam to the waterfall, where she climbed onto a wet rock to stand under the spray. Her back still to him, she spread out her hair to rinse away the muck and dust of the day.

He stared for a moment before coming back to himself, then picked up her clothes and laid them on dry rocks. With one last peek at the waterfall, he turned away and concentrated on the surrounding woods. He'd seen his share of naked women, of course, but this one… For some unknown reason, every time he looked at this one, even with her clothes on, his body reacted like a youth approaching his first communal bath. It made no sense.

Guard duty. He was on guard duty. What was wrong with him?

"They won't dry before the sun sets." It took an effort to watch the forest when all he wanted to do was watch her.

"No, but they'll be clean." Kiana's voice. *Too close.*

When had she swum back? He didn't dare turn around lest his body betray him. More splashing. Sweat slid down his face, and he wiped it from his eyes.

Concentrate. Don't think about golden skin, long legs… Concentrate.

Time slowed. How long had it been? Hours? At last the splashing drew closer until it stopped altogether. His imagination matched sound to vision, showed her climbing from the pool, scooping up her damp trews, struggling into them, then the shirt. He imagined the wet material sliding over her skin, clinging, caressing… *Odin's beard, how much longer*?

"Your turn." Her voice was laced with amusement.

He glanced at her, but lowered his gaze from her face to her shirt. Yes, sure enough, the dark nubs of her nipples pushed against the cold fabric.

He wanted to look away. He wanted to close his eyes. He did neither.

"Tor? I'm up here." Her voice came from a distance.

Why couldn't he move?

She set her hands on either side of his face and lifted his head. He raised his gaze. Was she furious? Embarrassed?

Her expression sparkled with amusement. "Do you like what you see?" she murmured in a low voice.

He opened his mouth, and she kissed him.

He stiffened. The last time she kissed him she'd almost torn his beard out by the roots, but this time…this time she stroked his cheek, snaked her hand around the back of his neck. Her tongue found his lips, and he thrust his own tongue to duel with hers while his hands shaped that lush bottom. He half closed his eyes, groaned when hers darkened. He trembled, skimmed his hands up her body. When he cupped her breasts, heat shot to his groin. Someone moaned. Him? Her?

She pressed closer and rubbed herself against him, then lifted a leg to hook over his hip, as if she wanted to climb him. He released one breast and ran a hand down her leg, back to that tempting bottom, so close to where he wanted it.

She murmured strange words, low and husky. Language deserted him. He didn't care. Who needed words?

She loosened her grip on his neck, then lowered her leg, gliding it along his. Finally she slid her hands to his chest and pushed away.

He moaned a protest. "Not yet."

She rested her forehead on his for a moment, then sighed. "You're getting me dirty, Tor." She pushed again. "I have to clean up again."

That was twice she'd said his name, addressing him directly instead of just asking about a word as she had that first time days ago. *Tor* sounded so…exotic…on her tongue. He drew back. The amusement was still in her eyes, but there was something else, deeper, something that tugged at his heart. They stared at each other, neither moving.

After a moment, Kiana blinked and backed away. Disoriented, Tor stood for another moment. Why were her clothes still damp and not bone dry from the heat they'd just generated? Surely she burned as hot as he.

Without a word, she returned to the pool, scooped up water, and rubbed at her clothes. "Your turn," she murmured after a few minutes, and she retreated to sit on a fallen tree and tug on her boots.

He waited until she rose and picked up her sword, then laid his own weapons on the ground. Before he changed his mind, he jumped into the pool. When he submerged, he wondered that the freezing water didn't turn to steam from the heat pouring off him.

Odin's beard, he was in so much trouble.

~ * ~

Kiana liked teasing the Norseman and had enjoyed that kiss more than she expected. When had she decided to kiss him again, for real this time? Why had she waited so long? *Not important.* His reaction was worth the wait, in particular when he jumped into the pool wearing everything except his weapons.

She took a step forward, concerned when his head disappeared underwater, but the lake was shallow there, and he soon emerged. He shook his head to fling the hair out of his eyes, then removed his clothes and tossed them ashore. They'd not dry in the few hours left of the fading sun. He flashed her a grin. "Like what you see?"

She chuckled, liking that he'd thrown her words back at her. She turned her back, listening to him swim to the waterfall. At once, she wanted to peek. Had he experienced this frustration when she was the one in the water? Had he resisted? She doubted it, so…why fight temptation? She glanced over her shoulder. Good, he hadn't noticed. Smiling, she made sure to observe everything she wanted.

Oh yes, she *did* like what she saw. Very much.

After Ajmal she hadn't expected to find a lover in these primitive Northlands. Ajmal had been one of the elite, a man of culture, of education. The kind of man she anticipated spending the rest of her life with.

If only he hadn't turned out to be a traitor.

No, don't think of that.

Tor… Well, if she took him as her lover she'd never take another. Just seeing him sent her blood to boil.

She made sure to face the forest when he emerged from the pool. He grunted and cursed while he donned his wet clothes. She had enough trouble with her own and wondered if his also chafed in certain spots.

"Clean now?" she asked instead, facing him again.

"I'll do." He tied his belt, strapped on his sword and knife. Water still glistened on his bare torso, but he didn't seem to notice. When he straightened and looked back at her, the memory of *why* they were bathing sparked wonder in his eyes. "I have a niece." He might have said *I have a unicorn* for all the joy in his voice.

She smiled. "You do. And you'd better get back to camp to look after her."

"True." He pulled her to him and kissed her again, then set her away from him. "Thank you."

With that, he strode away, leaving her speechless and…happy inside.

She hummed on her way back to the village, but when she passed the bear trail, she stopped. True, the animal hadn't attacked anyone yet, but no one in the Norse camp gave the danger the seriousness it deserved. Make noise to drive the bear away? More likely to attract it.

She studied the trail, looking for clues to how many and, more important, how big, this threat was. She'd been a good tracker back home, and here prints left an even better impression in the forest floor than on sand and rock. To her relief, the signs indicated a single animal. Bears were solitary creatures. Even so, one bear so close to the village and the encampment was one too many. If left to roam too close to people and it lost its fear of the hunters, more than the salted deer and fish were in danger of its hunger.

Time to do something about it and show the Norsemen what they were up against.

When she arrived at the village, Kiana located Soren and told him about the bear tracks. "These Norsemen don't know what the bears are like. May I ask some of them to come with the hunting party?" The more men, the better, when hunting the bears of this land.

"Yes, do that. I'll ask for volunteers at tonight's campfire to look for it. It may take a few days to find its den and map its territory. When we do, you can ask the strangers to join the hunt. We can prepare them for what to expect." While the well-being of the villagers was his responsibility, it was up to those who guarded the village to hunt down any danger.

"Lida will want to go." Kiana wasn't sure Lida was ready for the hunt, but the young woman had been practicing and was eager to try her skills.

Soren sighed. "She's grown up too fast. Very well, but keep her safe."

"Of course." *We'll see if Tor is as brave a warrior against bears as men.*

Chapter Thirteen

Ten days later Tor, Vider, and two of his men trailed seven village hunters through the dense bush. Alvar, introduced as their best huntsman, took the lead, followed by Lida and four other men, with Kiana behind them.

Tor glanced at his friend and grinned. He'd been in camp less than a day after the baby was born when Vider presented himself to ask for permission to court Runa. Now, every evening found him at the tent she shared with the other women, bringing her flowers…*flowers*, by the gods…and strolling along the beach with her.

The babe, named Astri in memory of their mother, was already stronger than at birth. She had lost her red coloring and the wrinkles Tor found so ugly, and now he glimpsed the beauty Runa insisted was there.

Some of the older boys wanted to come on the hunt with them, but Kiana had objected. "This isn't a game for children," she said with a frown. "Some of our best hunters have died or been savaged. Leave the boys behind."

As if to underline her warning, one of his men suddenly stopped, bringing Tor back to the present. "Gods, look at that."

They had come across a trail wide enough for two large men to walk shoulder to shoulder and was muddy in spots. The man stared at one patch and a paw print twice the size of Tor's spread hand. A chill slid up his spine. Not even soft mud spread that far. This was no ordinary animal. If this bear was as big as its paw print promised, it must be a giant indeed.

He let the village hunters take the lead—they were more familiar with this land than he and able to find a trail when he was sure it had disappeared—and with Kiana in front of him, he welcomed the distraction of her swaying backside.

Runa had confirmed Kiana came from the Southlands. That explained her black hair and dark eyes and the golden hue of her skin.

The shape of her eyes, round with a bit of slant, gave her an exotic look. She reminded him of the people who inhabited the lands east of Greece, or even farther south, in Egypt. She was a long way from home. What had brought her to this cold land where he suspected she'd never seen ice before?

Her clothes were different from her companions', but what fascinated him most was her sword. Bronze, she'd said, but from all he'd seen in the South, even the Nubians carried weapons of steel.

Vider nudged Tor's shoulder. "It's a pert enough backside, I admit, but it won't look any better from a distance."

What am I doing just standing in the middle of the trail? Tor cleared his throat. "Just checking," he muttered, but he remembered the sight of that backside splashed by the waterfall the other day…and his own cold walk home. Even the freezing water hadn't dampened his erection, and his wet trews had emphasized it. He'd had to slink into camp like a thief before changing into dry clothes.

He hurried to catch up with the rest of the group. They'd just rounded a bend and entered a small clearing when a roar sounded to their right.

Odin's beard, no bear could make a sound that loud or deep, but the creature that charged from the trees toward them was definitely a bear. In the few seconds it took for the animal to cross the clearing, the village hunters spread out, leaving Tor's men to fill the gaps between them. They had discussed this strategy before heading down the trail, and Tor now understood the value of it.

For this wasn't just a bear. This was a monster, a good three heads taller than Tor himself and as broad as two men. Its teeth were the length of his hand, and its claws…

He'd seen claws like that on Soren's cloak, the size of short daggers. These were twice as long.

Tor's first instinct was to leap in front of Kiana, but the bear was between them. He ducked a swiping paw, then danced back, studying how the other hunters handled the beast. Armed with barbed spears more suited to fishing than the leaf-shaped head of a hunting spear, they took turns stabbing at the creature, then skipping away.

Alvar took the lead, but the girl, Lida, wasn't far behind in adding her spear to the attack. When the bear spun toward one attacker, another pierced it from behind, forcing it to turn again. Catching the rhythm, Tor and his men joined the fray. The beast swung its paws, enraged at the attack but unable to catch any of its tormenters.

Kiana sliced a gash in its side. To Tor's horror, the beast decided to concentrate on its latest attacker. Ignoring the other warriors, it charged toward her. He ran after it and brought his sword down on the creature's leg just as it reached for her, but she wasn't where he'd last seen her. Instead she'd leaped and pulled herself onto an overhanging branch. From there she stabbed down at the bear's head.

As if sensing the strike, the bear jerked aside, but the sword bit into its neck. It roared, but before it retaliated Tor sliced again at its leg, cutting the foot. Off balance and unable to stop its forward momentum, the creature crashed into a tree. Deciding it had enough, it limped away, seeking cover.

Kiana swung down from her perch. "We have to catch it."

A wounded animal was a danger to anyone it came across and deserved a quick death. Despite its injuries, the creature kept ahead of them for the next mile until its luck ran out. It emerged from the trees onto the plateau where Tor and Kiana had met the gray man, and sure enough, the ghost appeared with its warning.

The village hunters skidded to a halt, staring at the apparition and gripping their spears so hard their knuckles turned white. Tor's men, pre-warned, slowed to observe the animal's reaction.

The bear swiped at the gray man, but when its claws passed right through it without damage, it kept running. Near the metal wall, it stopped and turned, a wounded creature at bay. Dangerous. Unpredictable.

One of the village hunters bent, lifted two rocks, and banged them together. The other warriors did the same. When the bear shook its head in obvious confusion at the noise, Tor drew his knife and slammed the blade against the blade of his sword. A satisfying clang echoed through the air. His men copied him, until the sounds of rocks and metal were deafening. The bear continued to shake its head and back away.

Until it backed into the wall.

Sparks erupted from the contact. The bear squealed, jerking and shaking like a broken doll, then fell forward. The sparks stopped. Knowing what to expect, both Kiana and Tor recovered quicker than their companions. They edged toward the downed creature. Burn marks scarred its back and smoke sizzled from the fur. Just to be certain, Tor raised his sword and cut off its head.

He tilted his chin at Kiana. "You were right. This is like no bear in my land."

She nodded, face pale.

Alvar came forward and drew his knife. Tor stiffened, but Kiana held up a hand. The hunter turned the knife and held it, hilt first, toward Tor.

"You struck the killing blow," she explained. "You may take the teeth."

Recognizing the ritual in the gesture, he accepted the knife with a bow of respect, then bent to cut the teeth from the beast's head. What was he supposed to do with them? He'd think of something later. Once he'd finished, he returned the knife.

The hunters descended on the body. In less than half an hour, the beast had been skinned, gutted, and declawed. The meat was cut into chunks and wrapped in leaves, then everything piled into the skinned fur, which had been spread open, fur side down, on the rocky ground.

"The meat is yours. We have plenty. You can have the fur, as well, if you wish it." Kiana gestured at the fur now folded into a bundle and tied to long poles for carrying.

Tor studied the huge skin, long enough to cover him from neck to ankle. "Do you have one?"

She chuckled. "I came here two summers ago and was allowed to hunt but once before. No, I don't have one. Not yet." The last two words were spoken with determination. Something she wished for, perhaps to prove she was as brave as the other hunters? She'd achieve her wish one day, Tor had no doubt.

His men lifted the poles onto their shoulders and started down the trail. Near the path that led to the gash in the sky ship, Kiana and the hunters split off to return to their village. He held back, letting his men go on ahead while something teased at his memory.

Vider stopped beside him. "What is it?"

"Shelves," Tor murmured, remembering how he and Vider had been unable to move them.

The space was enormous enough to make a good shelter if the shelves were removed. Was that what Kiana had been looking for? Those huts the villagers lived in didn't appear strong enough to withstand the winter storms he assumed hit there with the same intensity as in his homeland.

She said her chieftain wanted wooden walls. Why now? Even wood wasn't enough to make those huts strong enough. Did they stay there all winter or go somewhere else? If they were going to a more sheltered location, why hadn't they left already?

He turned to Vider. "Let's have another look at that village."

Vider frowned in confusion. "Why?"

Tor shrugged. "I'm not sure, but I think it's important we find out what's going on there."

~ * ~

Kiana trailed behind the hunters. She studied the sky, the trees. The crisp breeze stung her cheek. After two years, predicting the seasons came easily. Another month, if they were lucky, before the first snow. The new hut had to be ready by then.

She strode into the village and into chaos.

Attack? No. No blood. No bodies. But men rushed back and forth. Women wailed and wrung their hands. The healer ran past, and Kiana's heart leaped in fear. *Beren*.

The hunters, alarmed, followed the healer, who headed for the council hut.

Or what was left of it.

She skidded to a halt, as did her companions.

"Gods," Lida whispered in awe.

Kiana had to agree.

Where once had stood the framework of the expanded hut they all hoped to live in come winter, now lay flattened hides and broken poles. It looked as if a giant hand had crushed the center of the hut. Two poles remained upright at the far edge, bare of any hide or rope, but the rest of the structure lay like crumpled parchment.

Despite the addition of the axes and her observations, no one had been able to figure out how to use the new tools. She conveyed Tor's warning, but pride, she was sure, prevented Soren from asking for guidance. They managed to cut a few trees, and the trunks, thick and rough, now circled the edges of the hut like lonely sentries, attached to nothing.

Inga came to a halt at the edge of the collapsed hut and crawled beneath one edge. Some of the men held the hide up for her but after only a few feet she encountered more hide and had to retreat.

Kiana knelt beside her. "What happened?"

"We added five more hides this morning. It seems their weight was too much. This," Inga gestured at the mess before them, "happened a short while ago. Soren was inside, with his wife and their three youngest children. We can't get to them, but we can hear them calling. See there, that raised bit?"

A small area of the hide poked higher than the rest. Kiana brought to mind an image of the inside of the hut. That hump had to be where the chieftain's great chair stood.

Kiana studied the structure. "Have you tried cutting the hides?"

The men holding the edge stared at her in shock, and one blurted, "But we need the hides for shelter!"

Inga's voice dripped with sarcasm. "Do you really think we can still shelter in this mess?"

The man had the grace to bow his head. Before anyone else decided to object, Kiana drew her knife and signaled to Lida and her companions. "As I cut, you pull the sides apart. You," she pointed at the men who had dropped the edge at the healer's words, "start cutting over there. If you don't want to damage the hides, cut at the stitching where they join. Pile them over there." She indicated a piece of empty ground between the men and her.

She waited for them to start, then began herself. She found a seam, slit the leather thongs, and reflected how much easier it was to open a seam than to sew it together. Two women tugged one side away, and she stepped into the opening. The other three used their own knives to cut the hide free, widening the gap and tossing the separated piece onto the ground.

With the men working on one side and she and her trainees on the other, they soon settled into a rhythm. At last they reached the raised section. There they found Soren huddled next to the great chair. He shifted aside when they parted the last of the hides. Sheltered beneath his body lay his wife, her arms stretched under the chair. Their three youngest children crouched beneath.

All were alive. Inga pushed past Kiana and knelt beside them. The children crawled out and were gathered into their mother's arms. Soren sat back while the healer examined his family.

At last Inga turned to him with a cautious smile. "A few scratches, but nothing serious. Thank the gods this chair is so sturdy."

His face was white. "We wanted to see what space there was, if the roof needed to be raised higher. Then the walls collapsed. We were able to get the children underneath before the whole thing came down."

Men rushed forward to help him, but he waved them aside. Instead he signaled Kiana and led her away from the bustle around his hut.

"Time has run out." He lowered his voice.

Guessing what he was about to say, her heart sank. "But Chieftain—"

He held up his hand to silence her. "We have no choice. We will go to Suudrun."

But what about the Norsemen? Tor? And Runa? Kiana hoped she'd found a friend there, and she wouldn't abandon friends to sure death. She'd done that once before. Never again. Her mind raced. There had to be something.

"Is there a problem?" Tor said from behind her.

She turned. He stood a few paces away, his friend, Vider, behind him.

"You understood what we were saying?" Had he picked up the village language so quickly?

"I didn't need to. It's obvious." He gestured to the collapsed hut. "You were trying to build a large hut, and it didn't work. Your people don't stay in this village over the winter, do you? You live somewhere else. Caves, perhaps? Is that why you were interested in moving the shelves in the metal cavern?"

"What is he saying?" Soren demanded.

She repeated Tor's words, then added, "Chieftain, they'll starve if we leave."

Soren narrowed his eyes. "Then they shouldn't have brought the sky ship here."

"But they didn't—" She was sure of that now.

"Tell him to go away. We leave in three days." Soren turned and stalked back to his family.

Tor took a step forward, but she held up a hand to stop him. "I'm sorry. There's nothing I can do. We can't winter here so Soren has decreed we'll join his cousins in another village."

"And the food you were going to share with us?" From his pinched mouth and set jaw, Kiana guessed Tor already knew the answer.

She couldn't meet his gaze. "I'm sorry."

Chapter Fourteen

Tor shoved through the trees, heedless of the sharp needles and Vider's curses when the branches slapped him in the face.

"Slow down, for Odin's sake." He seized Tor's arm. "There's no need to take it out on the forest."

Tor whirled to face his friend. "They're going to let us starve!"

Vider dropped his hand and backed up a pace. "Now, calm down. I'm sure we can still make some trades with them—"

Tor ignored Vider's interruption. "You heard him, that so-called chieftain. He's taking his people away. Do you think his cousins will feed them? No. They're taking all the food with them."

"You don't know that." Again, Vider put a hand on Tor's arm, a soothing gesture that had no effect.

"It's obvious." Tor cursed and shook off Vider's hand, then continued toward the camp.

He sighed, followed several paces behind.

Tor fumed. All that visiting between his people and the villagers—for nothing. *If we become friends*, Runa had argued, *they'll be less likely to betray us*.

In the end he'd agreed, but that hadn't worked, at least not the way he planned.

A month ago, he would have assembled a raiding party to take the food they needed and woe to any who stood in their way. Now? Now he found it impossible to slaughter those he'd come to know and respect, but it didn't stop his anger.

He was still furious when he entered the camp, but overhearing one of his men describing the hunt, Tor put aside his anger for more immediate concerns.

"No one leaves camp without an armed guard," he ordered. "Stay away from any trails. There may be more bears in this area." He didn't want any of his people to face the bears this country produced.

"And stay away from the sky ship."

The men who accompanied him on the hunt had been graphic in their description of how the ship shot lightning at the bear, and Tor hoped even the most adventurous of the stripling boys stayed away. Of course, none of that mattered if they all starved to death over the winter. The reminder brought a return of his anger.

He headed for the forest. Chopping a few trees usually calmed him.

He passed the place where they were building the longhouse and paused. They'd made good progress, even in the short time they'd been here. Already the walls topped his head and some of the inner structure and support beams were taking shape.

The building was a good thirty paces wide and over two hundred long, the biggest great hall he'd ever seen, bigger even than Ottar's. It had to be. Everyone agreed one big place was better than several smaller shelters for all the people and animals.

The first day they were there he'd confirmed they were as far north as the home where he'd grown up, so it was safe to assume winters lasted many months. Although close quarters bred arguments and fights, the building was spacious enough to give everyone room. Why, the place was even big enough to take…

Tor stopped and stared at the structure for a few more minutes. *Yes, that might work. But first I need to talk to Runa.*

~ * ~

Kiana assembled the trainees not involved in clearing Soren's hut. While grateful she and Beren were assured a place over winter, she'd seen the dismay and anger in Tor's eyes and didn't expect the warrior to give up without a fight. The obvious response was to steal the villagers' stores, a tactic she'd choose herself in his place, so she posted guards around the food hut and watchers in the forest.

She wasn't surprised, then, when a trainee reported Norsemen approaching the village. But two men, not an army? That did surprise her. Giving orders to let them pass, she went in search of Soren.

He gathered his advisers and, with her at his side, met the visitors at the edge of the village—Tor and his friend Vider.

"We come here in peace," Tor said, and directed a respectful nod of his head to the chieftain.

Surprised by the courtesy and the formality of the words, Kiana translated, then waited for Tor to continue.

"We come to offer a trade." He held out his hands, palms up.

Soren grunted. "We don't need your furs now."

Tor pressed on. "We know that the people of this land have lived here for generations, from your fathers to their fathers to their fathers. The land has been good to you, giving you food and shelter."

He stopped and glanced at Kiana. She wondered who had taught him such diplomatic words since their first meeting.

"But with the coming of the sky ship, that is no longer true. The land is abundant, but your shelter…" He spread his hands. "…is gone."

Soren stiffened. "This we know."

Tor took a deep breath. "We still need your food to survive the winter."

"The food comes with us." Soren spoke with finality. Kiana's heart sank. "The ice nights are cold and hard, and we can't spare what we need to trade for shelter with our cousins."

Tor held up a hand. "We understand. But in exchange for your food, we offer in trade the one thing the sky ship took from you."

Kiana blinked. "What are you saying?"

"We are building a great hall that will withstand the storms and keep us warm during the…the ice nights." He stumbled over the unfamiliar words. "Our numbers are few and the space is great. We would be honored to share our humble dwelling with the people of your village."

Relief flooded Kiana's senses. *This solves all our problems*.

"Hmm." Soren tilted his head, a flash of satisfaction appearing and vanishing so quickly in his eyes Kiana wasn't sure she'd actually seen it. He turned away to consult his councilors, then straightened a moment later. "We thank you for your generosity and accept your offer. I will send someone to your camp to discuss the details."

Without waiting for a reply, he turned to Kiana. "I'll tell my people what is happening. As you speak their tongue, you'll make the arrangements It'll be easier than all this translating."

"As you wish."

She turned away but he laid a hand on her arm. "It's a good solution. My cousins are greedy and selfish and we'd not be welcome there. But don't tell these Norsemen that."

He gave a conspiratorial wink and turned back toward the center of the village, leaving Kiana speechless and wondering if this had been his plan all along.

~ * ~

"Well done," Vider murmured as they approached the trail.

"It was the obvious solution," Tor whispered back, but he smoothed the front of his shirt and resisted the urge to preen.

It *had* been well done. A great weight lifted from his shoulders. Yes, the longhouse would be crowded over the next few months, but there'd be food enough for all, and not even the eldest grandmother had to walk into the snow to leave more for her children.

"I thought you were mad not to bring Runa," Vider continued. "She has more patience with these things."

"That chieftain is proud," Tor explained. "He won't listen to a woman this time. There's too much at stake."

"You handled it well." Did Vider have to sound so surprised?

After a moment, Tor confessed, "This isn't normal trade talk. Runa gave me the words. There's much to say for ritual."

Someone touched his arm, and the snap of energy told him who it was. He stopped. Vider glanced back but kept walking.

Kiana dropped her hand. "Thank you. It's generous of you to share your home with us."

Curious, he held her gaze. "Would you have left us to starve?"

She lowered her gaze and stared at the ground. "It wasn't my wish, but I have to think of Beren."

"You're not part of this village, are you." He made it a statement. Aside from her coloring, there was a subtle distance between her and the others.

She returned his gaze, a touch of defiance in her eyes. "No. Beren and I came here two summers ago. We have no friends, no relatives in the other villages who'd take us in."

So why did this village? "They're generous in their hospitality."

She shrugged. "When it's useful."

Ah. "And what use did you bring?"

Now she smiled. "I have a gift for languages, as you found out—handy when traders come through—and I train anyone who wants to learn how to defend the village."

"Someday you must tell me how you came here." That would be a story worth hearing.

"Someday, perhaps." She took a breath. "Right now, though, we need to make other plans."

He straightened. "I'll tell the builders, make sure we've allowed enough room for everyone. We can always add side rooms if necessary."

She raised her eyebrows. "You can do that?"

He grinned. "If we can't, we'll find another way. We'll fit everyone in, don't worry."

"Soren will expect to stay as chieftain," she warned.

Tor wasn't surprised. "There's no reason we can't have two tribes in the longhouse. As for the rest, we can work it out with whoever you send to us."

"That would be me." She bowed.

He stared, then grinned. “Of course. When do you want to start?”
She considered for a moment. “Tomorrow?”
“Agreed.” With a lighter heart, Tor trailed Vider back to camp.

Chapter Fifteen

Soren encouraged the villagers to go more often to the Norse encampment, and the council made plans to relocate everyone there within the next two weeks. After an initial meeting to make the arrangements, Kiana's visits diminished while she helped prepare for the move. Some of the villagers went ahead of time to build temporary huts, including one to house the stores until the longhouse was finished.

The Norse camp was less than three miles away by sea, so the villagers loaded supplies and livestock into fishing vessels to be sailed around the point to the neighboring cove. Those villagers too old or weak to make the trek across the ridge also made the trip by boat, thus freeing up space in the shared huts so Kiana and Beren again had one to themselves.

Bit by bit, the village emptied. She recruited Beren to pack their few belongings. The boy now hobbled around with the aid of something called *crutches* one of the Norsemen had carved for him. More than just two sticks to support his weight, a cross-piece was fixed to the top, wrapped in leather bindings to soften the hard wood, and each stick was tall enough for the cross-piece to fit under his arms. A shorter cross-piece was fastened part way down the stick for handholds the boy grasped. The ingenious device allowed Beren to limp about almost as fast as his normal walk.

Of course, a normal walk was never fast enough for a six-year-old boy, but he stopped complaining when the healer reminded him of the alternative.

Ahead of schedule by five days, the last of the preparations was complete. With their belongings packed, Kiana led Beren toward the beach, where the final group of villagers waited to board the boats. They passed the skeletons of huts, their hide walls already packed and sent to the campsite to be used inside the permanent shelter.

Earlier, when the first hut was taken apart, she allowed herself to hope. True, they were abandoning the village, but they had a new winter home to go to, one where she and Beren might find safety. Now, seeing the empty skeletons of all the huts, a lump rose in her throat.

She hadn't expected to miss this place. The council hut alone remained, returned to its former size, a reminder the village was still their home. The chieftain's great chair also stayed behind, too big and heavy to carry to the camp.

"I've never been in a boat before," Beren confessed in a whisper as they approached the water.

"Yes you have," she whispered back.

He glanced at her, startled. "When?"

"When you were just a baby. I think it was your second summer." She smiled, remembering. Yasmin had been his personal guard that day, and she, too, had been nervous about boats. The memory still held sadness for Kiana, but she pushed it aside. "Your father had a grand lake built on the palace grounds and stocked it with golden fish. He let the people play in the waters there, near the shore. One day, he took you and your guard to the lake and showed you a boat with a bottom made of clear amber. The three of you rowed onto the lake and watched all the fish through the bottom of the boat."

Yasmin told Kiana later it had been as if the three humans were visiting the underwater world. It had fascinated and terrified Yasmin.

"In the middle of the lake," Kiana continued, "your father had placed a miniature underwater palace, with jeweled spires. The fish made it their home and swam in and out of the many open doors and windows. That part of the lake was so deep the people didn't venture out that far and didn't know about the palace. Someone needed to be in such a boat to see it."

"I don't remember." Beren stopped and looked up at her. His eyes filled with tears. "I don't remember anything about that time. I miss them. I miss my family." On instinct, she knelt and hugged him. He sobbed against her shoulder.

She struggled to hold back her own tears. "I miss mine too. But we are each other's family now." She drew back, stared into his wide eyes. "You and me. You are my family, and I am yours."

"But what if something happens to you? Arkin told me about the bear hunt. You could have been hurt. Or worse." Beren's voice had risen to a wail.

She cursed the older boy, but Beren was bound to hear about the hunt sooner or later. "Nothing happened to me, and nothing will." She rested her hands on his shoulders. "I'll never leave you, as long as there is breath in my body. I made a promise, and I'll take care of you for as long as you need me."

The tears still threatened, and he clutched her arm. "But—"

"No, listen to me." He'd worry if she didn't answer his biggest fear. She stroked his back. "If I'm not able to care for you, Eskil's parents will. I've spoken to them, and they'll be your family if I cannot."

His eyes opened wide. "I'd live with Eskil?"

"If that's what you want. If not, they'll help you find another family." She held him away from her and tipped his chin up until he looked at her eyes. "I promise this, Jenal of Zamad, you will always have someone to care for you. You will never be alone if you don't wish it."

His wide gaze took on a somber expression, and for a moment he looked more adult than child. He touched her shoulder. "I will hold you to that promise, Nahid, daughter of Eriacu."

A shiver raced through Kiana. He sounded so like his mother, and the words, with their true names, so like a vow.

She inclined her head in respectful acknowledgment. "Now, we'd best not keep Nils and his boat waiting."

"I know. It's not polite." He grinned up at her, and the child was back in his face.

Once he was aboard, she stood on the shore and waved until the boat rounded the headland. With one last glance out to sea, she turned away and began the final preparations for abandoning the village. The remaining villagers waited in front of the council hut. They carried bundles on their shoulders or tied to their backs like Kiana. She wanted to keep her hands free if they met with any dangers. People murmured around her, conversing in low voices, but all quieted when Soren joined them. His wife and children had left the day before, so he was alone.

He regarded the group with the gaze of a father looking with approval on his many children. At last, he gestured to one of the men, who handed him a bundle. To her surprise, its size was the same as everyone else's. He hefted it onto his shoulder, then led the way to the trail.

It took an hour, keeping their pace to those of the slowest in the group. Once, the back of her neck tingled, as if someone spied on her. She whirled, studied the surrounding forest. No one appeared among the trees. She hunched her shoulders, turned back, and resumed trailing the villagers. The sensation didn't return, but not until the group emerged onto the beach by the Norse encampment did she allow herself to relax.

Those who came by sea had already arrived. Beren sat on a boulder at the edge of the beach. Kiana hurried over.

"How was the boat?" She sat on the sand beside him.

He grimaced, his face pale. "My stomach didn't like it." Then he straightened his shoulders. "But other than that, it was *góðr*. That means fine or good."

"Very good." She ruffled his hair. "Who taught you that?"

"Dyre." A boy of eight ran toward them, Eskil dashing behind. "He went to smooth the path, so I won't trip."

The two boys reached them at that moment. Eskil grabbed Beren's hand and hauled him off the boulder.

Dyre offered Kiana a shy smile before handing Beren his crutches. "We have all the families in the tents." He pointed up the shallow slope to the three tents by the tree line.

Kiana shifted her gaze to the wood building. It had grown taller since last she'd seen it, and outbuildings were now attached to either side, like stubby wings on a clumsy duck.

"Go get settled," she said to Beren. "I'll join you later." Turning to Dyre, she gave a friendly smile. "Thank you for helping, Dee—Deeray." She stumbled over the pronunciation, but the boy just bobbed his head in answer, then turned to Beren.

With Eskil on one side and Dyre on the other, Beren hobbled up the slope. Neither boy touched him but remained ready in case he lost his balance. She smiled. She'd learned a lesson from those children. Give Beren enough freedom to discover what he can do for himself but stay nearby in case he needs help.

Assured the boys had no problem getting to the tents, she sauntered over to the wooden building. The two side pieces sloped away from the main structure on one side and another larger shed attached on the other side. Wooden roofs already covered all three.

She recognized several of the village women disappearing into one of the side rooms, carrying the last of the salted fish. They returned empty-handed. Curious, Kiana ducked through the doorway and stared at the rows of wooden boards, each stacked upon a shorter piece of tree trunk with space between to hold several baskets. She wandered down the spaces between the boards. They were organized with fish in one row, meat in another, berries and herbs in a third. Barrels held dried apples and fresh water. One, she saw with delight, held the tasty mead.

"Once the snows come, this room will be much colder." Runa stood in the doorway. Her silhouette filled the opening, but there was enough light to show she held her babe in one arm, wrapped in a blanket. "Nothing will spoil then, but your idea for salting was good. I understand they didn't do this in the village before you came."

Kiana shrugged. "They used to rely on catching fish through the sea ice, but sometimes it was too thick. Using salt to preserve the catch was a simple suggestion. After all, Beren and I rely on this food as well."

"So salting is common where you came from?" Runa shifted the baby to a more comfortable position and tucked a tiny hand under the blanket.

"For as long as I can remember," Kiana agreed.

"But it's hot in the South." Runa entered the room, letting in more light from outside. "You'd be able to hunt year-round, wouldn't you? Why do you need to preserve food?"

"There were dry years, when there was no rain," Kiana explained. "We had to be prepared for those, for no one but the seers could predict when they'd come."

Runa laughed. "Don't speak to my brother of seers."

"He doesn't believe?" She'd known many seers, and all had been true in their predictions.

Runa tutted. "He doesn't want to believe."

"Why? Was he given a bad future?" Why else disregard them?

"Oh, yes." Again, Runa laughed. "You'll have to ask him about it."

She wondered what was so amusing. "Perhaps I will."

"So…" Runa tucked her free arm through Kiana's and led her from the room. "Are you all settled?"

"Beren went ahead. I'll find him later." She stopped and studied the main building. "Will it take much longer? It looks done."

"Almost," Runa agreed. "Just one more level of boards, and then they'll start on the roof. It'll be finished in two, maybe three days."

"So soon?"

"Winter makes a good task master."

True. "Tell me about this great hall. What will it look like when it's done?"

A soft mewling sound drew both women's gaze to the babe. Runa sighed. "By Freya's tits, I'll swear this child eats more often than she breathes." At Kiana's grin, Runa chuckled. "Come, we can talk while I feed her."

They settled on a fallen log by the tents. Runa lowered the top of her dress. To give her privacy, Kiana stared at the clear sky. A moment later, the sound of eager sucking drew her attention back.

"What, uh, what are those two rooms outside the great hall?" The sight of the babe made her stammer. "Are they both for storage?"

"In a way. The one you were in is for the foodstuffs—meat and fish and grains. The other outbuilding on the same side is for the kitchens." The baby stopped sucking for a moment, and Runa stroked her cheek until she resumed. "A covered hallway will join the two, with an entry into the longhouse between."

Kiana struggled to envision it. "Won't the snow get into the hallway?"

"It'll be closed in, with a door solid enough to keep out the worst of the snow."

Smoothing out a space in the dirt at her feet, Kiana used a twig to sketch a long box with two smaller squares on one side, separated by a closed in hallway. "Like this?"

Runa studied the drawing. "Yes. The rooms are a little longer, but yes, like that."

"And the room on the other side?" She drew another box.

"Stables for the cattle and goats, an area for the chickens. We'll need milk and eggs for the children. There's one more building to be added tomorrow, by the stables. The woods are a good enough privy for now."

"Where will everyone sleep?"

Taking Kiana's stick, Runa stooped, careful not to disturb the feeding baby. She traced a line beside the inside wall of the main building, along both long sides. "Sleep benches. We'll use furs for bedding. The roof will have beams with hooks where we can hang the hides you brought to divide different areas for families." She added three jagged circles, one at each of the long ends and one in the middle. "Fire pits."

"Won't the smoke holes make it cold?"

"No, we have…" Runa paused, her brow furrowed for a moment. "Ah." She gave a crisp nod and grinned. "Chimneys. It's a new invention from the East. Stone tubes above the fire pits lead the smoke out. The tubes are bent, so the cold can't come straight in. It's still chilly, but not enough to notice."

"Amazing. I can almost see it."

Straightening, Runa settled the baby into a more comfortable position. "The huts in the village—they are very…simple. But I've heard the buildings in the Southlands are sturdier. Not wood?"

"No. We don't have many trees or stone in the desert, but lots of sand and enough water and straw and hot sun to make clay bricks." She paused. The palace was made of stone quarried from the nearby hills, but she didn't need to add that detail.

Her gaze was drawn to the far side of the camp where several men emerged from the trees carrying two deer on long poles. Tor, draped in a cloak made from the bear he'd help kill, led them, a brace of rabbits on a leather thong hanging from his fist.

"Tor's back early," Runa observed.

"They've been hunting." Kiana winced. Of course they'd been

hunting, but the sight of that Norseman took her sense and her breath away.

Runa shifted, moved the now-full child onto her lap, and closed her dress with an elaborate silver brooch. "I'm going to put this one down to sleep. Why don't you get settled in your tent? We'll have a feast on the beach tonight to welcome you all. You might want to get some rest ahead of time. Things can get quite spirited when the mead comes out."

Kiana grinned. "It's very good mead." She helped Runa to her feet.

"That it is. Since Vider found that beehive, we have even more now." With a grin and a chuckle, Runa headed to the closest tent.

Resisting a glance in Tor's direction, Kiana turned toward her own assigned quarters.

~ * ~

"By the Lady, what do you think you're doing?" Kiana strode across the tent to Beren lying on the floor. The boy's crutches lay on his pallet, several paces away.

"I wanted to walk by myself." His voice trembled, and she had to remind herself he was still just a child.

It took all her self-control, but instead of helping him up and back to the bed, she waited until he hauled himself to his feet, then offered her arm. "All right. You got this far by yourself, but your balance is still off. Lean on me. Can you make it back?"

He blinked, stared at her, then set his mouth in a stubborn line. Refusing to touch her, let alone lean on her, he took a wobbly step forward, shifted his weight, then lifted his other foot. Step by agonizing step, he made his way back to his pallet. Sweat stood out on his brow, but not once did he lean on Kiana.

He dropped onto the pallet with a sigh. "I did it!"

The grin he gave her spread so wide her heart stuttered with pride, and she had no choice but to grin back. "Yes, you did." She sat beside him and rubbed his shoulders. His muscles were so tense it took several minutes before they relaxed.

He sighed in delight. "I guess I showed Inga, didn't I? I won't lose my leg now."

"No, but it's still not that strong. You need to be patient." She rose. "So, where did you put our packs?"

"Beside the wall, over there."

Kiana lifted her pack and rummaged through it until she found the last of the hard sweets she'd bartered from the peddler last spring. The fruit pieces, boiled in honey, had appeared in Zamad a generation ago when explorers returned from the far eastern lands. Beren had developed a particular passion for the ones made with lemon and barley sugar. She paused. It *had* been foolish to fall for the peddler's temptation. Even now, the man might be back in the South, talking of a dark-skinned woman among light-skinned villagers and a boy with a taste for Southland sweets.

Foolish. Dangerous.

Yes, they'd stayed too long. Come spring, they must leave.

Refusing to worry further, she unwrapped the sweet from its soft leaf cover and held it out to Beren.

His eyes opened wide. "But you love those. I know it's the last one because you told me last month."

"It goes to the one who accomplished the most since then. That's the bargain, remember?" She placed the sweet on his hand. "You've won this time."

He placed the sweet on his tongue and closed his mouth and eyes in ecstasy. For a long time he savored the sweet, sucking the sugary confection until nothing was left. He reminded her so much of his mother, the gentleness of his nature, but at times like this, locked in his own blissful world, the lines around his eyes made him look very much like his father.

He would have made a good king, but he makes an even better little boy. The queen was right. In time, as the memory of his early years faded, he'd become a child of this place, these people.

It was a future she wished for all the little boys who perished in the attack on her city and the little girls, and mothers, and sisters…

With memory swamping her, Kiana stood, careful not to disturb Beren's contemplation of the sweet. She needed fresh air.

She shoved the flap aside and stumbled out, straight into a solid chest.

Chapter Sixteen

Tor didn't stagger when Kiana walked into him. He didn't even flinch. He opened his mouth to tease her about not noticing someone his size, but when she raised her face to him, her eyes glistened with tears and with such a look of grief in their depths, the words died on his lips.

She'd not appreciate pity, so instead of offering comfort, he took her arm to steady her. "We had a good hunt today. I left some men guarding the remaining carcasses. Do you want to help us bring them back to camp?"

"What?"

Her voice trembled, but he ignored it and repeated his question.

"Oh." Focus returned, she stared around, as if wondering where she was. She took a deep breath. "Carcasses. Yes, of course I'll help. We can't let the scavengers have them."

Instinct made him exaggerate a grimace. "That would be…annoying."

The corners of her mouth lifted, but the amusement didn't reach her eyes.

Tor released her arm and turned back the way he'd come. After a long moment, she followed. Two other men fell into step behind them.

They were well into the woods before Kiana closed the distance to walk beside Tor. "Is there really a carcass or did you make that up to get me alone?"

The attempt at humor eased the weight on his chest. "There really is a carcass, and I did want to get you alone."

She looked up at him, and he stopped, as did she. After a moment's indecision, their two companions slipped past them.

Kiana glanced at them. "Not alone."

"No." He stroked a hand down her arm. "You looked as if you needed a distraction. Do you want to talk about it?"

She studied him, her expression fathomless, then shook her

head. “I don’t think I can.”

He shrugged, trying to make the action imply he didn’t care either way. “Well, I’m here if you change your mind.” It hurt that she didn’t want to confide in him, but it was her choice. He’d be patient.

They arrived at the hunt site a short time later. Five carcasses remained, and the men had already stripped long branches of their remaining leaves and laid the poles next to the deer. Kiana turned one on its side and together she and Tor tied its legs over the pole. They took their time, making sure the animal was secure, then each took an end and raised it so the deer was on its back.

“Ready?” Tor asked.

Kiana nodded. “I’ll go first.” In one smooth move they lifted the pole and its burden. She turned so her back was to Tor and rested her end of the pole on her shoulder.

The others had finished before them and were already halfway down the trail. His first thought was to catch up with them, but something in the way she stood made him hesitate. She seemed braced for interrogation.

The last thing he wanted to do was upset her, so, acting on instinct, he held back until the others were out of sight before tapping the pole. “Let’s go.”

Kiana in the lead, they began the trek back to camp.

~ * ~

They walked in silence, but all the while Tor’s earlier question spun through Kiana’s mind. *Do you want to talk about it*?

She didn’t, hadn’t at the time. The sorrow had struck her without warning in the tent. For two years she’d concentrated on keeping Beren safe. She didn’t want to think about what had happened to her family, to his.

But this was Tor, the man who’d held his sister while she gave birth, the man who’d offered shelter to Kiana’s friends. The man she wanted with every fiber of her being.

Did she want to talk about it? Of course not, but before this went any further, he deserved to know the truth.

Oh, blessed Inanna, please don’t let the memories hurt too much.

If she didn’t look at him, if she didn’t stop walking, maybe she could get through this. She took a deep breath. “I was a member of the queen’s guard, as was my sister, Yasmin. There were six of us guarding the queen and her son. I…I wasn’t Kiana then. My name was Nahid.”

Yes, that seemed to be working. “We lived in a city, a town of so many buildings it spread over miles of desert. It was surrounded by a high wall, and guards patrolled day and night. We had enemies, of course, but our warriors were strong, and we had always beaten off attacks. Until one night…"

Memory threatened to swamp her. Perhaps if she treated this like a fireside tale, something that happened to someone else… She shifted the pole on her shoulder then forced her voice to take on a sing-song quality. "It was Yasmin's turn to stand guard over the prince, a child of four at the time. But she was in the midst of her first love affair and begrudged the time away from her lover. I was supposed to be off duty that night, but I agreed to change places with her. It was after midnight, and Prince Jenal cried out."

She had burst through the door, sword drawn, but no one jumped out of the shadows. "It was just a nightmare. He dreamt of monsters hiding in the dark. I wonder now if it was a premonition."

"Did he often have nightmares?" Tor asked.

Often. "He was afraid of the dark. A light, even a small flame in a wall sconce, would have been welcome, would have helped keep him calm, but the boy's tutor convinced the queen the child needed to face his fear." *The idiot.*

"Idiot," Tor muttered.

She had to smile at his echo. "Just so. Anyway, I sat on his bed with my sword drawn to chase off the monsters and waited for him to fall asleep."

She'd wanted to stride into his dreams and challenge any who dared to disturb his rest. He appeared so tiny, a lone figure among the silks of a bed big enough to sleep ten. Was this what it felt like to be a mother? How strange to think of such things now. Ajmal hadn't spoken of marriage, although she expected him to soon, and any child whose parents were in the royal guard had to wait to be born.

The memory of her lover brought his face to mind, that sharp, arrogant chin, the determined set of his lips. Every inch the captain of the guard, he was a strong man, capable of defeating an enemy or bringing a lover to fulfillment with equal ease.

Bile rose in her throat. She clenched her fingers on the pole. The memory of his touch made her want to throw up.

She pushed the vision aside and resumed talking. She'd never told anyone this tale before, but with Tor it felt right. "The window was open and there was a sound, a scrape of boot on stone. I'd not have heard it if I'd still been standing guard outside the door. The prince's chambers overlooked the outer courtyard. At that time of night, it should have been deserted, but there were shadows moving across it. Twenty, maybe thirty men. I shouted the alarm and slammed the shutter over the window before they could shoot at me." She continued to walk, lost in memory.

"Did anyone hear you?" Tor prompted after a moment's silence.

The question brought her back to the present. "Yes. The alarm bell has a deep, bone-shaking boom that can wake even the deepest sleeper. I made sure the door was barred, then woke the prince. I didn't want to frighten him, so I told him it was a test and that we needed to practice our hiding and escaping skills." She glanced over her shoulder at Tor. "We did that often at the palace. No king lives free of danger." *Or treachery*, she added to herself. "The boy didn't question it, so I got his travel sack from the chest at the foot of his bed. We kept it full of anything that might be needed in a hasty flight. He could dress later, once we were safe. The one item it didn't contain was his flute." She smiled at the memory. "He refused to leave without it."

"Was that the one you rescued from the cave-in?" Tor asked.

"He loved that flute more than any of his toys." She paused again but straightened her shoulders. The truth. He needed the truth. "I had a lover—Ajmal, captain of the guard. I expected he'd be defending the prince's parents, so when the queen knocked at the door, I was surprised he wasn't with her."

Queen Siri had rushed into the room. She'd been concerned not to find a guard outside the door, but as soon as she knew her son was safe, she'd resumed her mantle of confidence.

"The queen threw a cloak over Jenal and laced his boots," Kiana continued. "She told him he and I were going on an adventure."

"She wasn't coming with you?" Tor interrupted, surprise in his voice.

"No." This was the part she hated. "She was with child, close to birthing. She couldn't have run far, or even ridden a horse, and she couldn't—" *Breathe*. "She told us the Usali, our ancient enemies, had taken over the town and were already in the palace, that most of the guards were dead."

"Your sister was in the town?" Tor asked.

"And my mother. Father…my father was with the king. He died trying to protect him."

Again, she paused, and Tor asked the one question she dreaded. "What of this…this captain of the guard? This Ajmal? Where was he?"

Her mouth was suddenly dry. "Ajmal was the one who betrayed us, who killed the king and my father."

Tor sucked in a breath but didn't say anything. Kiana hurried on, eager now to get past the next bit. "He told the king he had made a pact with the Usali. His mother was one of the king's lesser wives, but Ajmal always wanted more power. The queen escaped, but he wouldn't be far behind her. Prince Jenal had to die if he wanted to be king."

The queen had doubted her, afraid her loyalties might lie with her lover. It had taken an oath to Inanna to convince her Kiana was as horrified by the betrayal as she.

"How did you get away?" Tor asked.

"There was a secret passage leading from the prince's rooms to the stables. It must have been made generations ago because part of the ceiling had crumbled, and the walls had narrowed the passage. The boy was small enough to fit with no problem, and so was I, but the queen…" She bowed her head. Even a few months earlier the queen might have fit into that narrow space. Not then.

"You had to leave her." Tor stopped, forcing her to stand still. After lowering his end of the pole, he took her end and lowered it as well, then turned her toward him.

I can't look at him. Not yet. I have to finish this. "She told Jenal she wasn't coming. He seemed to understand, even as young as he was." The queen had hugged him and whispered in his ear, but Kiana had heard the words: *Be brave. Live a good life. Make me proud.* "He went into the tunnel and didn't look back. She gave me her rings to pay for passage and made me promise to raise Jenal as a normal boy, without the burden of vengeance. And then she…she killed herself."

Kiana closed her eyes. *My fault. All my fault.* "I should have seen something in Ajmal. If I'd known… He betrayed us and opened the gate. Because of him, my parents died, the king died, the queen took her own life." Her voice broke on a sob. "Yasmin… I don't know what happened to my sister, but she must be dead. If we hadn't traded places, she'd be here now, alive—"

"Don't." He tightened his grip, and she broke.

She pressed her face to his chest. Her body shuddered with silent sobs while he held her. When at last she raised her head and wiped the tears from her eyes, she stayed in the comforting circle of his arms.

After a moment more, she managed to continue with the rest of her story. "That was two years ago. We went north, far from the city. We took horses from the stables, but abandoned them after a day or so. They were too easy to identify, too easy to follow. We traveled on foot the rest of the time, for weeks, months, and ended up here. I thought it safer if we had different names. so I became Kiana. Chieftain Soren gave us shelter. They've been very good to us, but they're not family." She sighed. "I miss my family."

Tor placed his hands on either side of her face, bent, and kissed her.

Chapter Seventeen

Kiana went still. Such tenderness, such…understanding—she hadn't expected that. Breaking contact, she drew back and stared at his face, but wasn't prepared for what she saw. Not the smug grin he'd worn the first time they'd kissed. Not the stunned surprise of the second. This time the corners of his mouth remained straight, serious. His gaze held compassion and something…else. It was as if, at this moment, there was no one else in the world. No one else mattered. No one else ever would.

She ran a finger over the scar on his cheek. He trembled under her touch, and she reveled in her power to affect him so.

He swept his hand down her back, cupping her bottom through her leggings. The chill air disappeared under the warmth of his touch.

His breath feathered across her cheek, and that was enough. She wanted, *needed*, to know she was alive, that the past had no power over this moment.

Kiana rose on her toes, pulled his head down to her, and kissed him back. Not a gentle kiss. This was hard, urgent, her tongue pressing its way into his mouth. Tor pushed it back with his own tongue. The kiss sent shivers down her spine. She'd wanted this for so long without even realizing it. Or perhaps she had. That first day they'd met, that first kiss she'd forced on him… It all led to this moment.

She wanted him inside her. *Now*. "Now," she demanded.

Then they were tearing at each other's clothes, ripping at laces, shoving cloth aside. Tor staggered them both to the side of the trail where he dropped his bear cloak on a bed of moss.

Sounds ripped from Kiana's throat, little cries of want, of need. "Now." Then again, "*Now*."

In a matter of moments they were both naked, and all rational thought dissolved into a tangle of legs and arms, skin slick with sweat, nips and bites, licks and kisses. When he plunged into her it was like coming home. This was right. This was perfect. This man was hers.

An endless time later, she opened her eyes. She didn't know how long they lay there, unable or unwilling to move. Tor sprawled over her, but not enough to crush, and she welcomed the weight of him.

She'd expected to be disappointed, but even Ajmal hadn't made her feel like this.

Alive.

Why had she told Tor so much? For that matter, why hadn't she told him about what the smoke had shown her that morning long ago in her mother's temple? When Kiana had first seen him in Soren's hut, her mother's constant refrain echoed in her mind, *Never doubt the gods.*

The gods hadn't helped her mother. Why believe they knew her own fate?

"Tor." She grinned, nudged his shoulder, but he grunted and settled more solidly atop her. She worked a hand free and tugged at his hair. "Tor, I can't breathe."

This time he did stir. He shifted, raised himself enough for her to take a breath, then nuzzled her neck. "You smell so good."

"I smell like sweat." Her sad mood of earlier had disappeared, leaving her with this…this contentment. This…love?

The grin vanished. No, not love. Love hurt too much when it was betrayed. She'd not risk it again.

But lust? Friendship? Want? Yes, those were allowed.

But never love.

With a sigh, she squirmed from beneath him, gathered her clothes, and dressed. The autumn wind nipped at her bare skin so she hurried. Tor stretched and folded his hands behind his head.

"We don't have to go back right away," he murmured with a lazy grin.

Kiana toed the deer carcass still trussed to the pole. "We still have to get this back to camp, and I promised Beren I wouldn't be long."

He said nothing until she finished dressing. "Beren is the young prince you spoke of, the one you helped escape from your city."

All Kiana's protective instincts raged to the fore. "He's just a little boy. He has no home in the South anymore. I promised the queen to raise him in a life of peace and not seek revenge or to win back his kingdom." She narrowed her eyes, her tone fierce. "No one must know who he is."

Tor's grin faded, but he gave a solemn nod. "I'll say nothing."

She waited for him to say something else, to ask questions, but he remained silent. He seemed content to stay like that all day. Naked. Aroused. She huffed out a breath. "I like the view, but aren't you cold?"

His grin returned, this time with a wicked gleam in his eye.

"There are ways to keep warm."

She had to laugh and turned her head away to keep from pouncing on him. "We need to get this deer back to camp."

He heaved a sigh. After he was dressed, Kiana returned to her position by the deer. "Did you want to take the front this time?"

"No" he said. "I'm fine back here."

She bent and shouldered the pole again.

~ * ~

The view from the back of the pole kept Tor in a high state of arousal all the way to camp. While the deer carcass hung between them, it swung with every step, revealing glimpses of Kiana's firm backside. He knew what that backside looked like under her trews and had every intention of seeing it again.

Her story of her past revealed more about her than he suspected she realized. It revealed her courage, her strength of purpose, her loyalty to her family, to her ruler. He was certain she'd wanted to stay and help her people, but she'd put duty ahead of her own wishes and instead ensured the young prince escaped. What must it have cost her, knowing she'd never go back to her home, never be with her family, even if they still lived?

She had already impressed him over the past few weeks. Now he'd not be content until he learned everything about her, until he had her in his bed again. Perhaps…yes, perhaps until he had her as his…wife?

He turned the word over in his head. *Wife*. Someone to always be there for him, to give him children. He imagined Kiana running after a brood of black-haired and golden-haired toddlers, teaching them all, girls and boys alike, how to hunt and fight.

The idea made him smile, but the reality drove the smile away. He'd not want his girl children to learn the ways of a warrior, a hard life and dangerous. On the other hand, he'd not worry as much knowing they were able to defend themselves from men like Ottar. Besides, if he raised a brood of daughters as strong and brave as Kiana, he'd be blessed indeed. She was a shield maid to rival the fiercest of Valkyries. Deep in his soul he knew she'd never give it up, never stand back and let him protect her.

Gods, how could *he* stand back and let her protect herself?

On the way back to camp, curiosity drove him to ask the one question that had puzzled him about her tale. "Where did you come up with your new names? They're not Southland names, nor from these parts."

She shifted the pole to a more comfortable position. "There was a couple, husband and wife, who took us in that first winter. We didn't know about snow, or how cold it got this far north. They found us huddled in their cowshed for warmth and took pity on us. We stayed with them three months. I didn't know how to milk a cow or cook a meal, but I cut vegetables and skinned rabbits, and Jenal was an extra playmate for their two children. When we left, we took their names to honor their help."

Tor tried to imagine his fierce shield maid in a kitchen. "So Beren and Kiana were farmers."

She nodded.

"Did you ever learn how to milk a cow?" He grinned at the image.

She scowled. "What do you think?"

He chuckled. She turned her back, but not before he glimpsed her tentative smile.

The camp came into view at the end of the trail. Ahead of him, Kiana stiffened, slapped a hand to her sword, and glanced around.

He drew his own sword. "Trouble?"

They stopped and studied the trees but all was quiet.

After one final inspection, she shrugged. "No…I thought I felt…but no, there's nothing."

"Thought you felt what?" His little warrior wasn't one to jump at shadows.

She was silent for a moment, then shook her shoulders and cast him a sheepish look. "Like I was being watched…but it's gone now. Maybe some animal afraid I was too close to its den."

She faced forward and proceeded down the trail. Tor stared at the trees. Was it an animal?

Just in case, he'd put the guards on alert. He didn't want anyone sneaking up on the camp without him knowing.

Chapter Eighteen

When the sun's edge touched the horizon on the first night the villagers spent with the Norsemen, three men thrust lit torches into the pile of wood gathered close to the beach above the water line, and a great fire flared to life. Kiana helped Beren maneuver over the rocky ground and settle on one of the many tree trunks Tor's men had laid around the fire pit.

Most of the Norsemen were there, claiming seats on one side of the fire. Tor's brothers sat with their families. Beade's wife had been one of Kiana's most enthusiastic converts to swordplay, and she threw Kiana a welcoming smile. The villagers took longer to arrive, some still unsure of their welcome, but happy to gather on the opposite side of the flames from their new neighbors.

Kiana studied faces, looking for signs of suspicion, of fear. Assured there were none, she allowed herself to relax. The Norsemen didn't plan trickery, but a lifetime guarding the royal family taught her to be prepared.

Not that it had done any good when the Usali attacked. She'd been blind then, ignoring the signs her lover was going to betray them all. How had she never noticed?

Beren tugged on her arm. "Look at the colors, Kiana!"

She followed his gaze. Indeed, the flames were different colors, shifting from orange and deep red to blue and even green. Such magic was common in the palace, but in an open fire on a beach? How did they do it? They didn't have the spices or powders of Southland magicians.

She studied the scene. The old man Runa told her was their seer circled the fire, tossing what looked like sparkling dust into the wood. Each toss brought a new color to the flames.

The answer came to her at once, and she laughed at her own slowness. If peddlers carried sugar sweets from the South, why not the powders of the magicians? Her father told her once the powders brought a good price in the North, where such things were little known. These Norsemen, then, must have trade with the Southlands, wherever their original home was.

Kiana nodded toward the old man. "Watch."

The boy narrowed his eyes in concentration, then laughed. "Oh, magic, like your father used to do." Then he shot her an apologetic glance. "Sorry," he muttered. "I didn't mean to remind you."

She ruffled his hair. "We'll never forget those who loved us. Don't you remember *your* father? Your mother?"

"No," he admitted, and shifted his gaze away from her. "Not even what they looked like."

Tears shone in his eyes. Going with instinct, she knelt in front of him. "But you do." She tapped his chest. "Here."

He swiped at the tears. "Not their faces. I can't see their faces, no matter how hard I try."

"Oh, Beren." She drew him into a hug. "Faces aren't important." She placed her hand over his heart. "In here, you remember their laughter and their joy in you, their love for you and for each other. That you will never forget."

He gazed at her, eyes wide in wonder and hope. "Truly?"

She gave him a confident smile. "Truly."

He stared at the fire. "I remember mama's hand stroking my back when I fell off my pony into the prickle-bush and had to sleep on my stomach."

The memory of that time brought a grimace to Kiana's lips. She'd been on duty that day and was terrified the king would dismiss her. He surprised her by taking her aside and admitting he'd done the exact same thing when he was a child. He'd eased her guilt, offered her understanding. Having no brothers, neither she nor Yasmin had experience with the mischievousness of small boys.

Just then Eskil and Arkin dashed over. "Oh," Beren cried in dismay. "I left my flute in the tent. We were going to play for the strangers."

"They call themselves Norsemen," Kiana reminded him, grateful for the distraction. "I'll get your flute."

Leaving Beren discussing music with his friends, she hurried back to their tent, dug out the flute from Beren's pack, and returned to the beach within minutes. In that time Beren's friends had claimed seats on the log flanking the boy. She handed him his flute and gazed in resignation at her lost seat.

Beren slanted her a hopeful look. "Can Eskil and Arkin sit with me?"

"Of course." She strolled around the circle until she found an empty log.

Big enough for two, it sat between the groups. No one from the village wanted to sit next to a Norseman, nor did the Norsemen seem willing to share close space with the villagers. That might change with time, but for now at least she had a seat.

No sooner had she settled than Tor approached. "Do you have room for another?"

She glanced over to Runa, who sat close to Vider with no empty space around them. It was the first time Kiana had seen Runa without Astri. Babies and young children remained in the tents with willing grandmothers, allowing mothers to have an evening free.

Kiana shifted to one end of the log. Tor sat, taking up more than half the space, and she bumped his hip. "Do all Norsemen grow this big in your land?"

He chuckled, raised his arms and flexed his muscles. Thank the Lady she was already sitting. Even so, her legs trembled. Tor lowered one arm to his lap, draped the other over her shoulder, and tugged her close. She stiffened, glanced around. Had anyone noticed?

Again he chuckled. "Come, is it so shameful to show we're lovers?"

She whipped her head round. "We're not lovers," she spluttered.

He leaned away to look at her, but left his arm in place. "So what we did this afternoon was…what…exercise?" He grinned when he said it, and the infectious laughter in his gaze had Kiana's mouth curving up.

She assumed the haughty expression of a lady of the court, straightened her spine, and managed to glare down her nose at him, even though he sat taller than she. "One encounter does not make a lover. For that one needs at least two."

"Two lovers?" His tone suggested innocent curiosity, but his eyes twinkled with mirth.

To her horror, heat rose in Kiana's cheeks. "No, idiot." She slapped at his chest. "Two encounters."

"Ah, then we must arrange a second very soon." He bent until his mouth brushed her ear. "Perhaps after everyone has gone to bed tonight?"

A shiver of anticipation slid down her spine. She had to swallow twice before answering. She intended to reject him. After all, she'd resolved never to give her heart again. But…she didn't have to give her heart to give pleasure. The logic stunned her, and she wasn't surprised when the word that came from her mouth wasn't "No" but "Where?"

"My ship." He gestured to one of the dragon-prowed ships that had been dragged onto the beach, silhouetted against the red sky of the setting sun.

She just had time to nod before one of the Norsemen strode to the center of the circle, beating a drum.

Once he had quiet, he bowed to Tor, paced to the other side of the campfire and bowed to Soren.

Women from both camps entered the open area bearing platters of food. They walked around the circle, serving everyone. Kiana hadn't been involved in the food preparation, but she recognized the roasted venison. Some unfamiliar cakes surrounded the meat, soaking up the juices.

Copying Tor's example, she took a cake, used her knife to cut a slice of meat from the roast, and slid it on the soaked side of the cake. She placed the combination in her mouth and was delighted with the taste of succulent meat, exotic spices, and herb-flavored bread.

When the women had circled once, other women approached with another course. This one consisted of bowls of broth made from the deer bones and filled with root vegetables, some familiar to her, some not. Again, the combination of Norse and local food was well received. In the meantime, cups of mead were handed out to the adults, goat's milk to the children, and older girls circled with pitchers to keep the cups filled.

Near the end of the feast, several boys not yet approaching manhood dashed into the circle with platters of fruit and berries resting in a lake of spiced milk. When the server reached Kiana, she discovered the milk was heated and thickened, providing a heartbreaking taste of home.

By the time the food was finished, the sun had dipped below the sea, full dark had descended, and the stars shone with a clarity and brilliance she had marveled at ever since she'd come north. A faint glow over the mountain hinted at the rising moon. Neighbor chatted with neighbor, and mothers settled children on cloaks or bedding at their feet. When the moon, close to full, cleared the mountain, its light joined the light from the campfire to brighten the clearing. Time for the entertainment.

Kiana sighed, patted her stomach, and rested against Tor. Replete, relaxed. It felt…normal…to snuggle against the big Norseman like this, and the mead made her drowsy enough to wonder if she'd even be awake for her midnight tryst.

The man with the drum again entered the circle and banged for silence. An older man joined him, and while the first man tapped on his drum, the second began…well, chanting or singing. "Listen, oh people, to the saga of Tor the mighty, the flaming sky ship, and the hole in the world."

"Do you want me to translate?" she whispered.

Tor squeezed her shoulder. "No need. The bard is skilled at his craft."

Puzzled, she turned back to the bard, who now circled the fire, gesturing at the same time he chanted the tale. The words were clear to her, but his actions were far from random. With his hands, his body, he drew the story in the air, drew his listeners in. Language was no longer a barrier.

As the story progressed, she cast glances at the villagers. All paid attention to the bard with an eagerness that told her they understood the tale as if he spoke it in their own language. Most had picked up enough Norse to understand some of the words, but the bard's actions alone told the story. Delighted at his skill, Kiana imagined herself standing beside Tor while he faced the raging storm, shared the bard's awe and fear at the appearance of the sky ship, his relief when they arrived in calm waters.

She was amazed at how easily the bard made her *see* the arrival from the Norse point of view. The tale continued with Tor's encounter with the villagers, the making of the truce, the fight with the bear, and ended with the arrival of the villagers to share the Norse camp over winter.

Finally the bard's voice died away, and the drum stopped beating. Everyone, Norse and villager alike, jumped to their feet and shouted their approval. Together with the others, Kiana clapped her hands overhead.

Tor leaned close. "I told you he was skilled."

"If he came to my homeland he'd be given bags of gold and have his choice of maidens eager to entertain him." She'd never met anyone so skilled at his craft.

He chuckled. "Then it's good he isn't in your homeland, for his tales are much admired by my people."

When the shouting stopped, everyone sat once more. Anticipation filled the air. The man with the drum remained by the fire while another handed the bard a mug and escorted him to a seat with the other Norsemen. A fast beat on the drum drew everyone's attention.

The drummer stopped, and without a word bowed toward the village side of the campfire and took two steps backward. To Kiana's surprise, the two boys sitting with Beren jumped to their feet, bowed to the drummer, then sat again. Eskil settled a drum in front of him, and Arkin held a strange-looking harp, unlike any she'd seen before, a flat piece of wood, the length of his arm, with a long narrow hole carved in the top half. Strings made of some sort of vine or animal gut stretched the length of the hole. She wondered if he'd borrowed it from one of the Norsemen. Beren already had his flute, and at an invisible signal, the three boys played.

Kiana had heard Beren before. Back home he practiced often and even more after they came to the village. It seemed he'd now taken up teaching, for the tune he and the other boys played was straight from the South, a sad lament for lost love. She didn't think Beren knew the words that accompanied the tune, but she did, and it brought tears to her eyes. When they finished playing, there was silence for one eternal moment. The boys looked around, uncertain, but then one of the warriors began banging his knife against his sword. Another picked it up, and another, and before long the whole camp was applauding the youngsters' performance.

Grinning now, flushed with success, the boys raised their instruments again. This time they played a tune that set the feet to tapping, a common harvest tune often heard in the village of an evening, and keeping to tradition, most of the village women jumped up and pulled their men into a lively jigging dance around the campfire.

On impulse, Kiana tugged Tor to his feet.

"I don't know the steps," he protested when she dragged him into the middle of the dancers.

She laughed. "There are no steps. Just stomp your feet." She demonstrated, and he copied her. She picked up the pace, held both his hands, and made him turn in a circle while she skipped around him.

After a few more awkward moments, he fell into the rhythm. His body relaxed, and he took the lead, spinning her around as they danced with the other couples. When they passed Runa and Vider, Tor waved them to join in. Kiana lost sight of them when she and Tor circled the fire, but when they returned to the Norse side, several Norse couples now jigged in place, including Runa and Vider.

After the dance, a Norse woman sang a sprightly song of spring and young love. Two of the village fishermen, drawing on their years of balancing in tiny fishing boats, performed an extraordinary combination of leaps and spins, walking on their hands, tossing each other to tumble head over heels and spring again to their feet. Not to be outdone, three Norsemen followed, demonstrating their own flexibility and dexterity. Soon others entered the area, village and Norse men competing to prove whose jumps and rolls were the most daring, the most outrageous.

When the men collapsed, exhausted and laughing, back in their seats, five village women entered the space. One held a drum, smaller than the Norse drummer's but with a sound lighter and higher as she beat it in a complicated pattern. The other four women used the beat to guide them in a circle dance, one hand linked to each of the others in the center while they dipped and spun, swinging their skirts wide until they appeared like summer flowers tossing in the wind.

Tor tightened his arm around Kiana's shoulder. When she looked up, his attention was on her, not the four dancers. "Do you have a skill to show us, Kiana? I'd wager you have a voice like the songbirds I have heard live in the South."

When he'd asked her about the farmers who'd taken her and Beren in last winter, their names hadn't made an impression. Now, though, her name on his lips sent tingles skittering down her spine. Kiana caught her breath, then forced out a chuckle. "Then you would lose that wager. My own mother once told me my voice reminded her of a sick camel." At Tor's surprised glance, she leaned closer, dropped her voice. "One day, though, I will dance for you." She put enough emphasis on the word *dance* to have his eyes widening in curiosity. Grinning, she returned her attention to the entertainment.

When the last of the singers and jugglers abandoned the central area, he sighed and squeezed her shoulder. "My turn," he whispered, "and then just you and me." He took her hand and pulled her to her feet. "Will you translate? I don't want to get this wrong."

Together they strode to the area in front of the fire, where he signaled to the drummer. A fast beat brought silence to those assembled.

Tor raised his arms. He reminded Kiana of a temple priest bestowing his blessing. "People of this land." He paused, glanced at Kiana.

"They call themselves the Norden," she murmured.

"Oh Norden, we of New Asgard thank you for welcoming us into your land." His voice rang loud and clear. "We in turn welcome you to this, our new home, and are honored you allowed us to invite you to stay with us over the winter and share your food. We hope by spring we will have become friends and allies, and that our homes will be open to each other."

He faced the fire, much lower now with the evening drawing to a close. "May this flame be our hearth fire, and the entertainments we have seen this night prove our mutual hospitality."

He lowered his arms. Norsemen standing at various points around the fire tossed sand and water on the remaining flames. In moments, fading embers glowed in the light of the full moon high overhead.

When the last of the flames disappeared, a great sigh spread around the assembled people. Tor turned his back on the fire pit, bowed to the people in front of him, then paced around the pit, stopping at the cardinal points to bow again. When he returned to Kiana's side, Soren took his place beside Tor and spoke similar words, again with Kiana translating, then repeated Tor's gestures, bowing to all.

He, Tor, and Kiana remained standing by the fire pit while everyone gathered themselves. The women and children dispersed to the shelter of the tents and the temporary huts, and the warriors and village men returned to the open-air camp near the training ground.

When all had departed, Soren bowed to Tor and followed his own family. Tor stood a moment longer, staring after the departing people, then touched Kiana's hand.

"My ship?" he murmured without looking at her.

Her heart sped in an uneven rhythm. "Let me get Beren settled, then I'll join you."

He glanced at her then, and the mischievous twinkle in his eyes caused her breath to stutter. "Yes, you will."

He turned away just as Kiana recognized the double meaning in her words. Her face flaming, she hurried up the beach to the tent she shared with Beren and several of the village women and children.

"I was a member of the queen's elite guard," she muttered. "I am a warrior and have led men in battle. I have killed, starved, protected. I have taken lovers. I'm not a virginal maiden to blush and stammer at the attention of a man."

Yet Tor made her blush, as no other had done, not even Ajmal. *But I will not stammer*, she vowed.

She remembered then that she'd promised to dance for him. Not tonight, though. The dance she had in mind required a more…intimate location than the deck of a ship, and when she danced… Her annoyance vanished in a soft chuckle. Ah, yes. When she danced, *he'd* be the one stammering and blushing.

Chapter Nineteen

Tor peered into the dark of the lower deck. No, not there. It smelled of privy and sweat—not the place for what he had in mind.

He stroked the bear fur at his shoulder. Possible. The cloak was big, good enough for a tumble on moss in the middle of a forest, but not as soft as he wanted for tonight. A pity they'd taken the tents to the shore. The deck now looked bare, uninviting. There must be something that hadn't been removed.

His gaze passed over a bale of rope by the railing, then caught on a half-hidden wooden chest, one of several his friends had hidden aboard the ships before they sailed. The gods were smiling on him tonight. He hadn't even missed his war chest the last few weeks in camp, and he knew just what it contained.

Striding over to the shadows, he then dragged the chest into the moonlight, unfastened the latch, and lifted the lid. Inside were furs and rich cloth, bags of gold he'd hidden from Ottar, sparkly baubles Tor planned to give to the children at midwinter, even a few books he'd managed to bring from his home when Ottar had driven them out.

Tor placed the books on the deck, withdrew the furs and cloths, then returned the books to the chest and refastened it. He'd store it in the longhouse once that building was complete.

The ships had been dragged onto the beach, above the high tide mark, and anchored to stakes driven into the hard earth beneath the sand, where they'd stay until spring. They were too big to turn over, so hides would be added in a day or so, stretched from side-to-side to protect from snow and wind. The prow faced inland, the high dragon head blocking the view of the casual observer and hiding what he and Kiana were doing. Perhaps not the most romantic of settings, but at least it offered privacy.

He spread his new bear cloak on the deck, then the furs in several layers on top, forming a bed big enough to keep him from falling off the sides and soft enough to avoid bruises. He was sorting through the cloths when a muted rustling drew his attention to the side of the ship.

Kiana slipped over the railing. In the moonlight her skin was flushed with exertion, or perhaps…eagerness?

Tor's heart jumped in his chest, then settled into a fast beat. His palms tingled in anticipation of running over that flushed skin. Once she stood upon the deck, he took a deep breath to compose himself, stood, and extended a hand. She sauntered forward, studying his preparations. Were they acceptable?

Her gaze slid to his face, and to his immense relief, she smiled. "You've been busy."

He nodded, unable to think of a single word to say to her. How did she have this effect on him?

She tilted her head to study him. "Well, and I didn't even have to dance."

He blinked and found his voice. "What?"

Her chuckle, low and sultry, sent a shiver down his spine. Strolling to the furs, she then turned her back to him, bent, and unlaced her boots. Once again his throat went dry. Odin's beard, why hadn't he brought some mead with him?

After kicking off her boots, she knelt in the middle of the furs and turned to face him. With a teasing smile, she untied the laces of her shirt and had them undone and the shirt half over her head before Tor remembered to breath.

Her shirt landed on the deck and she smiled at him. "Aren't you joining me?"

In seconds, he stripped off his own boots and shirt and now worked on his trews, anxious to be rid of them. Kiana undressed at a more leisurely pace, then lay back on the furs, naked and not at all self-conscious.

The lacings in his trews birthed a knot resistant to his already shaky fingers. He cursed, struggling with the knot while amusement lit her face. In frustration, he drew his knife.

"No, wait." Kiana rose to her knees and scooted to the edge of the furs. She reached for the laces. "Let me."

Fingers brushed like feathers across the front of his trews, and he cursed under his breath. He wanted out of them, *now*. He looked down. Her dark hair flowed over her hands where they tugged at laces, her bare back bowed in an arch he wanted to caress.

"Kiana," he breathed and closed his eyes.

"Yes." Her breath sighed over his hot erection. His eyes flew open. *Thank the gods*. His trews lay in a puddle around his ankles.

Kiana sat back on her heels, waiting. He kicked out of the

confining material, and then he was on her, pressing her back against the furs. She laughed, her legs sliding up his until she crossed her ankles behind his waist, latched her arms around his neck and drew him into her.

They groaned as one, and then her mouth was on his, devouring, demanding. Tongues fought, hands clutched, nails bit. She arched beneath him with a cry, then reared up and sank her teeth into his shoulder as he made one final thrust.

Breathless, slick with sweat, they collapsed. Tor had enough presence of mind to slide off her onto his side. He tugged one of the furs over them both, then drew her against him, tucking her head under his chin, but instead of relaxing as he expected, she began licking his throat, and her hands…

He sucked in a breath. "Are you trying to kill me, woman?"

She answered with a soft laugh and continued her wandering exploration. He caught her wrists before she arrived at her destination. She sighed but let him wrap her in his arms.

"I'm not sleepy," she murmured.

Gods. "Then just…wait a little."

She chuckled, but settled against his side. She watched the stars, and he watched her, fascinated by her features, willing to stare at her all night.

"The stars are different here." She spoke as if the subject held immense appeal. "I've never taken the time to look before."

He dragged his gaze from her face and glanced at the sky, then returned his attention to Kiana. "Different, how?"

"Oh…" She waved her hand. "Different patterns, I suppose you'd say. My father studied the stars. That's how we knew when to plant, when to harvest. We used to make a game, guessing what the patterns looked like—the dragon, the lion, the hunter, the lamp."

"Lamp? You mean, like a torch?" He visualized the shape, but nothing torch-like in the night sky came to mind.

"A bit. The flame is held inside a cage made of fine metal, with bars as thin as my smallest finger." She traced the outline in the air.

Tor studied the sky, frowned, then pointed to a single star. It wasn't as bright as he expected, but perhaps his memory played him false. At sea it might look brighter. "That one we navigate by. It's always there, in the North, even as the others move. Can you see it from your homeland?"

"All our stars move, from eve to morn, season to season." Shivering, she didn't resist when Tor eased her closer.

"I've been to the Southlands. All that heat." The cold must affect her more than most here. "Why did you come north and not go to another of the Southland towns?"

She shrugged. "The Usali were spreading. No matter where we went, they'd soon follow, so I thought this might be a better place. Safer for Beren. Even if someone came looking for him, they'd not expect us to come to the cold-lands."

Once more she shivered, and he drew the furs up to her shoulder. "Do you miss the heat?"

A chuckle escaped her. "Oh yes. In the dead of winter, of course, but strangely enough, I miss it more in the summer."

"Because it doesn't get as hot?" he guessed.

"No." She stretched the word out, as if thinking while she said it. "No, it's more the…the *smell* I miss."

"The smell?" Did summer have a smell? He'd never noticed.

"Mmm." She sniffed, memory sending fleeting expressions across her face: joy, wistfulness, wonder. "Figs left in the sun too long. Camel dung and people sweat. But sand, most of all, the kind that's so fine it clings to every wrinkle in your clothes and body, and the kind that's coarser, near the dunes. It's…salty, I suppose. And dry. So dry. Here, the damp gets in your bones."

"You could always wrap up in a fur." He pulled her closer to the heat of his body.

"I prefer to wrap up in a man," she murmured.

Her hand strayed again, and again he caught it. "Not yet."

She sighed, then turned her head toward him. "All right. I've told you about my home. Tell me about yours. Why did you leave your homeland?"

Tor went cold, but it was a fair question. She'd answered his, and if he wanted this to go any further than an…*encounter*…then why deny her? "It's a long story," he warned.

She patted his chest. "I'm not going anywhere." She slid her hand downward, but stopped when he sucked in a breath. There was a smile in her voice when she whispered, "But perhaps shorten it, just a bit."

He looked away. How much did he tell her? As much as she told him, so…all.

"The village we come from is now called Ottarshavn, but before it was Olafshavn, after my father, Olaf Strongarm. Ottar was the son of a distant cousin, vain, ambitious…treacherous." He paused, tamping down the anger that flooded his veins. When he continued, he was proud his voice didn't shake with the emotion, the self-loathing that accompanied the words.

"As the eldest son, I was expected to lead the trading expeditions, the raids. When I left, my father was chieftain." He clenched his fists. "When I returned, he was dead, and Ottar had taken over."

"He challenged a weak old man?" Kiana asked, incredulous.

Tor snorted. "Not so old, and not weak. In a fair fight my father would have defeated Ottar without breaking a sweat."

"Ah." That one word held all her sympathy. "You said treachery."

"Yes. It must have been that way." Was this how she'd felt when her lover had betrayed her people—a burning in the throat, a knot in the stomach, bands of iron around the heart? "They said my father was as if drunk, swaying on his feet, when he faced Ottar. He could hold his mead, could Olaf Strongarm, but Ottar was said to know a witch skilled in potions that can fell the strongest man. I believe he somehow fed a potion to my father, so it was easy to kill him."

"You didn't challenge this Ottar when you returned?"

Tor swallowed the bitterness. "My father knew he might be tricked. He feared for our lives and made my brothers promise not to avenge him and to make me pledge the same. So to honor him, we didn't. Until we found out about Runa."

Kiana stiffened. "Your sister."

The bands tightened around Tor's heart. "It was perhaps two months after my father died that she began to show, a thickness around the waist Beade's wife identified. But Runa refused to say who had fathered the child, no matter how we begged or threatened."

A sympathetic smile tilted her lips. "She's a strong woman."

"She's a stubborn woman," Tor grumbled. He remembered how frustrated he'd been, unable to learn who had defiled her.

"What changed?" Her tone was mild, soothing, as if trying to soften his memories.

"Ottar. He kept quiet, perhaps fearing our wrath, but when Runa was closer to her time…" Was it only a few weeks ago? "When Runa was closer to her time, she overheard him brag about how he'd raise his son—his, not hers—to be a great warrior like himself. *Great warrior.*" Tor sneered and clenched his fist. "Anyway, that was the last insult for Runa. She confronted him, told him he'd never get his hands on her child even if she had to strangle it herself. Everyone in the village heard her."

"You challenged Ottar?"

"I wanted to." The memory was still bitter. "Runa argued against it. She was afraid for us, just as our father had been. She knew what Ottar was capable of, and she also knew he wouldn't feel safe while I lived in the same village. I had powerful friends, honest warriors whose loyalty

Ottar needed. So she promised to give him what he wanted if he'd send me into exile instead."

To his surprise, Kiana kissed his forehead. "I'm glad you had the sense to go."

Against his better judgment he'd let Runa's pleas convince him. "My brothers stood by me and declared they'd go into exile with me. And so did our crews, their families. Ottar gave us one day to load and provision our ships. There wasn't time to bring everything we needed, and he wouldn't allow Runa to come with us, of course, but she fooled him."

A hint of pride had crept into his voice. "She snuck aboard before we sailed and hid in the tent with the other women. And not just herself, but the war chests Ottar had confiscated. We were a day out of harbor when she came out."

He chuckled. "I think Ottar would have been more annoyed at losing the war chests than my stubborn sister."

Kiana was silent for a moment. "Then you ran into that storm and the sky ship."

"Yes." He turned his head toward the dark bulk of the mountain. "And it brought us here." He turned back, brushed a kiss across Kiana's forehead. "To you."

She tilted her head so his kiss slid down her nose to her mouth. There he lingered, capturing her moans, until her hands wandered once more.

"Will you live this time?" she whispered.

He gave a dramatic sigh. "Perhaps. But if I don't, *you'll* have to explain my lifeless body to my people come morning."

Her body shook with laughter when she proceeded to test his readiness.

~ * ~

The next morning Tor forced himself not to stagger while he climbed the mountain the beach had become. Kiana left him a short time before sunrise, and it took him longer than usual to drag on his clothes. He hadn't had much sleep, if any. The night had been filled with mouths and hands and sighs. The woman was insatiable, but at least he'd kept up his end of the…encounter.

That was twice…well, a lot more than twice…they had *encountered* each other. He and Kiana were officially lovers. Now all he had to do was get her to say it.

The warriors were already on the training ground, practicing. Others worked on the longhouse. Cook fires were lit. Children rubbed sleepy eyes as they crawled from tents. An ordinary day, for everyone else. Tor grinned. A wonderful day for him. Nothing could possibly go wrong today.

"Storm coming." Jorvik sidled up to Tor, matched his pace.

Never dare the gods. He studied the clear sky and kept walking. "Are you certain?"

The seer darted in front of Tor and stopped, forcing him to come to a halt. Jorvik scowled and crossed his arms. "You may not like me, war-leader, or the things I know, but that doesn't change the future. I see what's there, not what I want to be there. Whether you believe me or not, that won't stop what's going to happen."

Reluctantly, Tor reminded himself the seer had never yet been wrong about weather, and that a clear sky could change in a heartbeat. He shifted his gaze to the longhouse. Three more days before they finished the roof, according to his builders. "How soon?"

Jorvik smirked, satisfied, it seemed, that Tor was now listening to him. "Not tomorrow, but the day after. There's time if you work faster."

Two days. Was it possible? He huffed out a breath. It had to be done. They had no choice. "I'll talk to the builders."

When Vider passed, Tor caught his arm. "There'll be a storm soon. We need to prepare."

Vider paused. "What do you want me to do?"

"Let me speak to the builders. I'll let you know." Before Vider moved on, Tor's mind turned in another direction. "Was Petter able to do anything with the metal box?"

"No." Vider's face lit in excitement. "It was the strangest thing. He put it in the hottest fire, but it wasn't even scorched when he took it out."

Tor frowned. "Pity. There must be some use we can make of those boxes."

"I'd like to look at it some more, if you have no other need for it now." Vider reminded Tor of an eager puppy waiting for a special treat.

He wasn't surprised at his friend's request. Vider loved complicated things and easily spent hours trying to determine how a bauble he'd traded for worked. "Go ahead. We can't do anything with the rest until the snows end and we can get back into that ship."

Vider grinned in delight and hurried on.

Kiana was speaking with a woman who sat at the mouth of one of the tents. She looked up when he drew near. "Inga says the weather is turning. There'll be a great snow in two days' time."

"So I understand." Tor gestured to the longhouse. "We're going to have to speed up the building. In the meantime, have everyone stay in camp for now. I don't want anyone wandering off and risk the storm coming sooner."

He didn't wait for her to agree, but trusted Kiana to spread the order.

After a brief word with the builders, he knew he'd been wise to ask her to keep everyone in camp. He drew his horn from his belt, strode to the open area where they'd held the welcome fire last evening, put the horn to his lips, and blew. His people recognized the summoning, and they assembled at once, bringing the villagers with them.

He motioned for Kiana to stand next to him. "Your people are picking up our language, but I don't want any misunderstanding. Will you translate?"

She nodded. As last night, his people stood on one side of the circle that surrounded him and the villagers on the other. One day, he hoped, they'd all mingle, but for now he faced his people and let Kiana face her villagers.

"The wise ones say a great storm is coming." He paused for her to translate, then continued, first him speaking, then her, "The longhouse needs one more level of wall before we can add the roof. If we all work together, we can have the walls up and the roof on before the storm hits, but we'll need everyone, Norse and Norden alike, to finish in time."

A murmur of dismay rose from the group. "What about the animals?" one man asked.

"We have stables against the east wall. Some of you will help finish those and get the animals inside." He allowed himself a grin, "And we'll also need a privy."

Others shouted more questions. He answered a few but at last held up his hands for silence.

"Time passes, and we need to start." He pointed to different people. "Vider, Havard, and Ivar will coordinate the work. Talk to the builders about what's needed. The center support poles are in place but we still need the roof beams so some of the men will have to cut those. Perhaps the women can cut up the hides and prepare the grasses we've gathered for flooring. The children can bring food and drink. There won't be time to break for feasting until we're done."

He studied the group, his people and the villagers. All had the same look. Determination. Having a definite plan went a long way to avoiding panic.

After everyone dispersed, Kiana touched his arm. "Thank you for including the villagers. They wouldn't like to be thought weak and unable to help."

"We're going to need everyone, even the weak." He frowned.

"The builders say we can't be done before end of day, day after tomorrow, no matter how fast we go."

"And the storm will hit in the morning of that day." She furrowed her brow in worry.

He nodded. "I intend to be ready by then, no matter what the builders say."

She straightened her shoulders. "Well, then. I'd better find out what my job will be."

Tor gazed after her until she was swallowed up by her friends, then strode off to his own job.

The next two days passed in a blur. Without the skills of a builder, Tor found himself following orders as if he was a mere crewman. He cut trees, shaped logs, dug holes, and watched the progress with anxious eyes at each spare moment. Plank by plank, the walls on the longhouse grew. By the end of the second day, the beams had been laid to support the roof. As the sun set, those men and women who weren't constructing the roof or caring for children stood in a circle around the building. Each held a torch, the ends wrapped in braided vines and soaked in oil. Tor ensured he stood beside Kiana. Two men each lit a torch using flint, then turned to their neighbors to light theirs. One by one the torches caught fire, and when the sun disappeared below the horizon, the many torches cast enough light for the men on the roof to continue working as if in daylight.

In this way they worked all night. Those holding the torches took turns resting, but the light remained steady throughout the dark hours. Tor refused to relinquish his torch. Rest could wait. He was responsible for these people, and wasn't surprised to see Soren a few paces away holding his own torch throughout the night. The two leaders exchanged silent nods of respect.

The first snowflake fell as the pale gray of dawn lightened the sky. Faces turned skyward. Clouds had appeared overnight, low and heavy with their burden.

Yes, it was going to be a bad storm.

A few moments later, a man shouted from the roof. The head builder straddled the peak, where the roof sloped away on either side. He was grinning.

Finished.

His shout was picked up by another man, then several more, until the entire camp shouted with triumph. Gratefully, Tor handed his torch to his neighbor and shrugged the cramp from his arm. This part he knew how to do. Raising his voice, he issued orders.

The torches were carried into the building and fastened to metal hoops that kept the flames away from the walls. Children were woken, possessions bundled, animals gathered, tents taken down. Before the ground was covered in a shallow blanket of snow, every man, woman, child, and animal had moved into the longhouse and the solid doors closed with a satisfying *whump*.

They'd made it.

Chapter Twenty

While Kiana hadn't spent the entire night holding a torch, and had even managed a few hours' sleep between shifts, she still felt exhausted. Gathering Beren and their few belongings, she hurried him into the new shelter, eager to get him out of the snow and cold.

For the first hour all was confusion. Families roamed the edges of the building, staking out their own areas on the benches. As Kiana expected, Norsemen found spots on one side of the hall and villagers on the other. A few families mixed together, but most weren't yet comfortable with their neighbors.

Kiana and Beren claimed a short length of bench between the door to the stable and the north fire pit. Ropes were flung over the roof beams, and hides and woolen blankets raised to separate each family area, with more blankets covering the front for privacy. The benches were deep enough for people to sleep with their heads toward the inside of the open space and their feet to the outer wall.

On the south end of the longhouse a longer area of bench was open on both walls, without the separating hides. There the single men and women slept, the men on one side, the women on the other. Thankful she and Beren were deemed a family, Kiana sympathized with those of her trainees who had to put up with the giggling Norse maidens.

Despite having no windows, the room was far from dark. Dozens of torches hung on beams at the edge of the benches, facing the open area. She'd expected it to be crowded, but everyone had their own place.

Norse women took over the north end of the building and drew out braziers for cooking. She learned trestle tables would be built later once the necessities of shelter and warmth were satisfied. Meanwhile, people ate from communal bowls or wooden platters in their sleeping areas. On one side was set up an area for the youngest children. Between the south end and the central fire pit, the Norsemen had organized a training area that she intended her own trainees use as well.

The storm hit in full force an hour later. All the outside doors rattled, sending children screaming to their mothers. Gusts of wind found their way down the tubes feeding the fire pits and howled around the roof. Torches flickered but didn't go out. After the initial assault, the wind settled to a constant drone through the rafters.

After a while, Kiana forgot about the storm. There was too much going on in the building to distract from what was happening outside. Last winter she and Beren had been similarly cloistered with the villagers in the caves. Most of the village men were fishermen who brought their nets with them for mending over the winter and wood for carving. The women had threads and beads for decorating their men's clothes. The villagers now established themselves far from the training area.

Fascinated, Kiana saw two of the Norse women peering curiously at the villagers' beads and eventually, after giggling discussion, they joined their new neighbors, displaying their own decorative pastimes. Other Norse women joined them and before long both groups huddled together, bent over clothing, blonde hair making them indistinguishable from each other. A good omen.

Although the men showed little obvious interest in the training area, she noted a few furtive glances from some of the younger men when Tor's warriors began their exercises.

By midday everyone was settled. Beren and his friends made themselves a comfortable nest by the center fire pit where the warriors practiced. Kiana assembled her trainees together on one side where they, too, began practicing.

After two hours, she called a break to drink some water and rest for the next session. A shout of encouragement from the other side of the open space drew her attention. The shout had come from Eskil, so she suspected Beren was involved, but she wasn't prepared for the sight of him standing in a clear space and holding one of the wooden training swords. Facing him was Tor.

Stripped to the waist, sweat gleaming on his torso, he looked the image of a warrior fresh from battle.

More curious than alarmed, Kiana wandered over, sipping at the mug of water one of the Norse women had given her. She sat cross-legged beside Eskil and watched Tor face off against the young prince.

At first, Beren swayed on his feet, trying to maintain his balance with only one crutch to support him. Once he managed that, Tor showed him how to brace himself on that crutch while holding a short sword in his other hand. With impressive patience, Tor led the boy through the moves of defense and attack, adjusting the instruction for one leg. After half an hour, Beren was winded but grinning at his growing skill.

Tor escorted him back to Kiana, and Eskil jumped up. "Me now, me!"

Tor laughed, the boy's meaning obvious in his excitement if not his words. He signaled to another of his men, who took Eskil onto the training floor and showed him the motions.

Beren snatched up his other crutch and, with a wave to Kiana, hobbled off to join some other boys playing a game involving stones and hoops.

She turned to Tor. "Thank you for teaching him. How were you able to figure out how to change the fighting tactics for one leg?"

He plucked the mug from her fingers and swallowed the rest of her water. "It's not unusual for a warrior to lose a leg in battle, so we've learned many ways to help them stay useful. One leg, one arm—all can still fight."

"Amazing." She looked to where Beren was gesturing with one hand, explaining to his friends what Tor had been teaching him. "Can you show me so I can help him practice?"

He waggled his eyebrows. "Is that all you want me to show you?"

She scowled and slapped his arm, but was unable to hold back her laugh.

Later, when she brought Beren a bowl of stew for supper, the boy stared at her while he ate. Unnerved by the intense scrutiny, Kiana lowered her own spoon. "What is it?"

"You like him, don't you?" It was more a statement than a question. He jutted his chin toward where Tor sat with his men across the open space.

She followed his gaze and her heart beat quicker. "Perhaps. Don't you?"

He considered the question, his brows furrowed. Then he smiled. "Yes. I do."

"I'm glad." She took another spoonful of stew.

The boy glanced at her sideways, not turning his head. "Do you think he likes you?"

Kiana choked on the mouthful she'd just taken. She grabbed a mug of water and gulped the contents. When she was again able to speak, she gave a non-committal answer. "Perhaps."

"I think he does." Beren nodded and spoke with certainty. "Yes, I think he does. And since you like him too, you must be friends, don't you think?"

"We are. Friends, I mean." What had brought on this line of questioning?

"That's good then." He set his bowl on the bench beside him and leaned back, resting on his elbows. "You need more friends." With that, he turned on his side and closed his eyes.

Children. She'd never understand them.

~ * ~

The next morning, the storm raged outside, but inside was light and warm. Rubbing sleep from his eyes, Tor noticed that some of the younger adults had begun tentative friendships, and a few couples eyed each other with interest. It seemed a good omen.

Beren sat on one of the log benches while his friends practiced with the wooden swords. He looked…annoyed, Tor decided. Every once in a while the boy's hand clenched on his leg, and he swung his arm in a shielding motion. Tor's lips twitched, but he held back the grin. He remembered the frustration of being injured and unable to play with his friends.

He wished he had more time to learn the boy's language and hoped Beren's lessons were further along, for what Tor wanted to say needed more than gestures.

"You'll be up there with them soon, lad." He sat on the bench beside the boy. "We can have another session later today if you like."

Beren's head jerked up in surprise, then he narrowed his eyes, concentrating. "Kiana say…says I heal…uh…quick."

Relief swept through Tor. The boy did, indeed, have a good grasp of the language, enough, at least, for Tor's purposes. "That's good in a warrior."

A grin of delight split the boy's face.

He relaxed. This wasn't so bad. "I believe your family would be happy you have found a home here."

Beren's grin disappeared. Wariness entered the boy's gaze, a wariness Tor had seen often in Kiana's. He let sympathy show in his voice. Sympathy, but not pity. "I lost my mother when I was but a lad, and my father less than a year ago. I know how it feels to lose those you love."

Beren swallowed, but the wariness never left his eyes. "My father and mother both…dead…two summers."

Tor ignored the urge to comfort the lad. Best for them both if he kept emotion from his tone. "And Kiana's family also."

"Yes." Beren lowered his gaze.

"So…" Tor continued, careful to keep his words simple. "You are each other's family now."

The boy raised his gaze. Wariness faded, to be replaced by speculation and curiosity. "Yes. Kiana say so."

He took a deep breath then every word he'd practiced disappeared from his head. Panic threatened. No. He *would* say this. Now. "You…you stand for Kiana's family now, as her father."

"Father?" To Tor's surprise and relief, the boy giggled. "No, just friend. I not old enough to be her father."

Tor licked his lips. "I need to talk to her father, but he isn't here so I speak to you. As family."

A puzzled frown creased Beren's brow. "All right."

He glanced around the longhouse. Kiana was on the far side working with her trainees. No one else was close enough to hear, but Tor discovered if he looked at the boy the words stuck in his throat, so he stared at the young trainees instead. *Is this how Vider felt when he spoke to me about Runa?* No wonder his friend had stammered so much.

Tor opened his mouth, closed it, then blurted, "I wish to take Kiana to wife and ask your permission to woo her."

To his utter astonishment, Beren whooped at the top of his lungs and threw himself at Tor, wrapping his arms around the bigger man and squeezing with all the enthusiasm of a six-year-old boy. "I knew it! I knew you liked her!"

Tor winced and quickly surveyed his near neighbors, but aside from some curious glances, no one showed any interest. Kiana didn't seem to have heard the shout. His heart slowed from its frantic gallop, and he wiped damp palms over his shirt, then returned the boy's hug before helping Beren sit back on the log.

"Thank you." Tor wanted this moment to be serious, but his own grin broke free. "But Kiana will need persuading. Can this be our secret for now?"

Beren placed two fingers over his lips. "I keep secret." Tor half-rose, but Beren touched his arm, holding him in place. The boy's joy had been replaced by a worried frown. He sat back, waiting for the question in the boy's gaze. "When you wed Kiana, will I live on my own?"

Tor treated the question as if it came from another adult. "No son of mine will live on his own unless he chooses."

"Son?" Beren's eyes were wide with wonder.

Careful now. "I know I can't replace your own father, but I'd be proud to have you as a member of my family. With my people, when we wed, we wed the family, not just the woman."

"But Kiana is not…" He frowned, searching for the words. "Is not…blood kin."

"Family isn't just blood." Nor did blood define family, but Tor didn't want to confuse the boy.

Beren scrunched up his forehead for a moment, then looked at

Tor from the corner of his eyes. "Do I have to call you father?"

Ah. That was one worry easily put to rest. "If you wish, but Tor is also fine, and proper between men."

The grin returned. "Tor. I…I believe you will make Kiana happy."

"I intend to." He turned away, his own grin threatening to explode again. *I intend to.*

~ * ~

On the second full day, the third day after everyone took refuge in the longhouse, Tor woke early. The wind didn't howl as much, and the walls no longer shook.

He was getting dressed when Vider rushed up to him. "Tor, you have to see this!"

Tor straightened from lacing his boots. "Can't this wait until later? The storm sounds as if it's easing, but it may just be a temporary lull."

"Now, Tor. It has to be *now*." Unable to keep still, Vider bounced from foot to foot.

Tor sighed. In the two days since they'd shut themselves into the great hall, he'd seen Vider perhaps a handful of times and not with Runa. What had he been doing? Unwilling to encourage his friend with too much curiosity, Tor offered a casual, "Fine."

"In the stable." Vider hurried in the direction of the outer shelters. Tor followed at a slower pace, in no hurry to leave the warmth of the main building.

The stables held a comforting smell, of cattle and warmth, mixed with the pungent scent of straw in need of cleaning. Vider had claimed the end at the back wall, separated from the animals by a wooden barrier. A leather hide hung over the opening, and Tor pushed through to the area behind. Vider had been busy.

This space held the fodder for the larger animals, but the piles of straw were shoved back against the walls, leaving a narrow space the width of the shed. A stool sat at one end, by the inner wall. On it rested the box Vider had taken from the sky ship. The broken metal stick was now lashed to a splinter of wood, keeping it straight.

"You fixed it?" Tor wasn't surprised.

Vider stood behind the box and pressed one of the colored circles. It lit up as if a fire burned behind it. At his gesture, Tor shifted to the side. "I call these *stangs*." Vider touched the metal sticks.

Tor had to admit they resembled small versions of the bars of iron Petter used as raw material for the swords. "What do they do?"

"Ah." Vider's face split in a triumphant grin. "Watch."

He pushed the bar forward, and a beam of light shot from the front of the box to stop short of the outside wall. Inside the light was the circle Tor and Kiana had seen with the strange stone room behind it. This time, however, the room wasn't empty. Two men in long white shirts hovered over the flagon on the trestle. Both were old, with gray hair tied back with red thongs and faces wrinkled and bearded.

Tor slapped his hand to his sword. "Who are they?"

At his words, the men looked up. They smiled at Vider and said something in a strange language.

"It's all right," he soothed. He stepped around the box and approached the circle. "I've spoken to them before."

"You've *spoken* to them?" Tor stared at the strange men. "You know what they're saying?"

"No, but we've been able to use gestures." Vider waved at the men and pointed to Tor, then himself, and placed his hand over his heart.

The men bowed, and one mimed raising a cup to his lips. Vider chuckled. He drew a stoppered horn flask from his belt and passed it through the circle. One man took the flask from Vider's hand. The other lifted a platter from under the trestle. On the platter were flat disks the size of Tor's palm, like oat cakes but lighter in color with darker bits embedded in the top. The man stretched his arm forward, and the platter appeared on Tor's side of the circle.

Vider took the platter. "Oh, sweet cakes," he exclaimed in delight, taking one of the disks and biting into it. "These black bits? They are called chok-let." He took a second and held it out to Tor, who shook his head.

The other man emptied the contents of Vider's flask into a jug on the trestle. From the color and smell—*he smelled the scent through the circle*—Tor recognized the liquid as mead. Vider scooped the rest of the disks from the platter and exchanged it through the circle for his flask. The men smiled and waved. Vider pulled the bar on the box toward him, and the circle disappeared.

Tor let out a breath. "So, it *is* a hole in the world."

Vider nodded. "Just like the one we came through."

"Like a shadow of our own world. A shadow world." Tor studied the box. "Will it swallow us up again?"

"The hole isn't big enough, and I haven't found a way to make it larger. All we can do is exchange food. Perhaps someday we'll be able to learn their language, or they ours. Just think of the trading possibilities." Vider appeared so eager Tor had to smile.

"Kiana can help us with the language. It's a skill she has. As for trade…" He paused and contemplated the box. "I wonder where the other boxes open to."

"Just so," Vider agreed. "I wish we had some now. It'd be good to explore them over the winter. Do they all open to the same place? Or to another land? Or—"

"Spring." Tor laid a quelling hand on Vider's arm. "We can't get more until then. And I want to know more about how this one works before we try any of the others. We have all winter for that."

Vider sighed then stuffed another disk into his mouth before pressing a coloured circle to turn off the light in the box. When he finished swallowing, he offered the last disk to Tor. "Try it. It's good."

Again, Tor declined. "Perhaps another day. I'm not hungry right now, not when the stables need mucking out." He sniffed and grinned. "Or hadn't you noticed?"

Vider chuckled and popped the last disk into his mouth.

~ * ~

Despite the evidence the villagers and Norsemen were more at ease with each other, Kiana wasn't content. Beren was settling in well and had friends in both groups.

Yet…yet…something was coming, something dark. She took time to speak with the village wise woman, and even with the Norsemen's seer, but although they both agreed there was darkness in Kiana's future, neither was able to tell her what. So she put it from her mind and concentrated on keeping Beren busy.

Had it been just three days ago the storm began? It seemed longer, and now the wind rattled less against the doors. Was the storm at last losing its strength?

Still Kiana was unable to settle. *What's out there*?

The wind died by evening, but no one wanted to venture out until daylight.

Kiana tucked a blanket around Beren. One more interminable night. She wanted to get out of the smoky building and breathe fresh air again. Of course, getting out was going to take time. She'd glimpsed the snow through a crack in one of the doors. Several men would be needed to clear away enough for anyone to leave. The stables had to be cleaned again—despite the efforts of the boys on stable duty, they'd soon run out of places to put the dirty straw, something that would have to be corrected before winter confined them for longer than a few days—and in her previous winter in the village she'd learned a few of the berry bushes survived the first storm. The villagers always harvested those before the next snowfall.

There was still tonight to get through, though. Glancing at where Tor chatted with several of his warriors, she sighed. As a single man he slept with his shipmates at the other end of the longhouse, but tonight, she didn't want him sleeping that far away. If she had a djinn at her command she'd wish Tor beside her, in her bed—but not with Beren sharing that same bed.

She'd never felt so…so *wanting*.

Frustrated, she stalked toward the west door and the kitchens. If Tor was out of reach, then she'd cool her need with water, or perhaps she'd find some mead someone had overlooked.

As she entered the short hallway she glanced to her left at the door to the dry stores. Berries? No, her first choice was better this late at night. She turned right into the kitchen.

The cook fires were banked for the night, but the room was still warm. She located the barrels leaning against the far wall, lifted the lid of one, and sniffed. The aroma tickled her nose, and she smiled. Not water. She lifted a ladle off a nearby hook and dipped it inside.

"Too much of that will give you a blinding head by morning," a familiar voice warned. His teasing tone sent a shiver of need through her. *Tor*.

She peeked at him over her shoulder. "I don't want much, just a little to help me sleep."

He glided farther into the room, and suddenly the space was too crowded. "I know a better way to help you sleep."

Her heart kicked up a beat. With exaggerated care she rehung the ladle and replaced the lid on the barrel before turning to him. "What did you have in mind?"

He took one more step and gathered her to him. She tipped her head back, giving him access to her lips. He didn't bend his head as she expected, but studied her as if she were a rare flower. Instead of impatience, she found herself mesmerized by the admiration in his gaze.

"We fit together so well," he murmured.

She nodded, unable to speak.

He ran a finger down her cheek, tucked a strand of hair behind her ear. At last, he closed the final distance between their lips.

Despite her silent urging, he was gentle at first, a whisper of a touch. She strained upward, eager, desperate, but he withdrew to keep the kiss soft. "*Tor*," she breathed, prepared to beg.

A chuckle, low in his throat, then—there was no other word for it—he swooped like a hawk diving for the kill.

Trapped against the wall, Kiana wrapped her arms around his neck and lifted her legs around his waist, crossing her ankles to anchor her there.

He swept his hands up her legs, found the ties on her leggings and loosened them, slipping his fingers inside. She moaned into his mouth. The world tipped, disorienting, until she found herself on her back on the floor. No longer needing her hands to keep herself upright, she put them to better use working on the leather ties of his shirt. By the time her leggings were around her ankles, she had his shirt open and was licking his chest.

They joined with a sigh of relief. Tor moaned and murmured something that sounded like, "Home."

For a long time the only sounds registering on Kiana's fogged brain were sighs and groans, names called in hushed whispers. They flew together to the heights, then drifted back to earth. When the world settled back into place, she gave one final sigh, unclasped her ankles, and let her boneless legs slide back to the floor.

"Do you think you can sleep now?" Tor murmured into her shoulder.

She smiled. "I might."

He rolled onto his back, took her with him so her head rested on his chest. "I can help you sleep like this every night."

"Hmmm." Then his words penetrated the haze around her brain. She jerked her head up, her body tense. "What?"

He smiled, but she sensed uncertainty beneath it. "We make a good pair. Like a…a family."

The languid mood she'd been lost in the last few minutes vanished. *Please don't say it. Please don't say it.*

He cleared his throat. "I would be honored if you consented to be my wife."

She closed her eyes. He'd said it. "I…" She stopped, cleared her throat, forced herself to look at him. "I expect there are many young women in your, uh, tribe, who'd be happy to be your wife."

His smile faded while he studied her. The warmth in his gaze cooled to hurt. "But not you?"

She slid off him and sat up, fumbled for her leggings. She didn't look at him now. *Couldn't* look at him. "I have a duty to Beren."

"He'd be part of our family." His tone was persuasive, but did she imagine the hint of desperation buried in it?

She finished tugging on her leggings. "You are leader of your people. You need to take someone to wife who will bring riches to your house. I bring nothing, not even a single coin."

He sat up, frowned, and tugged at his ear. "Is it something I did? Or said?"

The words sent a shiver of despair through her. She caught up her shirt, but he traced the bones of her spine with one finger, and she stopped with the shirt held, just held, in front of her.

He set his hand under her chin and turned her to face him. "Kiana, I don't need coin. I need *you*."

She closed her eyes. Need. No one had ever needed her, not in that way. Yasmin had needed her complicity. Queen Siri had needed her loyalty. Beren...well, Beren needed Kiana's protection.

Tor...for Tor to need her... *No, don't weaken.* Need wasn't love. She had sworn never to love another man, and she didn't. She didn't love Tor, but she wanted him, and he wanted her.

Needed her.

No. "I'm sorry. I can't...I just...can't."

He said nothing while she finished dressing, but she imagined the weight of his gaze. What would she see if she looked? Accusation? Disappointment? Lady, this was tearing her apart. She had no choice. When she straightened, she made her decision.

"We're leaving in the spring, Beren and I. We can't stay any longer." Tor drew in a breath but she forged on, "So you see, there's no future for us." She turned toward the doorway.

"Kiana—" He reached for her.

She kept her back to him. "It's best if we stop this now, before..." *Before I lose my nerve. Before I fall in love with you.* "Before it gets too serious." *Too late.*

"I *will* change your mind." It sounded like a vow.

"I'll not accept your offer," she whispered.

"Perhaps not yet. I'll wait until you do." Yes, without doubt a vow.

A tightness clenched around her heart. Blinking back tears, she fled.

Chapter Twenty-One

When the sun rose on the fourth day, Kiana woke to the chatter of excited people. The noise surrounded her, but one sound was missing. The wind no longer howled or even murmured under the conversations. The storm was over.

Men were already outside clearing paths through the snow. Every time the side door opened, the piles beside the walls had grown higher and the open space longer. Once the paths were cleared enough to get to the forest, the men planned to make one last hunting trip to check the rabbit snares they'd set up before the storm and, with luck, find a stray deer or two.

The village women were going to search for berries, since they'd spent their lives in the area and knew where to find the bushes without relying on the trails. The snow was never too deep between the trees. As for the Norse women, they'd stay and finish the preparations the storm had cut short. Kiana was part of the group guarding the village women on their berry hunt.

She was preparing to leave later that morning when Beren hobbled up to her. "I want to come with you." When she didn't respond right away, he continued, "I'm getting very good on my crutches."

With a sigh she straightened from tying the laces of her warm winter boots. "The snow is deep. Did you see outside when the doors were opened?" She'd discovered the easiest way to get the little boy to obey her was to treat him like an adult. Sometimes. Hopefully this was one of those times.

"But Tor said they were beating paths through it." Beren didn't whine, but his tone betrayed the underlying hope.

Studying his eager face, Kiana considered. She didn't want him leaving the longhouse. He was safe here, lots of people to protect him while she was out, but...there was still danger outside. Her unease hadn't gone away.

However, if she didn't convince him to stay now, he'd only try to follow her. "All right. Put on your cloak and come with me."

With a whoop of triumph, he snatched up his cloak and hobbled after her. She swung the main door open.

When Tor had opened this door earlier, a huge drift reached to the lintel. It took five of his biggest warriors two hours to dig their way through. Now a broad path of beaten snow led from the doorway toward the open area where the snow wasn't as deep, and from there toward the woods.

Beren halted beside her on his crutches, and Kiana stood back. She pointed to a tree stump halfway to the woods. "If you can walk to that stump, you can come with me."

He grinned at her and started out. Within two paces, his crutches were sinking into the path. Even the boy's slight weight was enough to drop them through the beaten crust. He struggled forward. After a few more paces, the snow was frozen enough the crutches no longer broke through. He shot Kiana a grin, then hobbled two more steps before the crutches slid sideways in opposite directions, tumbling the boy to the ground.

She resisted the urge to rush forward. She had to give the child credit for effort.

He dragged the crutches to him and managed to get back on his feet, his smug grin replaced by a set jaw and mulish determination. This time, he was careful to place each crutch before putting his weight on it. He was halfway to the stump now. *Dear Lady, he might actually make it*.

Then the crutches slid away from him again, and as he went down, he fell on top of one, snapping it in half.

Hiding a mixture of relief and worry, she hurried forward. She reached down to help him up.

He slapped her hand away. "I can do it!"

Pushing himself up using the unbroken crutch for balance, he clambered to his feet. Sweat beaded his brow and his eyes creased in pain, but he didn't complain. Kiana wanted to shout with pride at his effort, but held herself back.

Ignoring the broken crutch, Beren limped forward again. He was three quarters of the way to the stump by now, but it was clear to her, if not to him, that he'd never make it.

He tried, he really tried, for the next few minutes, but every step ended with him on the ground. At last, tears of frustration streaming down his face, he sat and glared at her.

"I'd have done it if the crutch hadn't broken," he muttered.

She knelt beside him. "Yes, you would, and one day you will. But not today."

He wiped his sleeve under his nose, sniffed, and straightened his shoulders. "No, not today." He glared at the crutch, then slid her a look from the corner of his eye. "But I did try, didn't I?"

"Yes, you did." She smiled, as much in pride as relief.

"So, may I have a sweet?" He grinned, as if that had been his goal all along.

She had to laugh. "Oh, Beren. I'd give you a whole bag of sweets if I had any, but you ate the last one a few days ago, remember?"

His face fell. "Oh yes."

"Never mind." Kiana held out her hand. "I'll bring you back some plump berries, all right?"

Beren loved the berries almost as much as the sweets. "All right."

After helping him back to the longhouse and getting him settled on a bench by the fire, Kiana retrieved the broken crutch and set it beside him on the floor. "Ask if Dyre's father can make you another one."

On her way back to the door, Runa hailed her. Kiana found the other woman fussing over Astri in the alcove she'd claimed. An older woman hovered at the side.

"If she cries," Runa was saying, "see if she needs dry swaddling or just wants to be picked up. Or try giving her a little honey on your finger." She caught sight of Kiana. "I decided not to take Astri with us today. I don't want her catching a cold."

Kiana opened her mouth to respond, but Runa turned back to the woman. "That reminds me, keep her well wrapped and away from the doorways. Some of the outer walls aren't sealed yet so keep her away from the walls as well. Maybe take her down by the central fire pit. Oh, wait. It might get noisy there with everyone coming and going. Maybe the north fire pit, with the other children. Or maybe—"

"Mistress." The other woman plucked Astri from Runa's arms. "I have children of my own. Several. I know how to care for a babe."

"Yes, but—" Runa's protest was cut short by the other woman.

"Go get those berries you promised me." She sounded like a mother admonishing a stubborn child. "The air will put some color in your cheeks."

Kiana approached, noticing how pale Runa was. "You're not well?"

"No, I'm fine. I just…" She paused, gave a rueful chuckle. "I'm just fussing." She brushed a finger over the baby's fine blonde curls, glanced at Kiana. "Froya is our wet-nurse and is in charge of the children in the nursery."

The woman's patient smile softened into affection. "Raised you, didn't I? You and that hellion of a brother of yours and all your other brothers. I'll take care of this little one, never you fear."

Runa withdrew her hand and turned to Kiana. "Well, let's go, shall we? I'm sure this nice sunshine won't last forever."

What was she talking about? "You can't—" Kiana began, but Runa brushed past her.

"Yes, I know." She picked up her cloak. "We're supposed to stay here, but if I don't get outside and walk around, I'm going to scream."

Kiana didn't like the idea, but as long as Runa stayed with the other women and didn't go too far, it might be all right. Still, it didn't hurt to remind her there was still a risk. "It may be dangerous. The trails won't be clear, and there may be scavengers looking for berries."

"In truth, I'm not interested in berries." Runa fastened the pin of her cloak.

"What?"

She gave an enigmatic smile, and with one last loving glance at her baby, wrapped her hand around Kiana's then led the way to the main doors. It took but a moment for Kiana to throw on her own cloak, then they were outside.

The air had warmed since Beren's attempt earlier. Runa raised her face to the sky and closed her eyes. "I love this time of year. Everything smells so…"

"Cold?" Kiana shivered. Even in fur-lined leathers, the chill seeped between the seams.

Runa laughed. "I was going to say crisp."

"Well, that too, I suppose." Kiana shifted in front of Runa, preventing her from continuing. "There's no use going on. I'm not taking you anywhere."

"Oh, but you must." Runa looked around, but no one was nearby. She lowered her voice. "I never did get to see the gray man who protects the sky ship."

So that was it. Kiana sighed. "No. You're not to leave camp."

Runa narrowed her eyes. "I'll go with or without you."

Kiana recognized a vow when she heard it. By the Lady, this woman was as stubborn as Beren…or herself. She had no doubt Runa would find a way. Better to go with her and keep her safe.

With a sigh, Kiana led the way to the edge of the woods. Runa trudged behind her, relaxed and humming to herself. They followed the other women for a while, then veered off at a fork in the trail. Kiana's trainees accompanied the others down the right fork, while Kiana and

Runa took the left. While the snow was still thick around the base of the trees, the more open ground had less. The wind that piled drifts against the tree trunks swept the open areas clear.

Although she knew the way to the caves from the village, coming from this direction took longer. In time, though, she came across a familiar trail and struck out with more confidence.

She was always amazed at the number of birds still singing in the treetops. She'd learned that many flew away to warmer climes for the winter, had even recognized some who spent time in her own homeland. Still, many remained, huddled fluffed up in bushes and hollows, pecking for hibernating insects and competing with the humans for the last of the berries.

"Do you think we'll encounter one of those bears?" Runa asked from behind her.

Kiana glanced over her shoulder. The Norse woman fingered a slit in her skirt where her short sword was fastened out of sight.

The question offered a perfect opportunity to argue for Runa's return to camp, but she'd not lie to her friend. "I doubt it. Once the snow comes, they find shelter and sleep until spring. Even this false summer won't wake them."

Runa lifted her hand away, but kept close to Kiana.

They traveled for another ten minutes, but Kiana's concentration wavered. That same prickly sensation in her neck was back. She found herself searching the trees, squinting into the darkness beneath.

They emerged in a clearing where several trails converged. Not long now to the plateau. Somehow the sky ship and the gray man represented security. Safety. She wasn't sure why, but hurried forward, eager to reach their destination.

She studied the trail ahead and the trees beside them, her uneasiness increasing. If she hadn't been so cautious, she might have missed the glimpse of scarlet cloth sticking through a pile of snow at the base of a tree. She stopped, her sword already in her hand. "Wait here."

To her surprise, Runa remained on the trail. Kiana pushed her way through the deeper snow to the tree, then bent and brushed away the white covering to reveal a man. His face, once as dark as her own, was now a waxy white. Frost clung to his hair and eyelids. She stared at him, frozen with sudden terror.

"Is he dead?" Runa called from the trail.

Kiana shook herself. Now wasn't the time to panic. "Yes."

Runa craned her neck. "Who was he?"

She wanted to grab Runa and run back to camp, but she needed to be sure. Her hands trembling, she cleared away more snow. The man was huddled into a light cloak well suited to desert nights but inadequate for the northern temperatures. The scrap of scarlet she'd spotted above the snow faded to a rusty copper where the drift had soaked through. What was he doing out there, so far from shelter? She stood, turned in a slow circle. Through the trees she caught a glimpse far below of the Norse camp. From there the man had a good view of the longhouse and everyone who came in or out. Whoever had put him on watch had no idea of the risk the snowstorm posed.

She took deep breaths. *Stay calm. Think.* Were there others? Yes, of course there were. How many? How close?

Runa remained silent during Kiana's investigation, but now asked the question Kiana feared most. "What was he doing here?"

Looking for Beren.

"We'd better go back. He won't be alone." Kiana paused. Was she leading an enemy to their camp? No, they already knew where it was. Her sluggish mind cleared. She, the villagers, the Norsemen, they'd need to protect the camp. The snow was deep, except where the men had opened narrow paths easy to defend. What if the hunters hadn't returned yet?

She didn't know where they were, but she did know where the women were harvesting. "We need to get the other women back to camp and warn Tor."

As they turned away, a stranger emerged from one of the trails ahead. Leather boots and leggings were all that showed beneath the black cloak covering him from shoulders to knees. The sword in his hand made it clear his intentions weren't friendly, but what sent a chill of ice through her body was the sigil embroidered on the shoulder of the cloak. She had an identical symbol on the scabbard of the sword she'd brought with her from home.

Pushing Runa behind her, Kiana crouched and drew her own sword.

"Don't be rash, my love," sneered a familiar voice behind her, in an all-too-familiar language.

Two more men emerged from the woods on either side. She straightened, turned to face the fourth man.

Ajmal.

Her past had caught up with her.

Chapter Twenty-Two

Tor shoveled another pile of the fouled straw and tossed it outside the stables. Although not his place to clean out the stalls, after Kiana rejected his proposal he needed to use up the stored energy. He'd gone hunting, but when his stomping through the woods frightened the deer away, and he almost beheaded the man who'd been brave enough to berate him, Tor decided he needed something more physical. None of the warriors were available for practice, so he'd volunteered for stable duty to the amusement of the youngsters whose task it was.

So now he sweated while he laid fresh straw in empty stalls, transferred animals to them, and cleaned out their old quarters. The work was heavy, tiring, and mindless.

"Lord Tor?" A young boy ran into the stables. By his clothes he was one of the Norse children, not from the village.

"Here," he answered.

The boy skidded to a halt in front of him. "Lord Tor, Jorvik asked that you come to him right away. He said it's important."

Tor sighed. "Not another storm, I hope."

"He didn't say, just that you must come at once." The boy bounced from foot to foot.

It must be important for Jorvik to send a boy for Tor. "All right. I'm coming."

When he strode from the stables, Vider fell into step beside him. "Had enough mucking out?" his friend teased.

"Jorvik," Tor muttered. He didn't have to say anything else. Vider's grin vanished.

They approached the seer who sat cross-legged on a fur outside the main doors, a selection of bones spread on the beaten snow in front of him, in a pattern he alone was able to read.

The seer looked up when Tor and Vider approached. The worry in the man's eyes made Tor reach for his sword. "Danger?" He didn't bother with a formal greeting.

Jorvik touched the bones. "Great danger, but not for us. For the old woman and your sister."

"Old woman?" *Sister*. Tor whirled, but Vider had already dashed into the longhouse.

A moment later, he returned. "Runa's not there. Someone saw her and Kiana leave with the berry pickers."

Tor clutched the seer's shirt and hauled him to his feet. "Runa is in danger? And what old woman are you blathering about?"

Jorvik wheezed until Tor loosened his grip. "The old woman you'll wed. She's with your sister. They're both in danger."

Vider seized Tor's hand and dragged it away from the seer's shirt. The old man dropped back to his former sitting position. Vider was as frantic as Tor about Runa, but he was able to hold his panic at bay long enough to get more details. "What kind of danger? Bears?"

"No. Men. Warriors." Jorvik ran a hand over the bones. "I cannot see them but they're not from here, from close by. They feel as if they come from somewhere hot."

"Southland warriors?" Tor remembered Kiana's story of escaping with her prince. "Kiana? Are you saying Kiana is the old woman?"

"Yes. Yes. Old. Very old. The bull isn't complete here." Before Tor could make sense of those words, Jorvik continued, "I threw the runes several times for her over the last few days. All was blackness, danger."

A shiver ran down Tor's spine. "She knew of this danger and went out anyway? Where are they? Are these men here for the boy?"

The seer shrugged.

Tor cursed the need for food that had taken the other warriors, save him and Vider, from camp.

Wait. The women Kiana trained. Some hadn't gone with the berry-picking group.

He clutched Vider's arm. "Go find Beren, make sure he's inside the longhouse. Then get everyone in camp inside as well."

"We can use the horn to call back the hunters," Vider reminded him. "And the women will hear it as well. There are a couple of our men with them and will know what it means."

Tor closed his eyes. Of course. He was addled indeed to forget the hunting horn. Opening his eyes, he drew it from his belt and blew three sharp blasts.

"You think this is about the boy?" Vider asked. "Why?"

No one save Tor and Kiana knew of Beren's true origins, and

Tor refused to break Kiana's trust in telling him. "If the men are from the South, it's logical to assume they may be after the boy as well as Kiana. Make sure he's inside, will you?"

Vider accepted the explanation and hurried off.

After a moment, Tor blew the horn again. The hunters ranged far and needed time to get back but some of the women trickled in. He studied each one, but neither his sister's familiar face nor Kiana's distinctive black hair were among them. Fear clutched his stomach. The last time Runa had gone out with the berry pickers, she'd not stayed with them. Had she wandered off again?

Now Kiana was missing too.

A moment later, Vider ran up. "Everyone is inside. I told them to bar the doors. But Tor, Froya said Runa was talking about the gray man."

Tor swore. "Of course. Kiana must have gone with her. We'll need a search party."

Yes, a search party, but who…? Ah. There. Lida strode into the camp behind the berry-pickers. He hurried over. After he explained his need, she organized several women. Three she sent to the longhouse with orders to protect Beren, the rest to set up guard around the longhouse until the rest of Tor's warriors returned in answer to his summons. She, Vider, and two other Norsemen moved to Tor's side.

He glanced at his small troop. "Does anyone know a fast way to the sky ship? Where we killed the bear?"

Lida raised her hand. "There are many paths, but the cliff trail is fastest."

"Good. Let's go." *And let us be in time*, The knot in Tor's stomach grew to a boulder.

~ * ~

Emotions swamped her—rage, hate, betrayal—but Kiana's arm didn't tremble. She held the sword firm.

"I'm never rash." Thank the Lady she was able to hide the worst of her rage. Her voice remained calm, cold.

She studied Ajmal's once-beloved face. He hadn't changed much in the last two years. Still as handsome as she remembered, although the arrogance she'd once put down to confidence now revealed itself. His clothes were richer than before. A warm woolen cloak covered a vest of fine silk, the leather beneath unmarred by nicks and scuffs. Even with the cloak, he must be freezing, but he was too prideful to show any weakness.

"No, you always analyzed everything to death." He strolled forward, sword dangling from his hand. His body seemed softer, rounder than she remembered.

His three companions sidled closer. With them in attendance he'd feel no threat from Kiana. Even without them, his confidence was justified. He'd always bested her in mock combat.

Runa reached for her short sword, but Kiana caught her friend's eye and gave a barely noticeable shake of her head before returning her attention to her former lover. She was as familiar with his weaknesses as he with hers. Or what used to be hers. She hoped she'd grown stronger since fleeing the palace, not as quick to anger or as easily taken in by smooth words. "Am I to believe you missed me so much it took you two years to track me down? Are you here to offer the marriage proposal you never bothered with before?"

He stopped, threw back his head and laughed. Runa stared between the two of them. Unable to understand their language, she had to guess at what was being said and from her frown Ajmal's reaction baffled her. However, she was sensible enough to keep her hand away from the hidden sword.

"Ah, Nahid, how I have missed your humor." He stopped laughing, but the amused grin remained on his face while he circled her and Runa. His men edged closer. Kiana tensed. Four to one were unfair odds, and Ajmal himself hadn't become captain of the guard just by being the king's son.

She, however, had never relied on strength alone. Even now her mind worked, searching and discarding plans. She indicated the body. "Who was he?"

Ajmal shrugged. "Just a useless guard. He was supposed to watch your camp, let me know when you left."

"He got caught in the storm." She wasn't surprised at the callousness of leaving the man there. Although none of them had experienced snow before, nor realized the danger of freezing to death, Ajmal just didn't care. She glared at him. "How did you survive?"

"There's an abandoned hut on the shore not far away. We lit a fire." Losing interest in the conversation, he dipped the point of his sword under Runa's skirts then began to lift them. She gave an inarticulate cry and shrank back.

"Leave her be," Kiana snapped, but she wondered at Runa's reaction.

The Norse woman was playing the role of helpless female. The women of Kiana's homeland fought beside their men, but every country she'd traveled through since leaving regarded women as helpless chattels to be protected and used at will. Ajmal probably expected the same from the Northland woman. Someone to be underestimated.

Advantage to their side.

He chuckled but lowered his sword. "Still the protector." He slapped Kiana's sword aside, his expression hardening. "Drop it, or the woman dies."

She let the sword fall to the ground. One of the men strode forward, kicked it into the surrounding underbrush, then drew her knife from her belt and sent it sailing after the sword. He also took her bow.

"The arrows," Ajmal ordered.

She slipped the quiver off her shoulder, and the man snatched it, then backed away.

"Why are you here?" she asked. Runa clung to her arm, and Kiana wanted to keep Ajmal's attention away from her friend.

He smiled. "We want the boy."

Of course, but best to play the dullard for a while. "Jenal?"

He scowled. "Is there another boy? You will bring him to me, and I'll let you and your companion live."

She knew better than to believe him, but the longer she kept him talking the more chance she had of coming up with a plan. "He's just a child, no threat to you."

"He is heir to Dagan. As long as he lives the people won't—" He broke off, perhaps realizing he may have said too much.

"The people won't obey whoever the Usali have placed on the throne in *King* Dagan's place." Kiana finished the statement. She had emphasized the title to remind Ajmal where he owed his loyalty.

His scowl turned thunderous. He slapped his chest. "I am also of the royal bloodline."

"A concubine's child." She blinked, then stared at him in astonishment. "You? They put *you* on the throne?"

"I have more right to it than that mewling brat." He paced the clearing, flexing his fingers open and closed. "The king was my father too. I have as much right to the scepter as the boy. And *I,* at least, don't run away at the first sign of trouble."

"He was a child of four, too young to fight."

"A coward," he sneered.

"He's still your brother," she reminded him.

"Half-brother." He pounded his fist on his chest. "And I'm still the eldest. The crown should be mine by right."

He's mad. He truly believes that. "Killing him won't make the people obey you."

"Oh, I don't intend to kill him." Ajmal regained control of his voice, but his hands twitched on his sword. "He'll spend his life in the dungeons and be paraded out on special occasions. If anyone disobeys, *he* will suffer with them. Soon they'll realize resistance hurts their *beloved* prince."

A chill sped down Kiana's spine. The people loved and respected the royal family and would never allow a child to be tortured because of them.

Desperate, she sought for some argument to dissuade Ajmal from his course. "The boy can sign a royal proclamation, declaring you king in his place."

He stopped pacing, whirled, and hit her with his leather-clad fist. "They won't believe it."

She fell to the ground, head spinning. Runa knelt beside her and eased Kiana to a sitting position. While their heads were close together Runa whispered, "What do they want?"

Kiana wiped blood from her lip. "Beren."

"*No*." Even whispered, the one word held all the horror of a mother imagining danger to her own child. "But why? We must do something."

"I know, but I can't think of anything yet." She spat blood onto the ground. "There's too many of them."

"Quiet!" Ajmal kicked Runa aside, seized Kiana's arm, and hauled her to her feet.

Runa scrambled up and clutched Kiana's hand again. "May lightning strike him where he stands." She kept her voice low so the others didn't hear.

Lightning. *Lightning*.

By the Lady, that might work. The idea was risky, but better than the situation they were now in. At least it gave them a chance.

Ajmal thrust his face close to Kiana's. "Next time, I'll chop off your friend's hand, then cut out her eyes."

She was grateful Runa didn't understand, for the threat might have made even the brave Norse woman tremble. Or attack him.

"Now." He strode away three steps, then turned and placed his hands on his hips. "You will get the boy and bring him to me."

The faint sound of a horn echoed through the trees. Three short bursts. Runa flinched but said nothing. One of the men shoved past them and stared down at the camp.

"Well?" Ajmal snapped.

"Nothing's happening. Just one man blowing a horn." The three blasts came again. After a moment, the man shook his head. "Still nothing. Some women gathered around."

"Hah. Calling his harem to him." Ajmal beckoned the man away from the edge of the trees.

Harem? No, most of the village women were harvesting, and the Norse women were supposed to be working inside. It had to be Kiana's trainees. Was the man so blind he didn't recognize women warriors? Perhaps not. Except for those who'd gone with the berry pickers, most preferred skirts when they weren't practicing. As for the horn, Tor had blown one when he'd warned of the coming storm. Did he know Runa was missing?

Perhaps help wasn't so far off. All Kiana had to do was keep herself and Runa alive, keep Ajmal distracted… But how?

Then inspiration struck. "Since when did a king come on such a quest? And…," Kiana glanced at the three other men, "…with so small an army to back him up." His words echoed through her mind. *As long as he lives the people won't…* Won't what? Obey him? But the invaders were in charge, not him. *Yet.* Then she understood. "The Usali don't trust you, do they. They sent you here."

Ajmal lifted his hand to strike her again, but Kiana stood her ground. She was right, she *knew* it. He had no power unless he returned with Jenal.

Ajmal lowered his hand and smiled. "No one sends me anywhere." But she recognized the lie in his voice, the stiffness of the smile. "Now." He glanced at Runa, then back at Kiana. "The boy or the woman. Your choice."

Play along. She raised her chin but allowed fear to show in her eyes. "How do I know you won't hurt my friend?"

Ajmal studied Runa. "I'm sure we'll find a way to entertain ourselves in your absence." His expression left no doubt what form that entertainment would take.

Instead of snarling defiance, Runa shrank against Kiana, turning away to conceal her face. "I'll gut him where he stands," she whispered, and Kiana struggled to hide her admiration.

She'd not leave Runa in his hands. If her plan worked, she didn't need to leave Runa at all. "I'll tell him you're ill," she murmured. "He's superstitious about illness." Making her voice tremble, she again faced Ajmal. "Please, don't harm her. She's weak and suffers still from childbed fever."

Ajmal recoiled, horror contorting his features before he regained control.

Kiana pushed her advantage. "I beg you, let me take her to a place where she can rest, near a stream. Please. It's not too far."

Uncertainty crossed his face. He aimed his sword at Runa's throat and looked at Kiana. "Very well. Lead on. But if you try to trick me, *she* will be the first to die."

Chapter Twenty-Three

Runa stumbled once more, going down on her knees and adding a few more seconds' delay.

Kiana bent to help her up. "Soon," she whispered.

In truth they were a good half hour from their destination on their present trail. She'd chosen the one that wound along the base of the mountain, rising in a gentle slope. Wide and for the most part free of drifts, this was the path taken by the elderly and store carts when the villagers made the move to their winter quarters in the caves. For the first time she thanked the Lady the sky ship had crashed where it did, for she knew this part of the forest well. If it had landed elsewhere she'd not have the means to slow her enemies.

The longer it took to get to the plateau, the better her chances. Unlike Kiana and Runa, the men weren't dressed for long hours in the cold. They might have been able to keep warm at a faster pace, but the trail and Runa's supposed weakness kept their speed to a crawl.

Already the three lower-caste warriors shivered in their cloaks and linen vests, blowing on fingers numb with cold. Ajmal's heavier woolen cloak kept more heat, but his occasional shivers told her he, too, suffered from the bite of the icy wind that had blown up over the last few minutes.

She and Runa also shivered, but theirs was feigned for the most part. Their leather and furs were more suited to the temperatures, but the wind found a way inside even their sturdy clothes.

Kiana hoped that by the time they arrived at the plateau she'd have a small advantage over her frozen captors.

Ajmal had been silent since they began moving, but she wanted to get him talking again. The more he spoke the more agitated he became, another weakness to be exploited.

She glanced over her shoulder at him. "How did you find us?"

He strode along, to all appearances relaxed. His sword rested on one shoulder, but his grip on the hilt showed he was ready to use it if she or Runa attempted to escape. His eyes glittered in satisfaction at her question. "It wasn't hard. I sent men in all directions, questioned traders who came from far lands. A peddler told me of a dark woman and boy in the north who had a fondness for Southland sweets."

As she'd feared. "That's all?"

He smirked. "He also told me the boy played a metal flute."

Ah. Beren's flute. When they ran, he'd refused to part with his treasure, the one apparently harmless possession from his past. "So the Usali sent you to find us, like a dog sent to retrieve a bone."

"I am no dog!" He took a deep breath and smiled, a smile that sent a shiver down her back. "Besides, I wanted to see your face when I told you what I did to your sister."

She spun to face him. "Yasmin?" Dread settled like a heavy ball in her stomach. He knew what had happened to her sister. "She lives?"

Ajmal stopped. His feral grin told her he'd waited for just the right moment to say those words. "For a while. It was supposed to be you, you know. I scheduled *her* to be in the palace that night and you in the barracks. I had it all arranged. Men loyal to me took the barracks. They had orders to keep you alive, but when they found Yasmin and not you, they brought me her instead." He gazed into the distance, as if reliving the scene. "Oh, she was angry. Spitting with it. Seems our friends had killed her lover. But she wasn't angry for long."

Greasy bile threatened to rise from Kiana's stomach at the glee in his voice.

Ajmal returned his gaze to her. "She wasn't you, but she served well enough for a while. I had to chain her down, of course, but it didn't take much to break her. After that she'd do anything to avoid the pain." His grin spread, and he lowered his voice. "Anything."

Kiana lunged at him, but he was ready for her and swung the sword between them. At the last moment she twisted and missed skewing herself. Panting, fists clenched at her sides, she blinked the tears away from her eyes. She hadn't meant to show him weakness, but Yasmin… *Breathe. I'm stronger than this.*

"Kiana?" Runa's voice, as if from a distance.

The three men had stopped. Runa had taken a step toward her before one man caught her arm and held her back. Kiana shook her head at her friend. This was between her and Ajmal.

His smile didn't waver. "Ah, but I have missed your passion, little Nahid. I had great plans for you." He tilted his head to the side. "After we get the boy, perhaps I'll take you back with me. There's no reason to abandon my plans when I have you again in my hands."

She forced herself to say the words, even though she dreaded the answer. "What happened to Yasmin?"

He shrugged. "She's not as strong as you. She didn't last long, less than a month. She threw herself from the same tower I tossed your mother off."

Kiana's blood turned to ice. "Mother? She lived?"

"For a few hours, after we took the town. She was trying to protect her priestesses. We had to question her where she hid them and the temple treasures." He gave an exaggerated sigh. "She wasn't as strong as she thought, but she was your mother. I'm nothing if not merciful. After she told us what we wanted to know, I gave her a quick death."

No. Kiana's legs threatened to give way, and she stiffened her knees. She refused to collapse, and though the tears threatened to fall, she turned away and blinked them dry. She'd not give him the satisfaction, though her heart shattered into a thousand pieces.

In all the time she had been running, hiding, protecting the young prince, she believed both her parents dead in the raid. She had never been as close to them as to her sister. Her father, as court magician, was often away from their apartments, busy serving the king. Her mother was high priestess in Inanna's temple, a gentle, quiet woman who deferred to her husband in raising two headstrong daughters, but she had always been there when Kiana had been ill, always had food on the table and an encouraging word when needed.

And she had given her less than a thought in the past two years. Guilt weighed on her, more for that neglect than learning her sister's fate. Yasmin had been a warrior. Such risks were known, prepared for. A priestess, however, expected to live a long life surrounded by peace and calm, serving her goddess.

Resolve abandoned her. Kiana had no more strength. A wordless cry spilled from her lips, and she doubled over, wrapped her arms around herself as if to keep from flying apart. She fell to her knees, rocked back and forth, unable to stand against this final blow.

She wasn't aware Runa had broken free of her captor until she dropped beside Kiana and closed her in a gentle embrace, a mother's embrace. All the grief that had built up over the last two years spilled over.

She'd grieved when she'd told Tor about her escape with Beren, but that was nothing to this…this emptiness. The queen's death, exile to the cold North, even that meant nothing next to the loss of her parents, her sister. She'd prayed they'd met a quick death. Now even that faint hope was gone. It was too much. She was going to shatter.

"Well, that was satisfying," Ajmal said after a moment.

Runa squeezed Kiana's shoulders. "It's all right. You're not alone. I don't know what he said to you, but you mustn't let him win." She shot Ajmal a venomous look and whispered, "Do you want me to gut him now?"

Kiana choked between a sob and a watery laugh. *Lady Inanna, thank you for friends like this.*

His voice hardened, and he poked her with his sword as he said, "Now on your feet, or I'll kill your friend right now."

She took a breath, another, but failed to regain her composure. Runa helped her up and she resumed walking, concentrating on placing one foot in front of another. Though her heart weighed like a lump of ice, her mind spun with one word. *Revenge.*

After a while, Runa started dragging her steps, as if fatigued. It gave Kiana an opportunity to take her arm for support. Runa's head was bent, her long braids hiding her face from their captors. She glanced at Kiana without turning her head, her gaze full of concern.

"Any better?" Runa murmured, too low for their captors to hear.

"A bit." All Kiana wanted to do was wallow in her sorrow, but her friend was trying to help. "I learned my family is dead." There. She'd said it. Oh, Lady, why did it hurt so much?

Runa's grip somehow became comforting. "Ah. I'm sorry."

Kiana struggled to speak. She needed to be strong now. They'd be at the plateau soon and she had to be ready.

They both would.

"Runa, do you still have your sword?" she whispered.

"Yes." She wrinkled her nose. "They didn't bother with me after you told them I was ill."

Kiana appreciated her scorn. Neglecting to search both women was a raw recruit's mistake. Ajmal must be more desperate than she'd imagined if he hadn't trained his companions better. "Be ready. When the gray man appears, give me your sword then run as fast as you can."

Runa stiffened. "I won't leave you."

"You must." Kiana sought and found the incentive she needed. "Astri needs you, and you have to warn Tor."

Runa was silent for so long Kiana was afraid she was going to be stubborn, but at last she nodded. "I'll be ready."

A few minutes later they emerged from the trees onto the plateau. Kiana gazed around in wonder. There was no sign of the ship. Snow clung to the sides of the mountain, covering the metal wall. Was the sky ship even still here?

"Stop." Ajmal shouldered in front of them and regarded the

snow-covered space. He turned to Kiana, eyes narrowed in suspicion. “Where is the stream?”

She pointed close to the cliff, making her arm tremble. “It’s over there.”

Cursing, he strode onto the plateau. Runa shifted behind Kiana, and a moment later the hilt of Runa’s sword slipped into Kiana’s hand. They both tensed.

The gray man materialized in front of Ajmal. “Warning. Keep back. This ship is guarded. Keep away.”

Startled, the guards leaped forward. She lifted the short sword. “Now,” she whispered.

With one reluctant glance, Runa fled into the trees.

One of the men attacked with Ajmal but both stumbled through the gray man when they met no resistance. Ajmal managed to stop himself, but like the bear that memorable day, the other continued.

The metal wall may have been hidden by snow, but its effect hadn’t diminished. The man struck the wall and sparks flew. He jerked, his scream like nothing Kiana had ever heard before.

She attacked while the other two were distracted, but whether by instinct or luck, the man she aimed for swung around and blocked her thrust. The clang of metal on metal rang through the clearing.

Ignoring the fallen man, Ajmal snarled an order, and the other guard turned with him to face Kiana. Three to one. Still too many, but she didn’t have a choice.

Crouching, she circled the edge of the tree line and avoided the longer swords. The forest promised escape, but Ajmal wouldn’t stop until he had Beren in his hands. She had to end it now.

The two remaining guards separated, forcing her to divide her attention between them while she backed away. One lunged, but Vider appeared between them, and his sword deflected the other’s.

At the same time, Tor emerged from the concealing trees to face the second guard. He glanced at Kiana, winked. “One each,” he called, grinning.

She straightened then turned until she faced Ajmal. His face twisted in hate, he stalked toward her. His eyes were filled with madness but his movements were those of a skilled warrior.

Although Runa’s steel sword was sharper, it was short, a trainee’s weapon. Kiana was smaller, slower. She hadn’t fought any battles in the last two years.

However, she’d kept up her training and had hunted bears larger than any seen in her homeland. If nothing else, she’d learned new skills from the Norse warriors. It had to be enough. She may not survive this fight, but, by Inanna, she'd make sure Ajmal didn't either. She raised her sword, ready to battle the man who'd destroyed everything she held dear.

Then she attacked.

Experience meant little when faced with determination and passion. Size and strength paled before agility and speed, and a bronze sword, no matter how long or sturdy, was no match for the steel of a Norse blade.

At first Ajmal held his ground, but when none of his tactics drew blood, when the tip of his sword flew into the trees, sliced by her blade, his eyes showed his confusion. She advanced, herding him toward the metal wall, but he sidestepped, and circled until she was the one backing toward the danger. She let him push her, gain confidence, then she sprang forward and sliced another thumb length off his sword.

Sweat threatened to hamper her grip. She clutched her sword tighter. They faced each other with the gray man between them, intoning his warning as their blades passed through his insubstantial body. Used to the gray man's appearance, Kiana ignored the unnerving sight. Ajmal, however, became more and more agitated, his attacks more clumsy, his defense erratic.

Encouraged, she leaped *through* the gray man. Ajmal backed away, gaze sliding left and right as if seeking escape. All was silent.

She spared a glance at the other combatants. The guards were on the ground bleeding their last, while Tor and Vider leaned against a tree, swords still drawn but aimed at the ground.

They weren't coming to her aid. They trusted her to defeat Ajmal on her own.

Tor, her new lover, trusted her to kill her old lover.

She'd not disappoint him.

She swung the short sword in a dizzying circle designed to confuse an enemy and advanced with relentless determination, driving Ajmal to the edge of the plateau. He stopped there, fear in his eyes. Confidence rising, she took one more step closer. In the heart. She'd skewer him like a pig through the heart.

He snarled. Triumph replaced the fear and he lunged toward her, not with his sword, which he still held as a distraction, but with his knife.

Fool. I should have remembered that trick.

She twisted, managed to deflect the blade from her stomach, but it slid into her side. The pain was like a shock from the metal ship. It burned through her blood, sizzled through nerves. Someone shouted. Tor? Then there was no more time.

Ajmal's attack was brutal, all his strength focused on beating her into the ground. She stayed on her feet, forced herself to ignore the pain.

Movement in the corner of her eye drew her attention to the side. Tor circled around behind Ajmal.

No. He was hers.

Words from her training instructor echoed in her head. *Legs are longer than arms, girl. Use them*. And she remembered one of the lessons she'd learned from the Norse.

She drew on the last of her strength and, after deflecting Ajmal's next thrust, angled her short sword to flash sunlight into his eyes. He staggered, blinded. She kicked high, and her foot connected with his sword, flinging it into the trees, then used the momentum of her kick to circle her own sword back. It bit into his side, every bit as deep as her own wound.

His reaction was unexpected. He stopped…just stopped…and stared at the blood. He raised an accusing gaze to her. "You weren't supposed to kill me."

"You're a traitor, Ajmal." Kiana straightened. "You deserve death." Aiming her sword, she plunged it into his eye. "For my father." Into his throat. "For my mother." And one final thrust into his heart. "For Yasmin." Her voice broke on the last word, but she made herself watch him fall, watch the blood spill onto the ground, watch the life leave his remaining eye.

Strong arms surrounded her, held her. She gazed into Tor's eyes and smiled despite the pain. "That felt… good."

She let the blackness overtake her.

Chapter Twenty-Four

Thank the gods Lida had known a shortcut to the plateau. After reducing the odds against Kiana, Tor made himself stand back while she faced the final enemy. Now he held her, praying the wound wasn't as bad as it looked.

Runa rushed from the shelter of the trees. "Is she dead?"

Tor tightened his grip, shaking when blood spilled over his fingers. "Not dead." The vow was as much to himself as his sister. "Not yet. We need to get her back to camp."

"Wait." Lida hurried toward him and dug in her belt pouch. She drew out a handful of moss. "The healer taught us to use this on blood wounds. It'll slow the flow until we can get her home."

Home. Yes, the camp is her home now.

He lifted his hand long enough for Lida to pack the wound with the moss. The blood slowed to a trickle. Kiana wouldn't bleed to death before they got back to camp, but she'd need to get there as soon as possible.

The two warriors he'd sent on the longer route dashed toward them, slowed when Tor held up a hand. "Deal with the bodies. Lida will show you. Vider, get Runa back to camp." Then, with Kiana in his arms, he ran.

He took the shortest path, yet time slowed. Hours, days seemed to pass before the longhouse came into view. He emerged from the trees, slid on the packed snow, and by an effort of will managed to keep from falling.

He shouted for the healer, for anyone. The doors of the longhouse opened, and people spilled out. Before Tor regained his balance, Beade plucked Kiana from his arms and carried her into the building. Tor staggered after his brother, brushing aside questions. Beade carried her to a pallet by the south fire pit, where the village healer had set up her herbs and instruments. Thank the gods they had formed an alliance with the villagers and now had a healer more skilled than Jorvik.

She drew a curtain between them, instructing all present to keep Tor outside.

"Peace, brother. She's in good hands." Emund gripped Tor's arm, and Beade wrapped him in a strong embrace.

Tor cursed and strained against his brothers. "I need to be with her. Can't you see? I need to—"

A small hand slipped into his and tugged. He stopped his struggles.

Beren, face pale, looked up at him with fear in his eyes. "Will Kiana die?" The boy's voice was so low Tor had to strain to hear.

He had forgotten there were others who cared for Kiana. He glared at his brothers to release him, then dropped to his knees before the boy. "She's strong, and the healer is skilled."

"Can…can you tell me what happened?" Beren straightened to his full height. "I am old enough. Almost seven."

How much to say? Did he tell him about the Southlanders? No, that was up to Kiana, how much she wanted the child to know. "Kiana and Runa were attacked by enemies, but Kiana fought them off and saved Runa." The truth, if not the complete truth.

"So she is hero?" Beren relaxed. "Dyre tells Eskil and me about heroes of Asgard, but I not hear of woman hero."

Tor had to smile. "We have many. Did Dyre tell you about Valkyries?" Beren nodded. "Well, Kiana is like that, a warrior, and the bards will sing the saga of Kiana the Hero at the next gathering."

He stared at Tor, hope replacing the worry in his gaze. "Can I learn with bard? I good at re…remembering words when I write them down."

"You can write?" The idea had never occurred to Tor. So few Norse children wanted to learn, even though Tor and his brothers had explained many times the importance of reading to them. Perhaps they needed a teacher more their own age.

"I read and write three languages." Beren held up three fingers and lifted his chin in pride, then grimaced. "But all Southland languages."

"Well, perhaps we can teach you to read and write ours, and then you'll have four." Tor remembered searching his war chest for furs. "I have several books you can read."

"Books? You mean scrolls? I never see full scroll, just pieces my mother—" Beren stopped, swallowed, then straightened his shoulders and continued in a stronger voice. "Pieces my mother write for me to learn." He glanced at the curtain. "I want to learn how to read your language, but Kiana not know how to read it, only speak it."

His eyes again wore the haunted worry visible at the start of their conversation.

"Books are not the same as scrolls," Tor said to distract the boy again. "They're like several pieces of parchment cut to the same size then tied together on one edge, like the leathers we use to open our doors."

Beren frowned, staring at the hide that hid Kiana. "I like to see one of those."

Silence fell, and Tor wracked his brain for something else to talk about. Beren's words came to mind—*Kiana not know how to read it, only speak it*—and that led to a question Tor had since his first meeting with his shield maid. "How did Kiana learn our language? She didn't seem to know it when we first met."

Beren shrugged, sat on the floor, and leaned against Tor's legs. "Oh, that is her magic. She just hear someone speak, and she know the language. I think…" He screwed up his face. "I *think* that was one of her duties, to speak other tongues for the—for my father."

Tor went still at Beren's words. "She has magic?"

"A little, for languages." He seemed unaware of Tor's unease. "Her sister had magic with animals. She tamed even wild ones. Their father was the real magician. He had great power and was court wizard for many years."

Magic. Witchcraft.

No, not witchcraft. She was nothing like the witch who helped Ottar trick his father. Witchcraft and magic weren't the same, as the elders of his tribe were forever reminding him. The seer's talents were rooted in magic, weren't they?

Just then, the healer held aside the curtain. She was one of the few who'd picked up the Norse language with ease, perhaps because she was also the village wise woman. She beckoned.

He leaped to his feet, Beren's hand once more clutched in his.

The healer smiled. "She'll live."

Thank the gods. "May I—may we see her?"

The healer stood back, and Tor entered the healing area, Beren beside him. The boy's crutch crunched on the clean straw when he limped forward.

Kiana lay pale and unmoving on the pallet. Her blood-soaked clothes had been removed. She was covered to her chin with a thin blanket, but the blanket rose and fell with steady regularity.

"She needs to sleep for a while to regain her strength." The healer slipped to the other side of the pallet. "Now you've seen her, I must ask you to leave her to me for a while longer."

Tor released Beren's hand and ran a finger down Kiana's cheek. "For a while."

~ * ~

Tor wanted to sit by Kiana's bed forever, but Runa dragged him away after sunset.

"You need to eat." She shoved a wooden spoon and bowl of barley porridge sweetened with honey into his hands. The heat from its contents spread over his palms, and the scent reminded him he'd had nothing since early that morning.

Runa had also taken Beren in hand, and the boy now curled asleep on a pallet near her. Tor took his bowl and rested against a supporting pillar, his gaze never leaving the hides that covered Kiana's sickroom while he lifted spoon to mouth. She'd heal, he knew that in his head, but his heart still ached for her. He'd have to find a way to persuade her to stay. If those Southlanders had found her and Beren, others might also, but they'd be protected here. Even if she didn't agree to be his wife, she *had* to stay.

Or I'll go with her when she leaves.

The idea jolted him, but the more he considered it, the more it felt right. He wanted to spend the rest of his life with her. It didn't have to be here.

Jorvik walked up beside Tor. "Do you still say I speak false?"

"What?" Tor lowered the spoon.

Jorvik smirked. "Didn't I say you'd wed an old woman?"

"I'm not wedding anyone."

"Not yet, but you will." The seer pointed his chin in Kiana's direction. "What of the shield maid?"

He glanced at the hanging hides. "You mean Kiana? Does she look old to you, seer?"

The man rolled his eyes. "She doesn't have to *look* old to *be* old, boy."

"Riddles," Tor complained.

Jorvik sighed. "Very well, let me tell you a tale." He leaned against the wall beside Tor. "I was raised in a monastery, did you know?"

Tor tried to imagine the old man as a child.

Jorvik grinned, the gaps between his few teeth making the expression more of a leer than a smile. "No, I see you didn't. Well, it's true. That's where I learned to read and write. But I shared my belief in the old gods as well as the new one. My teacher was also a man of curiosity and delved into things long past, old scrolls and sky charts. I told you some time ago the night sky wasn't right."

"Yes, it's an autumn sky." Everyone knew that now.

"But not our autumn," Jorvik replied. "I celebrate Mabon, the turning of the year, when summer turns to winter, day and night hold the same hours. This turning didn't happen at the time I celebrated in our old home. The bull isn't complete. The sky pictures are different."

"So, the skies are different in this land. We've seen it so when we travel to the warm climes."

Jorvik stamped his foot, a gesture so unlike him Tor paused in his scoffing. "Look for yourself, boy," the old man snapped. "The lodestar moves. Odin's Wain is fuller."

Tor held up his hand, worried now. "What do you mean, the lodestar moves? It's always been still, else how can we navigate?"

"How indeed? Yet it moves, not much, but enough to lose your way if you use it at sea today." A smug look crossed Jorvik's face, there for an instant then gone, replaced by a shake of his head and a hand on Tor's arm. "Don't fear. I've observed there is another light that sits still, fainter than the lodestar but enough on a clear night to help."

He had wondered why the brightest star appeared so much fainter than he expected. "But how can the sky change so much?"

"It's never still. My teacher said the lights and sky-pictures moved over time, more so than just from spring to autumn." Jorvik stared at the roof, as if the stars were visible through the ceiling. "Hundreds, no, thousands of years would it take to shift the lode-star."

"Thousands?" Tor was speechless for a few moments, until logic forced its way through the panic. "No, impossible. To come through so much time in just an instant? Even a sky ship can't open a hole in time."

Jorvik shrugged. "It sent us from spring to autumn, months ahead or behind. Why not years? There are also the ancient tales. Among those tales was one of a people who lived in the Southlands many generations ago, some say three thousand years."

Tor snorted. Nothing was that old. No one knew when the world had begun, but three thousand years? Ridiculous.

Jorvik ignored Tor's wordless comment. "These people were most advanced. They, too, had reading and writing. They knew how to manipulate numbers, how to read the stars, and they knew the secrets of metals. They made the strongest, most advanced swords and knives and bows of their time." He paused, made sure Tor was paying attention. "They worked in bronze."

He remembered the first time he'd seen Kiana, the bronze sword she'd worn, the swords of her enemies, and her boast that the weapon had been made by the most skilled blacksmiths in her country.

She'd never seen metal like his own sword, had never heard of steel.

The seer smirked again, but he continued with his tale. "These people lived by the inland sea, where the sun always shines hot. They built mighty cities, but because they had many enemies, their cities were walled by strong walls. Yet one by one they fell, until few remained. No one knows for certain how these last few fell, but many speculate treachery played a part."

"Ajmal," Tor breathed. It wasn't possible. It *can't* be possible.

Jorvik ignored Tor's interruption. "Eventually these people disappeared from common knowledge, their existence known only to a few dedicated scholars like me and tales of legend."

Tor's head spun. He was grateful for the wall, as it helped his legs hold him up. Everything fit, the bronze weapons, the tale of betrayal.

The changing night sky.

His mind took the final leap and his legs refused to hold him up any longer. He sank to his haunches, his heart beating a furious drum in his chest, his throat.

"But that means we fell…" Words failed him.

"We fell back over three thousand years," Jorvik finished for him. Tor's mouth worked, but nothing came out. Jorvik laid a hand on his arm. "You plan to wed a woman who is three thousand years older than you. Does that make you love her less?"

He glared at the seer for a moment, then his gaze trailed to where Kiana lay, and the world settled back into place. "No, it doesn't."

He took a few deep breaths, then pushed himself to his feet, thankful his legs agreed to support him this time. He glanced around the room. Runa sat beside Vider, her head on his shoulder, while the girl-child he insisted on calling his own snuggled in his lap. Families cuddled children, young men and women danced with bodies or just eyes. Already villagers and Norsemen were mixing, adding their strengths to each other.

The village chieftain sat with his family by the great fire pit at the north wall. He surveyed his people with a satisfied smile, pride mixed with concern, a sure sign the chieftain shared Tor's own opinion. There were too many alliances, too many friendships being born there. They were becoming one people, perhaps not yet, not this winter, but the next, or the next. Who ruled then, the village chieftain or the Norse war leader, only the gods knew.

It didn't matter. None of it mattered. Tor had brought his people to this land, to safety, and there they'd thrive, but for now…

His gaze strayed to the hides again.

For now, he had more important things to do, like make sure Kiana knew he was there for her, that he'd go with her if she decided to leave. He'd found the one person he intended to spend the rest of his life with, and nothing was going to change that.

Returning his attention to the seer, he bowed and pushed away from the wall. "You have given me much to think about, Jorvik. But not tonight. Tonight, I must sleep with my old woman."

He strode away to the seer's roar of laughter.

~ * ~

Kiana opened her eyes. Was she dead? She shifted, and the sharp pain in her side convinced her otherwise. Memory returned like a tide. Ajmal had found her, and he was now dead. But what had happened after?

She recognized the peaked roof above her. She was in the longhouse. Gray light seeped through chinks in the roof. Dawn or twilight?

A loud snore interrupted her speculation, and she turned her head. Tor lay on the floor beside her pallet, his head resting beside hers. She stretched out her hand and brushed the blond hair from his face. He looked exhausted, even in sleep, and while he slept, she took the opportunity to study him and to think.

An honorable man, but sometimes he was too proud for reason. She imagined his manner when they first met stemmed more from the insult of his capture—caught in a fishing net—than by her pulling his beard. She smiled to herself. Although *that* had brought a reaction.

Although he admired his sister he was overprotective at times. He had scoffed at Kiana's claim to warrior skills yet had accepted defeat during their demonstration on the beach with humor and curiosity to learn more.

When they brought in the deer before the storm he treated her as an equal. He trusted her to protect Runa and allowed Kiana to fight her own battle with Ajmal.

He let her be herself.

After Ajmal's betrayal she'd sworn never to love another man. Tor was her lover. Now? Was he also her love?

Love. What a strange concept. She believed she'd loved Ajmal, but that had been an illusion. She'd loved his strength, his authority, his confidence. He was captain of the guard, the most powerful man in the kingdom after her father and the king himself, and she believed he cared for her. At least, he pleased her in bed, but outside the bedchamber?

He spouted words of devotion, but over the last two years she'd come to realize they were lies. His interest in her wasn't for herself, but for her family. He was the most powerful man in the kingdom *after* her father and the king. The king had no daughters, but his grand magician did, and a connection, perhaps even marriage to one of those daughters, would bring Ajmal that much closer to the throne.

He hadn't proposed that alliance, though. Had he suspected Kiana wasn't interested in marriage at that time? She enjoyed his company, but she also enjoyed her freedom. She wasn't surprised he'd grown impatient and sought his goal in another way.

So no, what she felt for Ajmal hadn't been love.

What she felt for Tor…what he felt for her…

Yes, that was real. That was what love should be.

The snoring stopped on an intake of breath. Kiana stilled her hand on Tor's hair. He opened his eyes and smiled.

Oh, yes. This is real.

"Enjoyed your rest?" he asked, his voice casual and just a bit lazy.

She smiled back, lifted her hand. "As much as you enjoyed yours. Did you know you snore?"

He frowned. "I don't snore."

"Ah. My mistake." She brushed at his hair again. "How long was I…resting?"

"Not long. Overnight." Tor straightened, clasped her fingers. "You lost a lot of blood. The healer said you'd sleep longer."

"I feel fine." She started to sit up, winced again at the pain in her side, the dizziness in her head, and lay back against the pillows. "Well, almost fine."

He squeezed her hand. "Are you hungry? The healer said you'd be hungry."

"Not really." Her stomach gave a loud rumble. She glared at her midriff, then locked gazes with Tor. A moment later both were laughing. Grasping her side to keep it from splitting open, Kiana realized the physical pain was all she felt. *When was the last time I laughed without the pain of loss, of guilt*?

That stopped her. No loss. No guilt. All this time she'd assumed, deep down, there'd been a mistake, that Ajmal hadn't been the traitor the queen accused, and if she'd stayed her family would still be alive.

But he *had* been a traitor. Whether she stayed or fled, it made no difference.

Tor touched her cheek. "Kiana?"

She blinked. Her gaze had gone unseeing but when she focused, she was still looking into Tor's eyes. She blinked again. "It's over."

His eyes widened. "Us?"

To her own surprise, she grinned. "Oh no. Not *us*. We're just beginning." Remembering their joined hands, she returned the squeeze he'd given her earlier. "No, clinging to the past. That's over. I always assumed—" She shrugged, gave a rueful laugh. "Foolish, I know. But I assumed one day we'd go back. I'd take Beren back, and he'd live out his life among his own people. We'd find someone had rallied the king's troops, beaten back the invaders. My family—" She broke off.

Tor placed his other hand over hers. Strength seemed to flow through that touch. She shrugged and straightened. "But that's not going to happen. Not anymore."

"You called him by name, that man, this Ajmal. Is he the one? Did you love him?"

She smiled at his attempt to divert her attention, but the underlying uncertainty in his question softened her heart even further. "I thought I did, once, but he's nothing to me anymore." *Nothing*. She had no more doubts about that.

Tor licked his lips. "And killing him didn't make a difference to going back?"

She recalled everything Ajmal said and how he'd said it. "He didn't trust the Usali despite them setting him up as ruler. I don't believe he told them where we are. He wanted to bring us, or at least Jenal—Beren—back to prove his worth, but he was just a puppet to them. They'll find another to take his place, and if anyone else bothers to look for us, we'll be ready." She gazed into Tor's eyes, willing him to believe her next words. "I won't run anymore."

He was silent for a moment, but he stroked his fingers over hers even as he contemplated her words. "If you do, I'll run with you."

The simple statement shook her to her soul. He'd give up his home, his family…for her? Tears pricked her eyes, and her heart overflowed. She'd never loved him more than at this moment.

"So," he said. "You won't be leaving?"

Her cheeks ached from her smile. "I…*we* won't be leaving. This is our home now."

Home. Not just the place but the people. Friends she'd made, Lida and Runa. And Tor, more than a friend. She imagined herself ten years from now. Twenty. Beren grown into a strong young man. Children…a sandy-haired boy, a black-haired girl, perhaps more. No more running. No more looking over her shoulder for enemies who might not come, and if they did? She'd be ready. She wasn't alone. This was her home, these people her family.

She freed her hand, traced it over his lips. "I've decided to have you."

Again, his eyes widened. "Have…?"

She wanted to laugh but dared not risk jarring her side. Instead, she grinned. "If I were my sister, she'd ask if you would have her, but I *tell* you that *I* will have *you*."

He caught her hand, pressed the fingers against his lips, and kissed them. "I always said I'd wed a sensible woman."

She laughed. "And I expect to wed nothing less than a very smart man."

He frowned. "You didn't think me so smart when we first met."

"Ah, but a smart man learns by his mistakes." She pushed herself up, leaned toward him, and lowered her voice. "And you, my love, made so many mistakes you could only get better."

He gathered her close, mindful of her injury, and kissed her with a tenderness that made her heart sing.

Kiana sighed. *Yes, this is real. This is love. And he is mine.*

Epilogue

Two weeks later

Tor waited at the side of the longhouse while Kiana spoke with Beren at the other end. Gone were her leathers. She wore a robe of pale blue made of a soft wool that flowed with her every movement. Fastened by ties at her shoulders, it draped to her ankles and the sleeves fell to her wrists. A belt of gold links pinched in her waist, and whenever she moved, a muffled tinkle of bells accompanied every step.

He recognized the robe as Runa's, a wedding garment every Norse girl made when she came of age in hopes it brought her a good man, and one Runa planned to wear when she wed Vider at midwinter. In it Kiana looked…soft. Feminine. Her dark hair hung free of its usual tail, and someone had even found a few late flowers to weave together into a crown. He wanted to spread that hair out on their bed furs later on.

He'd fallen in love with her all over again when she'd walked toward him and the priest this morning.

Kiana still moved with care, but she claimed to be healed. Still, she hadn't shared his bed since her injury. Tonight, that changed. No one slept alone on their wedding night.

It hadn't snowed since the big storm two weeks ago, but neither had the snow melted. The false summer hardened it into ice, but that hadn't stopped the combined energies of the village and the Norsemen from finishing the outbuildings and expanding the back of the longhouse into several individual rooms. Most had been taken over by those with young children, but two rooms were reserved for the leaders of both groups, one for the village chieftain and his family, and one for Tor and his new wife and son.

His new wife. The grin Tor awoke with this morning had grown wider as the day progressed. He didn't think he'd ever stop.

~ * ~

"Are you sure you don't mind doing this, Beren?" Kiana asked for the tenth time.

Beren's impatient eye roll told her what the boy thought of her question, but this was important to her, not just for what she had planned for Tor, but for asking Beren to help her. She was a soldier, a lowly guard. It didn't seem right to ask a favor of the prince. But then he wasn't a prince anymore, was he? Or even a king in exile. He was a little boy she'd come to think of as a friend.

"If I minded, I'd not have practiced all week, would I?" His tone was of a patient parent to an eager child and did more than his words to reassure her. "Eskil's been practicing the drum part too."

"The drums?" Tears pricked the corners of her eyes.

She'd asked Beren for the flute music, knowing he'd heard it played many times in the palace. She hadn't expected the drum accompaniment. The boy had gone out of his way to make this night special for her, even though he didn't know what she planned to do behind those closed doors while he and Eskil played the song. She blinked until she had herself under control.

"I…" She coughed, swallowed the roughness in her throat, and tried again. "I am honored by your help."

She bowed her head in a gesture of respect. Beren returned the bow with equal solemnity, then spoiled the moment by bursting into giggles. Kiana grinned. He was still just a child.

Tor came up beside her, slipped a hand around her waist, and drew her close. "What's so funny?"

She kissed his cheek and dropped her voiced to a conspiratorial whisper. "Secrets."

He raised an eyebrow.

Beren giggled again, jumped to his feet with, "I'll go find Eskil," and ran off into the crowd.

Kiana smiled. "He's growing up so fast." The words tumbled unbidden from her lips.

Tor gave her a gentle squeeze. "He's growing into a fine boy. I'm proud to call him my son."

The word jolted her. *Son*. She gazed after the boy and realization slammed into her. No longer prince and friend, but more. What she said to him a few days ago was true. They *were* each other's family. Of course, she'd never replace his true mother, and didn't expect him to call her *bāntu*, mother, but perhaps, in time, *bāntiš*, like a mother, a title he used with the other women in the king's harem.

A warmth swept through her. Beren truly was her son, as the villagers insisted on calling him, and now she had a husband.

She turned in Tor's arms and studied his face. He examined hers in turn, an eyebrow raised in query, until she stroked her fingers down his cheek. *My husband. Mine.* "It's time I gave you your wedding gift."

The eyebrow rose higher. "A wife doesn't gift her husband. Her father gives a dower—"

"Which you won't get," she pointed out. "I have no father here and nothing to give if he were."

"He's given me you, and that's enough." He bent his head to kiss her, but she slipped from his arms and instead clasped his hand and tugged.

"But I want to give you my gift." She led him toward the chambers they'd been assigned and lowered her voice. "And it's best done in privacy."

The light that sparked in his eyes sent shivers of awareness down her spine, but she resisted the urge to jump on him right then and there.

"Privacy," she whispered.

Grumbling, he preceded her to their chamber. Behind his back, she signaled to Beren. He and Eskil hurried over, Beren carrying his flute and Eskil his drum. She closed the door before Tor noticed them.

The chamber backed onto the south fire pit, and was one of the warmest. The other occupied chambers had no heat of their own so the occupants slept and spent most of their time in the longhouse. They still had privacy if needed and somewhere to put their belongings without taking up room on the already crowded benches. Once the fires died down in the main room and Tor's room cooled, she'd be grateful for the bed furs piled on the pallet by the wall, but for now it was warm enough for her purposes.

The moment the door closed, Tor pulled her into his arms. Kiana allowed herself to fall into the kiss, but before it consumed her, she eased away. "Go. Sit." She nudged him toward the bench that served as a bed.

For a moment she didn't think he'd obey, but at last, with an indulgent smile, he complied. "Tell me," he asked after he settled on the furs, "why do you wear bells? They're not part of Norse tradition. What part do they play in yours?"

She laughed. "You're about to find out."

She backed to the door and rapped on it once. A slow drumbeat began, then the wail of a flute. Kiana positioned herself in the middle of the floor and kicked off her boots. Her bare toes curled into the furs she had the forethought to spread over the floor rushes. She loosened her belt and tossed it after the boots, then crossed her arms and tugged the ties at her shoulders.

The robe parted at the sleeves and floated to her ankles.

~ * ~

Tor stared, swallowed. *Odin's beard, the woman is naked.*

Almost.

A scrap of emerald material covered her breasts and another her hips. Around her waist she wore a belt of flattened silver disks, and a ring of disks hung from her breast covering. A chain of tiny bells ran around each ankle and she drew two bracelets from somewhere in that flimsy costume and slipped them on her wrists.

For a moment she just stood there, letting him drink in the sight of her. On the other side of the door, the flute and drum still beat.

Then she moved.

First her hips, a gentle sway to the left, then the right, and again. The disks rang against each other with a faint chime. She lifted her arms above her head and her upper body swayed with her, but in the opposite direction from her hips. She turned then, a graceful shimmy that sent the bells at her ankles jangling. She made two full circles, slow and mesmerizing, hips and arms undulating in a way that reminded Tor of a flat-head snake he'd seen once on a voyage to the Southlands. He had to remind himself to breathe.

After the second turn, Kiana stopped, caught his gaze and grinned a wicked grin. Then she rotated her hips, sending the disks to clashing. As if in answer, the drummer banged once, then pounded into a faster beat. The tone of the flute went higher, wailing in a way that sounded like voices.

Faster beat the drum. Faster snapped Kiana's hips, until she slapped her bare foot to the ground and began moving in earnest.

Tor felt his mouth drop open again and forced himself to close it. He clenched his fists on his knees. His breath came in ragged gasps as Kiana whirled around the room, her movements frantic, bells and disks clashing with each undulation of hips and arms and feet.

Sweat dripped into Tor's eyes, and he swiped at it with equally damp fingers. When did the room get so hot? He wanted to leap up, drag Kiana onto the bed furs, and sink into her, but he was frozen in place.

She said once she'd dance for him. He hadn't realized the dance might well be the end of him.

With a jangle of clashing metal, she swept past him, twirled once more, then collapsed at his feet, arms stretched toward him, head bowed. The music died with a suddenness that told him this was planned. Faint giggles came from beyond the door, fading as the players returned to the main room.

For a moment she knelt there, breathing hard. At last, she raised her head and grinned at him. "Did you like your gift, husband?"

Tor's breath exploded from him. "Odin's beard, woman. Are

you trying to kill me?"

Her laughter heated him all the way to his bones. "I'll take that as a yes."

Tor leaned forward, no longer frozen like a lump of lead, and shakily pulled himself upright. After helping Kiana to her feet, he ran his hands over her shoulders, down her waist to her hips, and gazed into her eyes. "That was definitely a yes. Do any of your grooms survive the wedding night?"

She laughed. "They grow up expecting this, just as we women grow up learning it. It's a simple dance—"

"Simple!" If that was simple anything more complex would kill him.

Her grin widened. "But achieves its goal." She turned to the bed furs then cast him a coy glance over her shoulder. "Are you going to stand there all night, husband? Or do you want me to show you what else we women learned in the Southlands?"

Oh, she was good, but two could play that game.

Ignoring the desperate heat in his lower body, at least for the moment, Tor scooped her into his arms. When she laughed in surprise and delight, he carried her to the bed furs and dropped her onto them with a jingle. He didn't fall on top of her…*gods, he wanted to fall on top of her*…but she was still healing.

Instead he knelt beside the pallet. "Much as I like the sound of these, they're too noisy for what I have in mind."

He slipped the anklet of bells off her right foot, then the other, then proceeded up her body until he had divested her of every single scrap of material and metal. At last she lay naked on the furs, her dark hair spread around her, her golden-hued body still shining with the exertion of her dance. Even the scar on her side, pink with healed skin, glistened with sweat.

He rose and began to remove his own clothing. He'd do it as slow as possible, to torture her as much as she'd tortured him. At least, that was the plan, but by the time he reached his trews he was unable to wait any longer. He shucked them off and tossed them into a corner.

She smiled when he revealed himself, then held out her arms to him. "Now?"

He growled. "Now."

Much later he drew a fur over their bodies and tucked Kiana against his chest. She snuggled close, pulling his arms around her.

"I'm going to like being married to you." Her words slurred as if on the edge of sleep.

"That's good." He brushed a strand of hair from her eyes.

"Because I plan to keep you for a long time."

She sighed. "I do love you, Tor the Norseman."

"And I love you, Kiana the Warrior." He kissed her forehead, then stroked her hair until she drifted into sleep.

A night bird hooted from atop the roof. Sounds of revelry drifted through the closed door from the main room. The celebration would last most of the night and into the morning. His people took any excuse for feasting, and a wedding was one of the best reasons. Next month and another wedding. Runa insisted she and Vider wait until Tor was wed before thinking about their own.

Feasts and celebrations. Less than two months ago, Tor had been fighting a storm, cursing the gods for threatening the lives of his people. Now he lived in a land that welcomed them all. Yes, perhaps that land was many years in the past from his own, but time meant nothing now that he'd found a woman—*this* woman—to love.

When he'd cursed the gods, he never expected them to respond by giving him everything he desired.

Kiana shifted in his arms, nuzzled his neck. He smiled down at her and eased her closer.

Yes, the gods had favored him with more than he deserved, and from now on he wouldn't doubt their intentions. He'd found his future, and it was going to be good.

Acknowledgments

Thanks go to all my friends and family who have listened to my crazy ideas, read snippets of scenes, and supplied invaluable suggestions. Your faith in me has been a constant encouragement.

Special thanks to Deb, who got me started on this journey way back in high school.

Thanks also to Romance Writers of America and RAMP (Romance Author Mentorship Program), through which I met my fabulous editor, Renee Wildes.

Thank you, Renee, for your patience while mentoring me through this process and for inviting me to officially submit to you at the end of the program.

Finally, to the staff at Champagne Book Group. Thanks for guiding me on this exciting journey.

About the Author

When Maureen started writing her own stories, she discovered that even her most serious suspense thriller ended up with a fantasy twist (in this case, a cameo from the Loch Ness Monster). Accepting the inevitable, but still determined to end with a happily-ever-after, she turned to writing science fiction and fantasy romance.

A recent experience directed her interest toward Vikings, so she began with a story about a strong Viking warrior who happens to encounter a crashing spaceship, ends up in the ancient past, and falls in love with a woman born three thousand years before he was.

Maureen is now busy researching more interesting facts about Vikings, the Bronze Age, and time travel.

To learn more about Maureen's work, to sign up for notifications of upcoming events and releases, or to send her a message, visit any of her links below.

Website/Blog: https://maureencastell.com/
Facebook: https://www.facebook.com/Maureen-Castell-Author-102629802446032

~ * ~

Thank you for taking the time to read *The Viking Who Fell Through Time*. We hope you enjoyed this as much as we did. If you did, please tell your friends and leave a review. Reviews support authors and ensure they continue to bring readers books to love.

Turn the page for a peek inside *Beneath the Destiny Stone*, a time travel that catapults the heroine into the life of a surly Scottish man.

A medieval Scottish blacksmith and a millennial from Detroit walk into a bar...

By the age of six Fiona could sink a bank shot.

By eight she could mix a perfect Manhattan.

By twenty-two she had a business degree and a concrete plan to save her grandfather's failing bar.

Then she was pushed through a time-portal.

Now Fiona is stuck in fourteenth century Scotland with no way home. There's a good chance time-soldiers are after her. And Henry, the guy she's shacked up with, is a grumpy son-of-a-bitch who doesn't get her at all.

He is hot, though.

And brave.

And most definitely the love of her life.

If the two of them can stop bickering long enough, Fiona just might be able to have it all—the tavern of her dreams and the first man who can actually keep up with her. That is, if they can survive the battles, murder, and mayhem of the Middle Ages and the time-soldiers who have a hand in it all.

Chapter One

My granda once met the devil himself.

At least, that was the story he was telling his friends. They sat at their usual corner table of the Caledonia Club—Old John, William, Robert, and Granda. Above them, an olive-green lamp illuminated a haze of cigar smoke and dust motes. A Scottish flag hung behind their heads, and on a pedestal in the corner sat a bust of Robert Burns, there to remind them what becomes of *the best laid schemes o' mice an' men*.

His voice carried across the club to my spot behind the bar, and I smiled to myself. Of all Granda's stories, I loved this one most.

"There I was, storming the shores of Normandy, gunfire blazing on all sides." He paused for dramatic effect. "But it wasna the bullets I feared. Nay. It was the man standing before me with fire in his eyes." He stared each of his friends in the eye. "Auld Clootie."

Jones, the Caledonia Club's shift manager and sometimes cook, laughed beside me as he counted out cash for the till. "What the fuck is a clootie?"

I gave the bar a final wipe and tossed the rag into sanitizing solution. "It's a Scottish thing. They don't like to say devil, so they've got a bunch of nicknames for him."

Jones smirked. "You sure they're not talking about their Depends? I bet John's wearing an old clootie right now."

I laughed despite myself. "Don't start. It's already bad enough I have to deal with that lot."

As if to punctuate my point, William knocked over his drink, and the rest of the table hooted and hollered.

Jones jotted down the register balance in an old-fashioned paper ledger and bumped the drawer closed with his hip. He raised an eyebrow. "You sure you want to do this now?"

I glanced at the old men and sighed. "Better now than after they've cashed that bottle of Glen Livet."

He put a hand to my shoulder. "I have complete and utter faith in you. You've got this!" He yanked his phone from his pocket. "Now if you'll excuse me, I'm just going to check out some job sites for completely unrelated reasons..."

I flicked him in the forehead and snickered. "Dick." He handed me the ledger, and I headed from the bar to join the old men.

"...so, I shot off his horns and shamed him back to hell," Granda finished with a grin. The old men laughed and nodded in approval.

"It takes bigger stones than Auld Clootie's to take on a Highlander," said Old John.

"Aye. Aye. True enough." William nodded.

I pulled a chair from a neighboring table and squeezed in next to Granda. He flashed me a wide grin. "Ah, Fiona, love. I was just tellin' the lads about the time—"

I gave him a quick peck on the forehead. "I heard you, Granda."

He patted my cheek. "Such a bonnie lass." He beamed at his friends. "Isna my granddaughter the bonniest lass ye've ever seen?"

Robert raised his glass in salute. "Stunning."

William winked. "Like a young Audrey Hepburn."

I rolled my eyes. Sure, I looked exactly like Audrey Hepburn, except for my face full of freckles and head full of curls. I supposed we were both brunettes, though, so there was that.

"Oi, Poof." Old John waved an empty whisky bottle at Jones. "We need another."

I grimaced at John's words and snatched the bottle from his hand. "What did I tell you?"

His brows crinkled. "What? I just said—"

I glared down the bridge of my nose at him. "Do I have to call your wife and make her come get your old homophobic ass?"

Jones sauntered to the table with a fresh bottle. "It's all right. We all know why he likes to suck on them cigars all day." He winked at Old John and set the bottle in front of him.

Everybody burst out laughing, except for Old John who flushed purple. I slid the ledger in front of Granda.

He held it at arm's length and squinted at the numbers. "What am I lookin' at?"

I gnawed on my cheek. "We didn't break even this month."

He gave a half-hearted shrug. "Aye, well…business'll pick up."

I took a deep breath. "No, it won't. We have three customers, and they're all at this table."

William lit a cigar. "Aye, but Robert drinks as much as five men."

"Used to say the same o' your mum," Robert shot back, and the old men cackled.

I looked Granda in the eye. "We need to bring in a younger crowd."

"How should we do that? Turn the place into a disco?" Granda gestured around the empty bar. "Bring in a few go-go dancers?" The old men laughed.

I narrowed my eyes. "Be serious."

"All right, all right." He patted my hand. "What is it ye're wantin' to do?"

"A lot of bars sell craft beer now." I licked my lips. "Stuff that's locally produced. I've been researching it and—"

"Christ Almighty." Granda put a hand to his heart. "Yeh want to sell bathtub ale?"

William raised his pint. "Why should ye when the good Lord's seen fit to bless us with Guinness?"

Lord, there were more beers in the world. "Not everyone likes Guinness. We should have a variety."

Robert's mouth fell open. "Who doesna like Guinness?"

Granda's lip curled. "Tories and communists, that's who."

"Ye didna find all these namby-pamby drinks in Scotland." Old John waggled his pointer finger toward me. "Guinness and whisky, that's all we needed."

"First off," I scoffed, "Guinness isn't even Scottish. It's Irish. And second, how do you know what they drink? You haven't been there since 1945." Granda and his friends immigrated to our little town south of Detroit right after the war, but the way they talked, you'd have thought they were here on holiday and fought in the Battle of Culloden themselves.

Old John swayed, whisky in hand. "Aye, but my soul will return to the mountains and glens once I'm good and dead,"

"Aye. Aye," they agreed.

I turned my attention back to Granda. "Hear me out."

"By yon bonnie banks, and by yon bonnie braes," Old John sang.

"Where the sun shines bright on Loch Lomond," the rest joined in.

My lips tightened into a grimace. "Really? We're doing this now?"

"Where me and my true love will never meet again."

"Christ." I snatched the whisky bottle off the table and chugged.

"On the bonnie, bonnie banks of Loch Lomond."

I returned to the bar, head hung in defeat. Jones disappeared into the kitchen, and with no customers to serve, I kept myself occupied scrubbing the already spotless countertops and dusting the already dustless shelves. I was in such a mindless daze that when my phone rang, it startled the shit out of me, and my duster knocked into Granda's prized possession—an old message in a bottle he kept next to the top-shelf liquor. I had to sacrifice my phone to save it.

"Shit. Fuck. Dammit." I righted the bottle and swooped the phone off the floor. "Hello."

"Did I catch ye at a bad moment?" came my best friend Sean's amused voice.

"No. Yes. I don't know." I laughed. "I'm sorry. What's up?"

He took an audible breath. "Oh…nothin' much."

I snorted. "And by nothing, I assume you mean lots of cool stuff you refuse to tell me about."

Sean worked in some kind of Special Forces unit for the British military, so he was always tight-lipped about his job. Which I understood…theoretically. But in my opinion, there should be a best-friend loophole for super awesome, secretive government stuff. It seemed only fair.

He gave an awkward chuckle. "Never mind all that, how's it going with *you*?"

I scanned the nearly empty bar. "Great…Your great granda's being a homophobe, my granda won't listen, and I'm pretty sure I'll need to sell a kidney to pay the next electric bill."

He laughed. "Anything else? Your granda didna mention…uh…something special?"

"No." I narrowed my eyes at Granda's table. "Why? What are you two up to?"

Anticipation-laced silence radiated from his end of the line. "I shouldna say. It'll ruin the surprise."

I let out a bark of laughter. "They're two bottles in. I doubt he remembers the surprise."

"You're coming to Scotland!" he blurted as if he couldn't contain it any longer.

"What?" I squealed. "When?"

"Tomorrow." His voice rose an octave in his excitement.

My stomach twisted. "Tomorrow? I can't leave tomorrow. What the hell, Sean? Why would you wait until the day before to tell me?"

He huffed. "And give ye time to find an excuse not to come?"

"No," I said with forced patience, "but you could have given me enough time to, I don't know, make sure the Club doesn't tank."

He heaved a weary sigh. "For Christ's sake, Fi. It's a pub, not a hospital. Nobody's going to die if you're gone for a week."

I gritted my teeth. "So you say."

"Look, we've got it all planned." The sound of a running faucet and clanking dishes muffled in the background. "Your granda has your shifts covered. Plane tickets already bought. And I'm on leave. All ye have to do is pack and get on the plane."

I pinched the bridge of my nose. "It's not that simple. We can't afford for people to cover my shifts. I'm salary. Everyone else is hourly."

"Please. If your granda doesna have ten grand stuffed in that ol' mattress of his, I'll eat my bonnet." When I didn't respond, his voice softened. "It'll be fine, Fi. I swear. Ye worry too much."

"I'm the *only* one who worries around here."

"Fine." His voice turned petulant. "Dinna come and see me. It's only been two years…"

I groaned. "Christ. You're as bad as the old men. Is that a Scottish thing, or do I just invite emotional blackmail?"

The worst part was his guilt trip was working. I missed the hell out of Sean. Every summer growing up his mom used to ship him across the pond to stay with Old John, and the two of us raised all sorts of hell together. On one memorable occasion, we nearly burned down the Caledonia Club after an incident with Barbie and the deep fryer. In our defense, it was really Captain Hook's fault. He's the one who made her walk the plank into the French Fry Sea, not us.

"So ye'll come?" Hope colored his voice.

I bit my lip. "If I can get everything arranged in time."

"Come on, donkey…" Fondness filled his voice, and my heart swelled at the old school nickname.

Growing up during the height of the Shrek era with a Scottish best friend and the name Fiona, we had heard nonstop Shrek jokes for most of our youth. When I threatened to beat Ashley Wilson's ass after she called me an ogre, Sean teased it was stupid to get mad, because, really, I was much more like Donkey than the Princess. The nickname had stuck ever since.

I sighed. "I'll try."

"Ye'll come." He sounded certain now. "We'll have a grand time, ye'll see. The adventure of a lifetime."

I hit end call and joined Granda, his eyes sparkling as he told another story. "…and when she told me she'd stick the needle straight in my eye if I didna sit still and let her stitch me, well, I kent—"

"You knew she was the woman you were meant to marry." I slid into the seat next to him.

He raised an eyebrow. "Have ye heard that one then?"

I grinned. "Just a time or ten."

"Ah, well, good." He polished off the last of his whisky and raked a sleeve across his mouth. "Ye could stand to learn a thing or two from your ol' granda's tales."

I flashed him my cheekiest grin. "Like what? If I ever meet the man I want to marry, I should threaten to poke out his eye?"

"Now you listen to me, girl." He picked up his cigar, ready for a lecture. "To be with your gran, I crossed an ocean. I gave up kin and country and all I held dear. And I never once regretted it. Not for one second." He stared at me, unblinking, as if determined I absorb his message. "If you're ever lucky enough to find a love like that, let nothin' stand in your way. Nothin'."

The old men raised their glasses. "*Slàinte.*"

Granda's gaze fell to the ring on my hand—Gran's wedding ring. She had given it to me not long before the cancer took her.

I kissed his cheek. "I miss her too." He squeezed my hand. "So…" I licked my lips. "I just got off the phone with Sean…"

Old John made a disgusted noise. "But the lad canna be bothered to call his great grandfaither, now can he?"

"I'll have him call you tomorrow. Apparently, I'll be able to relay the message in person." I shot Granda a glare. "How could you not tell me?"

He raised an eyebrow. "Seems an odd way to thank your ol' granda."

"I'm grateful. I am *so* grateful. You know I've always wanted to go. It's just—" I scanned the Club and bit my lip. "Granda, there's so much to take care of. I've got to make arrangements before I go somewhere."

"Like what? Tell your ol' Granda, and I'll fix it for ye."

"How will you get around? And what about your pills?" I met his gaze and held it, so he knew how serious I took his health. "You always forget if someone doesn't remind you."

His eyes narrowed. "What do ye take me for? Some bairn just weaned from his mither's teat?"

I swallowed. "No, I—"

"You listen to me, girl." He smacked his hand on the table. "I've looked Auld Clootie in the eye and lived to tell the tale. I brought down a hundred Nazis with my bare hands. And I survived sixty years o' marriage to your grandmither. I think I can manage just fine without your hen-pecking."

William leaned forward. "My daughter'll drive him to the Club."

Old John tilted his head toward Jones in the kitchen. "Put the poof in charge o' his pills."

"The boy wants to see ye, lass." Robert sniffed. "Ye'll break his heart if ye dinna go."

"Oi, John, maybe she'll come home with a great-great-grandson for ye." William snickered.

I wrinkled my nose in disgust. "I'm not going to sleep with Sean, you old pervert!"

But it was too late. The table devolved into bickering, with Granda defending my virtue, and Old John arguing that any lass would be lucky to have his great grandson. I just shook my head and extricated myself from the table.

Back behind the bar, I glanced at the clock. Two hours left to figure out which bills weren't getting paid, and how to keep Granda alive while I traveled.

"Jones," I yelled into the kitchen. "I need you to dose Granda's whisky while I'm gone."

"Roofies or dick pills?" he called back.

"Heart pills." I let the door swing closed, then thought better and stuck my head back in. "How do you feel about switching to salary?"

Jones put his hands on his hips. "With all this overtime coming up? Hell no."

"Please," I whined. "I'll cover ten of your shifts. Whichever ones you want. You'll make more in the long run, I promise!"

He threw a handful of fries at me.

"So that's a yes?"

He threw another handful and turned his back on me—a yes.

Chapter Two

"Holy shit, Sean!" I said after a mammoth, rib-cracking hug at the baggage claim.

I gestured from his chin-length hair to his ridiculously muscled arms and chest. "When did *this* happen? You look like if Kurt Cobain ate Arnold Schwarzenegger."

He gave a wry smile and slung an arm around my shoulder. "Ye'd be amazed what a diet o' nineties action stars can do for the physique." He hoisted my suitcase. "Shall we go?"

"I don't know, man. I'm not about to find Sylvester Stallone all tied up in your fridge, am I?"

He sucked air between his teeth. "About that…"

I laughed and knocked into him with my shoulder. God, I missed this. We hadn't seen each other in two years, not since he got his super-secret, mystery job. We still talked on the phone all the time, but it wasn't the same.

We left the airport, and rolling, green pastures turned to pine thickets, then sprawling, suburban houses. I hoped this meant we were close, because I hadn't eaten since I'd picked over my airline meal of gray meat in red sauce.

As if on cue, my stomach growled. "What about food? Can we stop somewhere?"

"My flat's above a chippy. We'll grab a pizza on the way up."

I wrinkled my nose. "Pizza from a fish shop?"

He scoffed. "Says the lass who buys her knickers at the grocery store."

"Oh my god." I huffed an audible breath. "It's *not* that weird." Sean had never gotten over his first introduction to Walmart. He couldn't wrap his head around being able to buy a bicycle and a piece of fruit at the same place. "Besides, I don't normally get my underwear there. It was an emergency."

"Emergency?" He scoffed. "It was bloody two in the morn'."

"Yeah." I shrugged. "And I didn't feel like doing laundry. So…emergency."

He snorted, and the two of us fell into a comfortable silence. After a time, he turned down a brick road lined with shops.

"Now *this* feels different!" I couldn't get over how close together the buildings were.

If the shops didn't have different colored facades, I wouldn't have been able to tell where one building ended and the next began. I supposed bigger cities in the US might be equally cramped, maybe New York or Boston. But I was used to the Midwestern sprawl, where buildings came with attached parking lots and enough space between them nobody dreamed of walking from store to store.

Sean led me to his flat, the smell of fried foods wafting from the chippy below. He tossed my suitcase on the floor. "Make yourself at home. I'll be right back." He disappeared out the door, and I walked about, inspecting his apartment.

It was strange. I had known Sean as long as I could remember, but this was the first time I'd seen how he lived. His decorating style fell somewhere between rich executive and twelve-year-old boy. A black leather couch and two matching chairs framed a stone fireplace with a television above the mantle. An upscale rug in shades of gray, white, and black covered a spotless wooden floor. In the corner, a bookcase boasted hardback books, mostly biographies and boring-looking history tomes.

But then there was his artwork. Framed and matted pictures of superheroes ran along the walls, a few of which I recognized from years ago when we'd gone to the Motor City Comic Con. I paused in front of a picture of Spiderman. I ran my fingers over Stan Lee's signature and smiled. Sean might have an important job and expensive taste in furniture, but he was still the same old dork he had always been.

The door creaked open, and Sean entered, a tied plastic bag and a six pack in his arms.

"You know," I said, "I think I've got it figured out."

He set his bags on the marble-topped coffee table. "Oh, aye? What's that?"

"Your super-secret military job." I nodded at a picture of the Avengers. "They've given you some kind of Hulk juice. That's why you're all big and muscly now. They've turned you into a super soldier."

"Hulk juice?" he said with mock affront. "First off, Bruce Banner became the Hulk because of *Gamma radiation*." He cracked open a beer and handed it to me. "Second off, if you're going to guess super soldier, the obvious comp is Captain America. Have I taught ye nothing?"

I took a sip of beer. "Well, if you'd just tell me what you do, my guesses wouldn't be riddled with terrible analogies, now would they?"

He didn't laugh like I expected. His face twisted into a strangely nervous expression, and I stilled, surveying him. His eyes were red-rimmed and bagged, and his skin looked pale even for him. I was about to ask what was wrong, but my phone rang.

I put it to my ear. "What's up?"

"Jukebox died." Desperation laced Jones's voice. "The old men are about to riot."

"Christ." I put a hand to my temple. "Can't you stream them something?"

He moaned. "And eat up all my data?"

"Whatever." I laughed. "Tell you what, you go over, and I'll pay your bill." Jones huffed, which I took for assent. "Love you." I made kissy noises into the phone. He grumbled something about not being paid enough for this shit and hung up.

Sean raised an eyebrow. "New beau?"

"No, just Jonesy from the bar." I raised an eyebrow. "Why'd you say it like that, though?" He sounded almost irritated.

His jaw clenched. "Because ye have terrible taste in men."

I scoffed. "Please. It's the men who are terrible, not my taste." In fact, most people thought I was *too* picky.

Jones gave me shit for months when I broke up with my last boyfriend. Apparently not knowing how to change a tire wasn't a good enough excuse to end a relationship. But the way I saw it, a girl had to have standards, and I just couldn't respect a man who lacked basic life skills I'd managed to master at the age of eight.

Sean snorted, and I tossed a pillow at him. "Whatever. Don't act like you're any better. Remember Vanessa?" One summer a few years back, Sean had a fling with this girl Vanessa. Apparently, she hadn't appreciated Sean meeting me at the bar after one of their dates, and she wound up slashing my tires.

"Aye, well, she wasna my finest conquest…" His eyes narrowed as his gaze fell to the phone in my hand. "Let me see that contraption."

I snickered and handed it over. "Okay, old man."

Sean hated technology. He absolutely refused to use social media, still read a print newspaper, and, for all I knew, probably had an abacus tucked away in the closet. He stuck my phone into his pocket.

"Hey!" I snatched a toss pillow from the couch and wielded it like a weapon. "Give back the phone, Sean. Don't make me hurt you."

He tossed his hair over his shoulder. "Ye're on vacation. No more calls from work."

I lowered the pillow. "All right. I hear you." I held out a hand. "Now give it back."

He nodded toward the bagged food. "After ye eat."

My stomach growled, and I acquiesced, even though my fingers itched to text Jones for an update. Instead, I peeked inside one of the Styrofoam boxes. "What the hell is this?" It wasn't pizza, and it wasn't fish, but it was deep-fried and vaguely resembled a giant empanada.

He opened his own box and inhaled the smell of cheese. "Pizza crunch."

My jaw dropped in reverence. "Do you mean to tell me this is a deep-fried pizza!" I took a bite and moaned with pleasure. "That's it. I'm staying here forever."

"Aye?" His eyes lit with hope.

"No." I sighed. "But it's tempting."

Sean plucked the remote off the coffee table and clicked through channels until he landed on a show about a book club. We ate our pizza crunch and drank our beer in silence until I realized something about the main character.

"Holy shit! That's The Hound!" My head nearly exploded at the realization my favorite Game of Thrones character had once been sexy as hell.

I turned to Sean to commiserate, but he was staring off into space, looking all broody and pensive. I nudged him with my foot. "Hey, what's your deal?"

"Huh?" He blinked and gave a forced smile. "Nothin'. Uh, yeah, it's The Hound."

I narrowed my eyes. "Sean…"

He ran a hand through his too long hair and averted his gaze.

I kicked him again. "Out with it."

His shoulders slumped, and he took a deep, audible breath. "I don't know." His shoulders slumped. "Ye ever look back at your life and realize ye made all the wrong decisions?"

I pulled my legs onto the couch and twisted toward him. "Like what?"

He shrugged and didn't seem inclined to say more.

Concern tightened my chest. He clearly needed to talk about whatever was bothering him. Maybe if I got the ball rolling, he would open up.

"Sometimes I wish I skipped college and put that money into the bar instead." I bit my lip. "I mean, what's the point of a business degree if the place fails before I get started?"

His eyes softened. "Maybe it's a sign ye were meant for somethin' else…"

"Like what?" I stared at him, puzzled. Taking over the Caledonia Club was the only thing I had ever wanted to do. My dreams centered around bustling crowds and house bands and newly felted pool tables, stuff that might seem silly to others, but meant the world to me. And one day, I'd make it happen. At least, I would if it didn't tank before Granda retired.

Pink tinged Sean's cheeks, and he waved the question off. "Sorry. Here I am getting all philosophical, when I'm supposed to be showin' ye a good time."

I grinned. "Does that good time involve a bottle of single malt and me cruising for dudes in kilts?"

"Even better." Sean disappeared into a bedroom and returned a few minutes later wearing a pair of hunter green, skin-tight leggings and a burnt orange, belted tunic, which altogether gave him the look of a medieval pimento olive.

I burst into giggles. "Hey, Robin Hood, you know, your shirt's supposed to cover your ass if you wear leggings."

"They're not leggings," he said primly. "They're hose."

This made me laugh even harder. He tossed me a shopping bag, and I rummaged through, pulling out a white linen dress, a green, wool sort of over-dress thing, and a pair of odd leather shoes.

"Oh my God." I paused between each syllable. "You're taking me to a ren-fair, aren't you?"

He grinned. "To a castle."

My eyes went wide. "A ren-fair at a castle!"

He shrugged. "In a manner o' speaking." His eyes lit with mischief. "That's not all."

I cocked my head. "What?"

He leaned in. "Tonight, I'm going to tell ye all my secrets."

Eyes wide, mouth open, I froze. "Don't you fuck with me." His grin broadened. "Don't you fuck with me!" He nodded, and I flung my arms around him. "You're really going to tell me what you do?"

"Aye." His grip tightened. "It's time ye kent everything."

Chapter Three

"Are you sure we didn't miss it?" I asked, as we neared the bridge to Edinburgh castle. The esplanade we had just crossed had been conspicuously empty, and the sun already neared the horizon. "I don't think most ren faires go this late."

"About that..." Sean's voice turned sheepish. "It's not *exactly* a ren faire."

"It's not?" I stared up at his face. "Okay...What is it?"

He adjusted the belt around his tunic. "A surprise."

I laughed. "Now you've got me really curious. Is it a private tour?" He shook his head. "A themed ball?"

His eyes sparkled with mirth. "Ye'll have to wait and see."

I tugged at his shirt sleeve. "Well, come on then. You know I can't stand a mystery."

"Hold on, there's just one thing." His gaze fell to his feet. "I ken it sounds strange, but I need ye to not talk when other people are around."

Tilting my head, I studied him. "Are you serious?" He nodded. My brow furrowed. "Okay. Why?"

"Trust me, it'll be easier if ye don't." He put a hand on my back. "It'll all make sense soon enough, just bear with me until then." He gave me a gentle shove toward the bridge. "Come on. Our castle awaits."

Two guards manned the gate on the opposite side of the bridge. They wore bright red uniforms and tall fuzzy bear hats like the ones you see in pictures of Buckingham Palace.

"Are they for real?" I couldn't decide if they were guards or elaborately costumed ticket takers. Either way, I found them adorable as fuck.

At least, I did until they raised their guns. We froze. One of the guards crept forward.

"What the fuck, Sean?" My voice came out waspish with fear.

"Shut up." He kept his eyes trained forward.

"That you, Cameron?" called the guard.

"Aye, mate." Sean strode forward. "Stand down will ye? You're scarin' the new recruit."

The guard lowered his gun. "Apologies. Wasna expectin' anybody 'til shift change."

Sean inclined his head in my direction. "Seems they've decided *her* training is more important than *my* vacation."

The guard winced. "Called ye in on holiday and e'rything? That Eugene's a right bastard."

"Aye, he is that." Sean handed over a piece of paper and a pair of IDs, which the guard scanned.

"First trip is it?"

It took a second for me to realize he was talking to me. I bit my bottom lip and gave a nervous shake of the head. I didn't know what was going on, but Sean's advice about remaining silent seemed pretty fucking apt right about now.

The guard's features softened in sympathy. "Dinna be so nervous, love. It's not as bad as ye think. Ye ask me, worst part is the clothes. All that wool'll have ye walking about like ye've got a case o' the jock itch."

Even if I could speak, I wouldn't have known how to respond. And not just because I had no "jock" to itch. What the hell was he talking about? What trip? And what did Sean mean when he said he was here for my training?

Sean took an innocuous step between us. "She's posing as a nun who's taken a vow o' silence." "They want her to get used to not speaking."

"That's a good role." The guard sounded impressed. "Hard to mess things up when ye canna speak."

I didn't know about the nun part, but I hoped the rest was true, because I couldn't seem to settle on a facial expression that didn't scream liar-liar-pants-on-fire. Fortunately, he wasn't paying attention to me anymore. He had his eyes glued to the slip of paper Sean had given him.

"All right, then. Everything seems in order." He called over his shoulder to the other guard. "Open up."

He returned our paperwork, and Sean and I walked unimpeded through the gatehouse door.

Once the lock clicked behind us, I tugged on Sean's sleeve. He bent, and I whispered in his ear, "Can I talk now?"

He nodded. "Aye, but keep your voice low, just in case."

"All right." I slapped him upside the head.

"Ow." He rubbed his temple. "What was that for?"

I ground my teeth together. "Are you kidding me? What the hell, Sean? How did we start the evening going to a ren faire and wind up breaking into a national monument instead?"

He snorted. "We dina *break in*. I got permission from the colonel himself to bring ye." He patted his pocket. "How do ye think I got the paperwork?"

I glowered. "If I'm allowed to be here, why do I have to pretend to be a…a—" I gestured at his costume, "whatever the hell you are. And why can't I talk?" I narrowed my eyes. "Just be straight with me."

"I will—I am." A blush tinged his cheeks, and he dropped his gaze. "We've a bit of an arrangement, me and the colonel. Bringing ye was part o' the deal."

My fists clenched. "What does that even mean? Sean, I swear to God, if you can't do better than that, I'm out of here."

"Ye canna go!" His gaze darted about. "Listen, it's taken a lot of work to arrange this. Can't ye just trust me?"

His eyes pleaded with me to comply, and I softened. Whatever this was, he had obviously gone to a lot of trouble to make it happen. And honestly, how bad could it be? We were dressed like extras in a Monty Python sketch, for Christ's sake.

"All right." I poked him in the ribs. "But if I wind up in a Scottish prison dressed like Maid Marion, I'm whooping your ass."

He ruffled my hair. "Fair enough."

I always thought of a castle as one big building, like an oversized stone mansion, but this was more like a miniature city. Buildings loomed in every direction—a cafe, a hospital, the governor's house. Sights I might have found interesting if Sean weren't hustling me forward like we were late for a court appearance. We looped past cannons and museums and a little pet cemetery until we came to a stop in front of the Royal Palace.

"There'll be armed soldiers once we get inside." He put a hand on my shoulder. "Dinna freak out. It'll be fine, so long as ye stay quiet."

"Umm…you telling me not to freak out, just makes me want to freak out even more." I clutched his arm. "Why can't I talk? At least tell me that."

As if considering his words with care, he tilted his face toward the sky. "I told ye I had a deal with the colonel." I nodded. "Well, no one else kens about it, and it's just easier if they dinna realize ye're an American."

"Uh, yeah, that sounds shady as fuck." I put my hands on my hips. "Are you blackmailing him or something? Why would this colonel help you trick a bunch of soldiers?"

He shot an anxious look toward the palace door. "I'll explain later. It's nothing like you're thinking, but it's too complicated to go into now." I didn't budge. "Dammit, Fi. The soldiers dinna matter. The colonel is the highest-ranking man in there, and he's given ye his permission. Now will ye quit bein' a pain in my arse and do as I ask?"

I stared at him, shocked. Sean never snapped at me. I mean, *never.* It was so out of character, it made me question whether *I* was the one being the asshole. Hell, maybe I was. I kept jumping to every worst possible conclusion when Sean was trying his damnedest to do something special for me.

I licked my lips. "All right, fine, but you have to promise you'll explain later."

His head bobbed in agreement. "I will. I swear. It'll all make sense soon, I promise."

Reluctantly, I followed him into the palace. Half a dozen armed guards stood stationed inside. I didn't panic since Sean prepared me this time, but I still felt uneasy.

A man, who I assumed must be the colonel, marched forward. He was a severe looking man with sharp eyes and a trenched brow. He wore full fatigues with insignia around the collar and an emerald green beret.

"Stand down." When he spoke, everyone in the room stood taller. The soldiers lowered their guns. "Johnson, man the door. Cameron, bring the recruit and come with me."

He strode into the adjacent room, and we followed into an enormous chamber with oak-paneled walls and a painted mural border. Geometric, plaster designs covered the ceiling, and a large, stone fireplace filled most of one wall.

"The king's dining room," Sean whispered in my ear. Impressive as the room was, I didn't understand why he had brought me here. Then the colonel stepped into the fireplace. What the actual fuck. I hadn't been in Scotland long, but that didn't seem normal.

His head disappeared behind the stonework, and he pushed onto his tiptoes.

I raised my eyebrows at Sean in silent question. *Just wait* he mouthed. Keys jangled from the vicinity of the fireplace, and a few seconds later, the back wall of the hearth swung open.

My mouth fell open. Sean tugged me close. "There are secret passageways all over the castle." His voice was little more than a breath, but the excitement in his words rang clear. "There's a whole network of underground vaults and tunnels."

Part of me wanted to throw on a fedora, grab a whip, and barrel into the vaults like Indiana Jones hunting for the Arc. But what in the hell? This serious man, an important, respected colonel, agreed to show me whatever lay hidden in those tunnels. Clearly, this wasn't typical tourist fodder. Whatever Sean had on this guy; it must be big. I glanced at Sean. Excitement lit his eyes when he met my gaze, and the knot in my stomach loosened. This was Sean. He'd never put me in danger. I was being ridiculous.

Sean nudged my back, and we followed the colonel through the secret passageway, into a darkened room. The musky air was cool and damp against my skin. Sean closed the hearth door, and as soon as the latch clicked, bright, fluorescent lights hummed to life.

We stood at the top of a set of ancient stone stairs, rough and irregular, as if carved from the earth with a hammer and chisel.

He caught my elbow. "Watch yourself. The steps can be slick."

I managed all right, despite the lack of traction on my weird medieval shoes. The stairs emptied into a small room, empty except for an industrial vault door that formed the back wall. In its center hung a large metal wheel with combination dials on each side. He went to one dial, the colonel to the other, and they each twisted in a combination. It must have been a long string of numbers, because it took a good minute before they finished. After a series of high-pitched beeps, the colonel cranked the wheel, and the vault door opened.

Sean ushered me through, and I about crapped my pants…or hose…whatever.

"The Honors of Scotland." He gestured to a velvet draped display. "The oldest surviving crown jewels in all the British Isles."

Goosebumps erupted on my flesh. Mere feet stood between me and millions of dollars' worth of ancient gold and jewels.

He waved me toward the display. "Go ahead."

I inched forward. A gold crown, rimmed with fur and studded with gems lay next to a silver gilt scepter topped with polished rock and pearls. A silver sword adorned with oak leaves and acorns rounded out the collection. I circled the display to get a better view of the last item—a large, flat, rectangular stone with iron hinges on its side. I stared at it, puzzled. For the life of me, I couldn't figure out why they'd place a dusty old rock next to the finery of ancient kings.

Sean joined me. "Do ye ken what that is?" I shook my head. "The Stone of Destiny." He ran a hand along its surface. "For centuries kings of Scotland were crowned atop this stone. Some claim it's the verra stone Jacob used for a pillow in the book o' Genesis."

"Enough with the history lessons." The colonel's voice cracked like a whip. "Help me send it up."

I jerked at his voice. I'd been so distracted by the jewels, I'd forgotten we weren't alone. The colonel stood in front of a control panel on the far wall, his features carved into an impatient expression. Sean scampered over, and the two punched in more codes.

"Stand back." Sean's warning came moments before the display rose from the ground. He returned to my side and pointed at the ceiling. "See where it looks like elevator doors? It opens to a shaft that leads to the crown room. They keep the jewels there during the day and secure 'em down here at night."

The colonel rapped a key on the control panel, and the display stopped its rise. The platform hovered ten feet in the air.

Sean pointed to a trap door in the floor where the display had just been. "The most important treasure the vault protects lies beneath the Destiny Stone."

Next to the trap door sat twin dials, same as the vault, and again, the two twisted in numbers. I watched in disbelief. What could possibly require more security than the crown jewels?

An office, it turned out. Not even a nice office—just a musty room with a small computer desk and a handful of chairs. A whiteboard, covered in complicated-looking math equations, spanned most of the far wall, and a world map, studded with pushpins hung to the left. The only other objects in the room were a tall, rectangular frame, bolted to the floor, and a couple of leather duffel bags.

The colonel tossed one of the bags at Sean's feet. "Get it booted. I'm going to change." He climbed back through the trap door.

Goosebumps prickled my skin. "What is this?"

"Give me a second, and I'll explain." Sean slid behind the desk and tapped away on the keyboard.

I busied myself studying the map. "Holy Roman Empire?" I chuckled. "I think your map's a little out of date." Red light flashed across the map face, and a strange, humming noise filled the room. It was a low, menacing sound, like a swarm of angry bees. The frame lit up like a Christmas tree, a series of bulbs glowing along the top.

Sean pressed a final key and waved me over. "All right. Ye wanted to ken what I do." He nodded to the frame. "Well, this is it."

The buzzing grew louder, and the lights along the top changed from red to yellow. Sparks shot between the frame.

I swallowed, my lips suddenly dry. "What is it?"

"The British government's most powerful weapon."

The lights turned from yellow to green, and the sparks became full on lightning bolts.

The hairs on my arm stood on end. Nausea churned in my belly.

“Sean, I don’t like this. Let’s get out of here. You can tell me the rest later.”

The door swung open, and the colonel returned. He wore a ruffled shirt and doublet with a leather jerkin over top. My mouth fell open. What the fuck?

The colonel looked down the bridge of his nose at Sean. “Ye ready, soldier?”

Sean strapped the leather bag to his back. “Almost, sir. I just need to give her the rundown on entry protocol, and we’re set.”

The colonel’s expression was at once disappointed and piteous. “Ye had to ken I’d never allow this, lad.” He gave a clenched, half-smile and pulled a small pistol from his jerkin.

Sean leaped between me and the colonel. “No! Ye canna! Ye promised!”

“I promised to send her through…and I will. Ye can bury her on the other side.” The colonel tilted his head. “Now step aside, lad.”

Sean remained frozen in place.

Anger flamed in the colonel’s eyes. “I don’t have time to mollycoddle you, solider. Either ye believe Scotland’s worth the sacrifice, or you’re a liability. Which is it?”

Sean waved his arms. “No, wait—”

The colonel raised his gun. I screamed. Sean dove in front of me, shoved me back, and together we fell, into the crackling frame.

Out Now!

What's next on your reading list?

Champagne Book Group promises to bring to readers fiction at its finest.

Discover your next
fine read!
http://www.champagnebooks.com/

We are delighted to invite you to receive exclusive rewards. Join our Facebook group for VIP savings, bonus content, early access to new ideas we've cooked up, learn about special events for our readers, and sneak peeks at our fabulous titles.

Join now.
https://www.facebook.com/groups/ChampagneBookClub/

Printed in the USA
CPSIA information can be obtained
at www.ICGtesting.com
LVHW010115220923
758957LV00028B/255